The Weightless World

The Weightless World

World

Anthony Trevelyan

First published in 2015
by Galley Beggar Press Limited
37 Dover Street, Norwich,
NR2 3LG

Typeset by Kerrypress Ltd, Luton, Bedfordshire
Printed in the UK by TJ International, Padstow,
PL28 8RW

A CIP record for this book
is available from the British Library

ISBN 978-1-910296-41-7

To my dad,

Robert Trevelyan

the work attaches itself to the person not the place

Diane Coyle

PART ONE
The Blue Sky

1

Raymond Ess is going to kill me.

This is the thought I can't stop thinking. One way and another I've been thinking it for years, though I used to mean something like *Raymond Ess is going to be annoyed with me* or *Raymond Ess is asking too much of me.* I don't mean either of those things now. I just mean he's going to kill me.

One night soon, when he finds out what I've done, Raymond Ess is going to slip quietly into my room and murder me in my bed. He's going to stab me through the sheets with a kitchen knife, crush my throat with his speckled hands, and he's not going to do it because he's mad, though he is (stark, staring); he's going to do it because it's what I deserve. Because it's the only punishment that fits the crime.

When I said all this to Alice, one night last week, she did her best not to laugh. 'You don't mean that. You're being fantastic, you're being *interesting…*'

'I'm not being fantastic. I'm not being interesting.'

She gave me a complicated look – amused, pitying, maybe just starting to be worried. 'Then why are you going on this trip with him?'

'Because there's nothing else I can do.'

On the hotel roof terrace Raymond Ess and I are working through breakfast. We've been in the country for eight hours, at least five of which I've spent asleep. I don't know, and would fear to guess, how long Ess has spent asleep. It's possible he hasn't slept at all.

He sits eagerly hunched over the mosaic of paper he's spread across the entire table surface, relegating our cups and plates to the free chairs on either side of us. His hands are pressed together between his knees. He talks quickly, laughs often, often for no reason I can make out. He is in giddy high spirits; he seems to be trembling with excitement.

The roof terrace with its swept tile and faux-imperial architecture – columns, pillars, Greek nymphs, Roman busts – isn't really suitable for this meeting. The sun is so bright, insanely flashing, we can barely see what we're doing. Ess spends long moments with his nose in his notes, struggling to extract a word or a number from the field of dazzle the light makes of any page. I've had similar difficulties with my tablet; held at the wrong angle, the screen is an oblong of blinding fire. I tried shading it under the table, but the table is a latticework of metal, all chinks, and the pattern it threw onto the screen was ornate but not legible. The best I've come up with is to sit with my knees high, feet on the seat of my chair, the little computer steeply balanced in my lap, one hand round the upper edge of the screen, the other scrolling, dabbing at the virtual touchpad.

I would like to suggest we find somewhere else to hold our meeting. But Ess seems happy, more than happy, where we are.

Every few minutes he pauses. He shuts his eyes, tips his head back and sits silently smiling. At first I assume he's thinking, strategising. Then I realise he's just sunbathing.

Finally the eyes flip open and he says, 'Right. Where were we?'

And we turn back to our notes, our proposals, our plans.

We are, after all, here on business.

Raymond Ess is fifty-six, a senior executive, an important man. I'm twenty-eight, his personal assistant, not important at all. We work for Resolute Aviation and we've come to India to buy an antigravity machine.

'You're going to have a brilliant time. A brilliant and a – you know – hugely successful time.'

This was Alice, two days ago, before I left for the airport.

'You don't have to tell me,' I said. 'I'm pumped for this. Did you ever see anyone so pumped?' Probably I was trying to put her mind at rest.

'Mmn. And you're not thinking any more about that silly stuff, are you? About Ess or anyone wanting to kill you, or…?'

'God, no.'

She wasn't fooled. Alice isn't really foolable, or not by me she isn't. 'It's not healthy, carrying all that round with you, all that whatever it is. I wish you'd told me…'

'I did tell you.'

'Mmn.'

'And I'm not carrying it round with me. I'm not carrying anything round with me.' I held up my empty hands to illustrate the point, and she slapped them, one after the other, in the manner of a tribal greeting, or a tribal rebuke.

'Ess would never hurt you. He's a good guy, he'll understand. He'll see you didn't have a choice.' Her confidence, her authority. Alice has met Ess once.

And anyway, it's not true. I did have a choice. I could have stood up for him, stood by him. Instead I did what I did and I'm doing what I'm doing.

What I said to Alice, though, was, 'You're right.'

She looked at me for a long time then. Pressed her forehead, hard, into mine, as if trying to see inside my eyes. Inside hers, golden cities, hidden worlds.

Then she pulled away from me, gave a brittle sniff and said, 'Change of plan. You're not going.'

'Alice...'

'Nope. It's too weird. You're not going. I'm not letting you go.'

But she did let me go, in the end.

'Enough,' Ess says now, leaning back in his chair and stretching his arms above his head. 'If that doesn't satisfy them, I don't know what will.'

By *them* he means Resolute's board of trustees. Actually he means Martin Cantor, the board's thirty-six-year-old chair, and his nemesis.

'It's good,' I say, looking down at my notes. 'There's the same issue with some of the uh, fine detail, but there's nothing...'

I trail off. Ess isn't listening. He's frowning, thinking – a small, neat, dapper man; tanned and handsome, in a game-show-host sort of way, with dark, silver-wired, side-parted hair, fondly crinkling blue eyes and beaming, too-good teeth. Today he's wearing a white linen suit, a yellow silk shirt open at the throat, and incongruous scarlet Italian leather shoes.

On the other side of the table I'm tall, sprawling, thinning, jug-eared and odd-eyed (Alice says my eyes are 'fizzy'; I have no idea what she means by this, but I'm assured she means it nicely), in a T-shirt, shorts and trainers. We're here on Business but we're dressed for Pleasure. This is part of Ess's plan.

'Right,' he says, sitting forward. 'I'll give Asha another go.'

Asha Jarwal: our guide out of the city, into the countryside. Ess employed her on his previous visit to India, at the end of last year. He talks about her constantly, keeps telling me she and I are going to be 'great mates'.

'Oh,' I say, 'have you already tried her?'

He is silent. He takes out his phone, brings it close to his face and starts pressing buttons, peering intently at the screen. It's a weird, jaggy moment. I might not have spoken. I might not be here. We used to get moments like these a lot, though recently he's been better. Then, still peering at his phone, he says, 'I had to keep myself occupied somehow, while Goldilocks was getting her beauty sleep.'

A dig. I was half an hour late for breakfast. Relief. 'Goldilocks *did* need her beauty sleep,' I agree.

'You don't mind if I…?' He points to a corner of the terrace, I make shooing gestures, and Ess climbs to his feet and goes to stand in the corner with his phone clamped to his face. After a while his posture changes and he starts talking to someone.

And I look down again at my notes – my crazy estimates, my lunatic sums.

In fact the only calculation that matters is the one that says Resolute is finished. That says the company is done for and we're all going to lose our jobs.

Early last year Martin Cantor and the board announced their intention to dissolve Resolute Aviation. We all pretty much got it. We howled, we ground our teeth and rent our garments, but we got it. The company had been in trouble for years.

The only holdout was Ess. Two decades earlier he and three friends had founded Resolute, and while his co-founders had long ago gone on to better things (consultancy work, retirement), Ess had held firm. And firm he held still. Soon he was clashing with the board, privately – then, less so. Ugly scenes in the boardroom, then in the corridors, the car park.

In July things came to a head. Ess became unwell. It was suggested, fairly gently, that he should take some time off. And that's what he did. He packed a suitcase, boarded a plane, and spent six months travelling round India.

Six weeks ago he came back into work. He seemed fit, healthy, a man transfigured. He was loud with the subcontinent's praises. And that wasn't all.

On his travels, he said, he'd discovered the solution to all our problems. He'd met a man, a genius, a recluse of the Indian wilds who had invented an antigravity machine. He was going to return to India and buy this machine. In this way, Ess said, he was going to save Resolute, save our jobs, save us all.

On the roof terrace Ess is still standing in his corner, still speaking into his phone. It strikes me that he could talk for another ten minutes or another hour, and on an impulse I close my tablet, stand, and walk a few paces to the roof's nearest edge.

From here, nine floors above street level, the city is a vast and gnashing wheel, dusty, speed-lined, turning so quickly in the morning sun its details are hard to make out. Here, a futuristic office complex, all intangible tapering. There, a ramshackle tenement block, crazily corseted with strings of bright laundry. The rest is a blur.

I turn to face the bay with its ranks of covered boats waiting to ferry out tourists on to the water. I'm just beginning to comprehend it, the immense level of the Arabian Sea, when Ess strides up beside me.

'Magnificent, isn't it?' he says.

'It is.' I glance at him, and I realise he doesn't mean the view of the city, or even the view of the sea, but the view of the sky. With a broad, shallow smile, he's gazing up into the sun-flashed blue. And I know what he's seeing: this self-same sky awash with transit and industry, with gliding tankers, floating liners, pleasure ships and cargo craft of every variety, and swarming everywhere round everything countless thousands of human dots, commuters, caterers, deliverers, traders, all the workers of the world in graceful (affordable, sustainable) flight... I know he's seeing this, because Ess's recent conversation tells me he's seeing this sort of thing most of the time. What's funny is, over the last few weeks I've started seeing it too. Airborne crowds, ascended multitudes...

'Right.' Ess detaches his gaze from the sky and turns to me. The way he does this causes me to notice the faint scar on his cheek, crosshatched lines, like graph paper, catching the sun along their cellophane slits. A strange scar: sometimes there, sometimes not. As he moves his head almost imperceptibly in the bright air, it blinks on, blinks off. 'Fair news on the Asha front, I'm glad to say. Just now she's finishing up her current job and looking to join us this evening. All being well, she'll meet us for dinner here at the hotel. Which should mean a late briefing then an early start in the morning. Which isn't bad. Better than I was expecting, to be honest.'

'Okay,' I say. But the thought that early tomorrow morning a woman I've not yet met is going to lead us into the countryside, into the Indian wilds, is alarming, terrifying.

But then (this is to calm myself) I remember I have fairly good reason to suspect that the woman doesn't exist – that Asha Jarwal isn't a real person, that there is no guide and no one is coming to lead us into the Indian wilds, or anywhere.

Still smiling, he dips his head and urges it forward – an Ess gesture indicating a confidential disclosure. 'Sounds like she's up against it with this one. Great mob of Spanish clergymen wringing their hands over the slums. Rolling their eyes to the heavens, beating their breasts. Asha says they keep wailing at her, "How can this be?" And she tells them, "A slum is a slum. Life is hard." I can just imagine her saying that. "Life is hard." Not much nonsense in Asha.' He chuckles. It's the sort of chuckle

9

that makes people who don't know what he does for a living think Ess must be an entertainer, a late-night DJ, a croon-the-hits club singer. Then he straightens, claps his hands together. 'So, Mr Strauss, it rather looks like we've a day to kill. What say you to heading out?'

'Heading out... of the hotel?'

'It's a bold thought, I know. Come on. We'll explore, we'll shop. It'll be good for you. For your jetlag, or whatever's wrong with you.'

'There's nothing wrong with me.'

'*Ooh*. That's what they all say.' He slaps me on the shoulder then crosses back to the table to pack up his notes, the great mosaic of his pads and folders and binders. I stand watching him for a while, then privately purse my lips and step forward to help.

My jetlag. Or whatever's wrong with me.

We flew Bristol to Doha, Doha to Mumbai. On the second flight, the shorter one, Ess mostly slept, which was a relief, because on the first flight (the longer one) he'd talked the whole way. For a while I kept an eye out for warning signs – there are lots of them, and I know them all well – but I didn't see any and after an hour or so felt I could safely tune out.

The most reliable of his signs was the nose-twitch. He'd always had it, a brisk shrug or bob passing from the tip of his nose to the point of his chin, a rabbity realignment of the mask of the face, usually brought on by sustained thought or anxiety, but for years no more than one of those harmless quirks that made Ess Ess. It was only round March or April last year that it stopped being a quirk and started being a sign. First it increased in frequency: he'd be sitting there talking to you, his nose constantly jigging up and down, his top lip sliding continually over his teeth. Then it increased in severity. At his worst he looked as if he were trying to gnaw his own face off, to bite it, to tear it away.

But it was all right. On neither flight did any of his warning signs appear. Also, on neither flight did we travel Business. We travelled Economy. This was another part of Ess's plan. 'We'll be coming in under the radar!' he had said, with satisfaction. 'They won't even know we're there!' In this context, I had only the most general idea who he meant by *they*. But that was all right too, because I wasn't thinking about it.

We landed at Mumbai in the middle of the night. As soon as we entered the airport it was clear that something had happened. The Arrivals section was full of people, flight after flight of people, all apparently shouting. I talked to a group of women standing a little way in front of us who explained that the airport had been blocked for hours. When I asked why, they were incredulous. 'Haven't you heard?' one of the women said, with a pitying, piercing note. 'There's been another bombing. Bangalore this time.' It had happened while our flight was in the air. For now, the woman said, there were no other details.

I relayed this information to Ess, who tightened his lips and gave a single bleak nod. After that I didn't raise the subject of the bombing with him again. I sensed that if I did he would take it as something very close to a personal insult.

From the roof terrace we take the lift down to the ground floor. It's a slow, bumpy ride, the confined space of the lift resounding with the screech of unseen cables and feeling all the more confined for the presence of a uniformed attendant perched on a stool, a spry, quick, thinly grinning man with whom Ess keeps up a stream of garrulous conversation. When the doors finally smash open, the attendant taps the peak of his cap at us. Ess salutes in return. I raise a hand to my brow, weakly brush my fingers across it, and sidle out of the lift after Ess as quickly as I can go.

In the reception area Ess launches into conversation with the man at the desk, then hands across his papers so the man can lock them into the hotel safe. Presumably this is a measure to ensure *they* don't get their hands on his notes. So far Ess hasn't suggested that my tablet needs to be locked up. Does this mean his notes are indispensible, but mine are not?

As we approach the entrance a turbaned doorman bows and pulls open the door for us. Not looking at the man, swaggering in his glamorous white linen, Ess throws off another salute. I stare at the tiled floor.

At the top of the steps outside, Ess pauses. When he looks at me his face seems full of the noise, the light, the heat, the panting life of the street below.

'Well then, Mr Strauss,' he says, 'are you ready for an adventure?'

Funny: because two weeks ago I was asked the same question by Martin Cantor.

On a Friday afternoon, while Ess was off-site doing who knows what, Cantor invited me to his office. He was friendly, and welcomed me in among the film posters, the games consoles and pinball machines of his executive demesne. I had never been in his office before, though I knew Ess referred to it as the *Playpen*. It was pretty nice. A change at least from Ess's office, with its Chinese screens, its Viking maps, its oil burners and incense sticks. I mean Ess's office was nice too, in its creaky, fragrant way; it just wasn't so much my thing. In my head – and occasionally to Alice – I referred to it as the *Perfume Counter*.

'So Steve! Looking forward to your big adventure?'

'Oh, absolutely. I'm absolutely looking forward to it.'

'Great.' Cantor grinned and leaned towards me in a way that kept making me think he was going to tap my knee, though at no point did he do that. 'You know, I couldn't go to India. The States, anywhere in Europe, no problem. But India? Rather you than me.'

'Because of the instability? The uh, political instability?'

'Because of what I've heard described as the persistent and ubiquitous reek of shit.'

We laughed. It was the end of the working day, of the working week, and we were sitting on deeply comfortable reclining chairs, not quite facing each other, no desk between us. In fact I couldn't see a desk anywhere in the room. I tried to imagine Ess's office without a desk and it was like imagining a church without an altar.

'Anyway,' Cantor went on, 'I appreciate your coming to see me, because I'm keen to get your take on all this. All this Ray stuff. All this… Indian… antigravity… stuff.'

I thought: There's a *ray* now? Then I realised he just meant Ess. 'Okay,' I said.

He smiled, sat forward in his deep chair. 'So… what is that?'

'What's my take?'

'Yes, exactly that.'

I blinked, opened my mouth to speak, then a while later closed it again. I blinked and blinked. But there was nothing I could say.

'If you don't mind…?' Cantor was smiling at me now as if he thought I was close to bursting into tears. Oddly it was true. I *was* close to bursting into tears. 'I think it's like this. Put me right, jump in at any point. But basically I think it's like this. I think you're extremely fond of Ray. You've worked with him for a long time, and you've certainly been loyal to him. You respect him, as we all do, and you feel sorry for him, as we all do, especially in light of his recent health issues. Am I on the right lines so far?'

I nodded, careful not to dislodge the tears trapped all round the inside of my eyes.

'So there's that. At the same time you're a sensible guy. You hear him talking about this... stuff, and your heart sinks. Because you know all it means is he's not really well. Not really himself again yet.'

After a while I nodded again, slowly, cautiously.

'So there's that. At the same time you're thinking, "What's Martin Cantor playing at? Why is he letting Ray go ahead with this?" That's what you're thinking, isn't it?'

I tried to look at him, but couldn't. I managed a gradual shrug.

'Steve, like you I know this trip, this whole thing is madness. I don't know what a doctor would call it – a symptom, an ailment. Why am I letting it go ahead? Because I believe it's in Ray's best interests for it to go ahead. I genuinely do.'

Now I did look up at him. He was still wearing that rippled smile.

'I genuinely believe the best thing for Ray is to let him work through his issues in his own way. Let him take his own path through whatever he's dealing with. Ideally with a good man at his side, a good friend, looking out for him at every step.'

I gave a low laugh. It sounded surprisingly normal.

'And there's another reason.' Cantor's manner abruptly hardened or flattened: he seemed to be speaking to me from behind a screen of glass. 'You don't know this, no one does yet, but next month we're taking the big step and putting Resolute into administration. It'll be a painful process. The end of the company, basically. I'm sure you can see why it would be in no one's interests for Ray to be around while this happened.'

I stared at him, squinted at him – screwed up my completely dry eyes.

'You know what he's like.' Cantor gave a metallic laugh. 'How he always has to *get stuck in*... but he can't fight the administrators.

This is a battle he simply can't win. So I think we can agree that it would be no bad thing if next month, while we see to this administration business, Ray weren't around. If Ray were elsewhere, happy, happily oblivious, pleasantly distracted. I think we can agree on that. Am I right, Steve? Can we agree on that?'

2

The street outside the hotel is either slowly disintegrating or slowly knitting itself together. The slabs of the pavement are shattered, scattered, widely separated by ashen black pits, as if blown apart by aerial bombing. I can hardly keep my footing but Ess is already at the end of the street, grinning and waving, waiting for me to catch up.

When I do, we turn the corner into a sort of bazaar. Mouldy-looking shops on either side of the street, shoe shops, clothes shops, jewellery shops, seem to have spilt a silky lining of their innards onto the pavement, masses of veil and awning under which stalls form a seamless rickety bank, an endless wash of shawls, scarves, bracelets, novelty T-shirts, Taj Mahal key-rings, Mahatma Gandhi oven gloves. Every few feet a smart young trader tries to take you into an embrace with one arm while evincing the range of his wares with the other. Ess loves it. He stands with these guys for minutes at a time, for quarter hours, half hours, talking and laughing with mutually clutched forearms. Well, this is what Ess is like, has always been like – meeting people, talking to people, making friends.

Still, he manages to buy a lot of stuff. When he shows me his purchases he's like a stage magician conjuring an impossible string of handkerchiefs. It's soon apparent that even with all our hands we're not going to get everything back in his satchel. He tips his head back and laughs. Cramming pashminas into each jacket pocket, he says, 'Seemed silly not to take the chance while we had it. But I see I may have gone rather overboard!'

'Who's this even for?'

'Oh, there are always people. Cousins, nieces. The usual leeches and hangers-on.' He doesn't mention either his daughters, Kris and Esther (twins, owlish, unearthly), or Eunice, his ex-wife, and the girls' jealous protector. But then (I think) why would he mention them? Filling his trouser pockets, he says, 'I see I may have gone rather mad. Yet we're here to buy, are we not? Besides, it's good practise. You know, with the old haggling.'

'That's what you were doing? When you were touching up those guys? Haggling?'

"You have to do it. They expect it. They'd be offended if you didn't.'

'If you didn't take the piss out of their gear then offer them a pittance for it?'

'It's not taking the piss. And it's not really a pittance. These chaps aren't daft. They know what they're doing. Think of it as a ritual, a *dance*...' He shakes his head, changes the subject. 'Who's on your list?'

'I haven't got a list.'

'No? Didn't think you might pick up an oddment or two for your folks? Couple of tea towels for those great big brothers of yours?'

'Nah. Though probably I should get something for Alice.'

'Alice! Darling Alice Darling! A lady of the most scrupulous discrimination. No stall-rat's tat for such as she.' His conviction, his certainty. Ess has met Alice once. 'Happily I know just the place... along here a way, come on...'

While we're waiting to cross the road, jammed into a pack of tourists at the edge of the pavement, a kid in stained jeans and an oily long-sleeved shirt presses against me. He mutters hotly into my ear, the same sound, over and over again. I step away, glance at him sideways. He's grinning but his face looks as if it's been carved out of very soft chalk.

18

'What?' I say. 'Sorry?'

'Hash,' the kid says, keeping his voice low. 'Hash, my friend.'

'No,' I say, 'no thanks. I'm not interested.'

He shrugs and moves on to another section of the tourist pack, muttering hot and low: 'Hash, hash, hash, hash, hash…'

We're here to buy. But buy what?

Ess made it sound simple. On his previous visit to the country – which he referred to as both his *sortie* and his *sabbatical* – he met a man, an inventor named Tarik Kundra. He got along very well with this Kundra, who in due course took Ess into his confidence and agreed to demonstrate for him his greatest invention: an antigravity machine. A machine that cancels the effect of gravity. A machine that severs objects from the billion chain-links of gravity.

Ess asked Kundra to sell him the machine. Kundra demurred. Ess insisted. They negotiated – they haggled – and finally they came to an agreement. For 'a sizeable sum' (nothing more specific than that) Kundra agreed to sell the machine's schematics, its sole working prototype and exclusive rights to reproduce it, to Ess and to Resolute.

It was as simple as that.

Except it wasn't, couldn't be.

'But why?' I asked. 'Why would he just sign the thing away like that?'

'You heard my talking about "a sizeable sum"? Don't worry, Tarik will get his due.'

We were having this conversation in The Hanged Man, Ess's favourite pub, where we had most of our conversations after Ess came back from India. He refused to discuss Tarik Kundra in his office – as if he feared *they* had bugged the telephone, the light fittings, the scented candles of the Perfume Counter. Each morning we arrived at Resolute, met in his office, twiddled our thumbs for a bit, then skulked back to the car park, piled into Ess's car and drove for fifteen minutes out of Yeovil until we came to the green hills and The Hanged Man. It was a bit of a codger's pub, with its Toby jugs and horse-brasses, but I didn't mind it. And Ess was happy enough, lording it over the cloth-faced yokels.

'Okay,' I said. 'Why you? Why us? Why Resolute? Or any British company, or foreign company? Why doesn't your pal Tarik want to sell in India?'

'My pal Tarik is no great fan of his homeland, no patriotic model Indian. He feels his country has used him somewhat ill, let us say, and leave it at that.'

No, I wanted to say, let's *not* leave it at that, let's *talk* about this, because this doesn't sound right, this doesn't add up... Then I had to catch myself. The entire subject was – something other than real. None of it was going to sound right. None of it was going to add up. I realised I would have to form a new habit: the habit of letting Ess say and do whatever he wanted. Which would be difficult. After all, I'd spent the last five years forming precisely the opposite habit.

'Applications!' Ess now announced grandly. 'And I don't mean the bloody, jump-the-rope, count-the-slices-of-pizza playtime pissiness you kids are hooked on, I mean solid, real-world facts, light-of-day concretions, cash-value incorporations.' He clapped his hands. No one in The Hanged Man looked round when he did this, though they really should have. 'What have we got? Transport, obviously, freight, naturally. These are areas perhaps too massive for us to think about at this early juncture, so we may be best moving on... casting our net wide rather deep, so to speak. Remember, there are no limitations. None.'

This was how Ess liked to talk: wild, fast and loose, without the inertias of detail. He wouldn't even say definitely how much he thought the machine was likely to cost. One day he suggested that once it was in full production a unit could probably be sold at about the same price point as a mobile phone – and not a smartphone such as I had, but a dumb-phone such as he had, with its grainy green screen and twiddly physical buttons. But on other days he suggested that a typical unit could cost roughly the same as a paperback novel, or a desktop computer, or a family car.

The one detail he kept straight was that the machine was a circuit and a wire – a circuit and a loop. When you closed the circuit, any object encircled by the loop was freed from the dominion of gravity. The wider the loop, the larger the object you could so liberate. The size of the circuit remained the same.

'About as big as your hand. Well, not *your* hand, a proper man's hand. But you get the idea. Lampstand or battleship, it doesn't matter. One flick of a switch on a device about the size of an adult male's hand, and up it goes! Up into the wide blue yonder! Or rather, let's say, up and wherever you like. Ironing board or oil tanker, you can steer it to Timbuktu with a hand fan.'

Now in The Hanged Man he said, 'When you get right down to it, it's a question of seeing. It doesn't matter any more what we think, what we say, what we do, only what we see. What can we *see*? That's the question, the only question left, the question of shapes, forms, embodiments. Which is to say, the question of applications.'

As he said this I was sharply aware that he was wearing a cravat, a plush burgundy affair plumped up at the throat. It was a new affectation, and it looked ridiculous. Altogether, in this grimy, low-lit gaffer's pub, he looked completely absurd. But at least he didn't look old, as he had looked old. In April, May, June, he'd looked very old. The soft crinkles under his eyes had dried and hardened, grown into ridges, bitter bone-lines. His lips had been the lips of a shrunken head. He'd looked mummified, fossilised. But there was no trace of all that now. He looked a strong, ruddy fifty – forty-five, even.

And, while he went on and I sat nursing my glass of orange juice, I considered what Martin Cantor too had pointed out: wasn't this better? Wasn't this Ess a better Ess, quick, keen, fully alive, than the Ess you'd get if you shut him down, said no, called the strapping male nurses to peel him out of his chair and carry him shrieking to the ambulance, the quiet country hospital, the injections, the bed? Wasn't this better than the creature you'd get then – blasted, hollowed, with trembling lips and druggy dithers?

It was. It was better. Obviously it was.

Later that day he said, 'Here's a curious thing. The other morning I was leaving the house, it was Sunday, I was going out to fetch the paper, and a car screeched to a dead stop in front of me. It wasn't an accident, just some idiot driver who'd come the wrong way up a cul-de-sac. But that *screech*... awful sound. The tyres just screaming, *screaming* like they knew they shouldn't be here, like they knew they shouldn't exist any more.

'And that was it. For the first time I understood, truly understood the magnitude of what we're doing. Only one of the many terrifying implications of this project is we're putting an end to the wheel. Do you see that? We're making the wheel obsolete.'

Now we're dragging round the crowded bazaar, harassed by heat, by thudding car horns, by a brightly wrapped little girl who won't leave us alone, who toddles patiently between us, dabbing her fingertips to her lips and looking up at us, each in turn, with crater-wide eyes.

Stumbling on the broken pavement, I suddenly feel it: the click in my back. I keep walking but soon it's coming strong and fast – *click-click-click* – working like the needle of a sewing machine, piercing, puncturing. It's painful, at about the level of a stubbed toe, and I go along with hunched shoulders and gritted teeth until Ess pats my arm and with a swiping glance at his watch says, 'No point wearing ourselves out. What say you to a rest?'

'I'm okay.' I shrug.

Ess tips his head at me. He knows all about the back-click thing.

'Really,' I say. 'We're looking for a present for Alice, aren't we?'

'And the lovely Alice shall have her gift. Only now it occurs to me that I did say at about this time I'd call in with the fellow who runs Adventurers – you know, the tour company we're using. Dreadful bore I shouldn't doubt, but it may look good for Asha if we make nice, if we "touch base" so to speak, with her gaffer. Don't mind, do you? And anyway, you may not need a rest, but I bloody do. Happily I believe the appointed place is not far…'

This is the first I've heard about a meeting with the fellow who runs the tour company. Probably I would have something to say on the subject – points to make, objections to raise – if it were not that my teeth are welded into a single piece.

The place appointed for the meeting is a surprise. I'm expecting some clammy shack but instead Ess leads me to a large, airy, Western-looking bar, all coffee-culture murals and retro signage. A man standing at the entrance nods to us as we step in among the crowded tables. As Ess hunts for a free space I glance back and see that the man at the entrance has halted the little girl who was following us. He speaks to her, with an emphasis that I'm not accustomed to seeing when people speak to children. Then she ducks her head and toddles away.

At the back of the bar we crush ourselves round a table still loaded with its previous occupants' detritus, hot chocolate mugs, milkshake glasses. Ess goes to the bar to order and I sit concentrating on the sensations in my spine, not thinking about the fact that I've travelled without insurance, not thinking about the likely condition of the local hospitals, not thinking about anything but the needly click in my back until Ess is again sitting next to me, nudging my shoulder, saying, 'Here we go.'

He seems to be indicating the man seated at the next table, a large shaggy elderly guy with a bald head and a straggly white beard. My first thought is that Ess has been at it again – meeting people, making friends – then I recall that we're here to meet someone. The fellow who runs the tour company. Asha's gaffer.

'Raymond Ess,' says Ess, thrusting a hand at the man.

'Harry Altman,' replies the man, in one of those American accents that sound at first like a fairly serious speech defect. Then he brings his hand angling towards me, and I have no choice but to shake it too.

'Steven Strauss,' I say.

'Raymond. Steven,' says Harry Altman, as if assimilating our names into his accent. 'How very nice to meet you gentlemen.'

'You won't mind my asking,' says Ess, with a narrowing smile that makes me fear the worst, 'but are they… they are, aren't they? Look, Mr Strauss! They are, aren't they?'

I look at Harry and Harry looks at me. Still I'm at a loss. What is what? Harry is wearing trainers, jeans, a green sweatshirt, a slightly flashy pair of specs. Then I get it.

'The specs,' I say.

'You've seen these before?' Ess is excited.

'They're smartspecs. They're new, but I've seen them.'

'I expect you have,' Harry says, smiling with a sort of wan humility. 'They've been around for a while. Maybe not out here so much. These I had shipped from the States.' He takes pleasure in telling us this. The pleasure, like the specs themselves, sits somewhat absurdly, even grotesquely, on his ancient wreck of a face.

24

'So it's a computer?' Ess is virtually bouncing in his chair. '*Inside* your specs?'

'I've got internet, email, video, apps, pics, docs. Pretty much the whole show. Only no keyboard, no physical controls of any kind. Totally voice-operated.'

'It just listens to what you want, then beams it into your eye?'

'Beams it smack into my eye.' Harry's smile broadens and there it is: a flaming white square where the pupil of his right eye should be. The effect is unsettling. After all, how old is this man? Sixty-five? Seventy? Two hundred and ten?

'That's fantastic. You know, my young associate here loves this kind of thing. Don't you?' But before I can answer Ess is addressing Harry again. 'He gets all the gadgets. The second some new toy comes out, he's first in the queue. Crack of dawn in his duffel coat. At the moment he's forever pawing his... what is it?'

'Tablet,' I say.

'His tablet. His tablet computer. Forever fondling it in his lap, like a kitten.'

'Sure,' Harry says. 'Tablets are cute.'

I nod, smile. But I'm pissed off. I point at his computerised specs and say, looking very directly at Ess, 'It has a camera.'

'A camera? Good lord!'

'Still and video. You can just sit there filming people. You can have a conversation with someone and film them the whole time and they've no idea you've done it.'

'Is that so.' Ess's grin stalls; his excitement falters. For the first time he seems to register a proper wariness of our unkempt interlocutor. 'That's... ingenious.'

Harry taps his specs, indicating a black clip. 'Lens cap. Courtesy cover.'

'So people know you're not filming them,' Ess supplies unnecessarily.

'It should be bright red or something, I know. They're still working out the detail.'

'Have you been here a long time, Harry?' Ess asks.

'You mean in the country? Or in this bar?' The two of them laugh at this in a way I just have to go along with. 'Yes to both. I adore this bar and I adore this country. It'll be five years in October. Gone native.' He spreads his arms, as if in surrender.

'And now you run a tour company.' I'm smiling as I say this.

'I do, though I wouldn't say that's all I do. Sure, I have interests in Adventurers, but I have interests in a number of areas. I guess I like to think that primarily I'm a builder.' He slumps his shoulders and dips his head, all bullshit humility. 'I used to be a software guy. That's why I first came out here, tech conferences, the Asian Future, so forth. Then one day I decided I didn't want to go back, so I didn't. I stayed and I became a builder. Among ah, other things. That's kind of the life-arc for me. From America to India, from software to hardware. From the abstract to the concrete.'

'Is that what India is?' I ask, still smiling. '"The concrete"?'

'For me it is. I know for other folks it's metaphysics, mythology, but for me, yes, it's the concrete. A brick between my palms. Grit under my fingernails.' A smooth bullshit chuckle. 'How about you gentlemen? My role at Adventurers is pretty hands off, so I've barely had a glimpse of your itinerary. What brings you to these shores?'

I'm ready to field this one – to trot out the cover story Ess outlined on the plane: we're workmates, in the country to celebrate a former colleague's wedding at a somewhat remote location – when Ess says, 'Would you believe we're here on business?'

I open my mouth then shut it again.

'Isn't everybody?' Harry snorts into his cappuccino. 'What're you selling?'

I open my mouth.

Ess says, 'As it happens, we're here to buy.'

Shut it again.

'No kidding.' Harry nods thoughtfully in his smartspecs. 'You're kind of against the traffic, aren't you? I thought it was all sell, sell, sell with you guys. I mean it's the same with my guys. No one in the States buys a plane ticket to India unless they know they're coming back with like a hundred IT contracts.'

'Not us,' Ess says. 'We're buyers. Ardent buyers.'

'May I ask, buyers of what?'

I slump in my chair. What's the use?

'Oh… *boring* stuff.' Ess laughs, discreetly nudges my shoulder again. Great. He's messing with me. 'We're in aerospace. Resolute Aviation. You might have heard…?'

'Wow. You kids are in the shit. I mean *wow*.'

'There's no doubt some truth in that,' Ess says, with strained neutrality. 'Down but not out, I would say.'

'Down but not out. Yes, sir, sign me up to that.' Harry holds his cup out between our tables and we clash it with ours. 'I guess you heard about the bombing? In Bangalore?'

I'm ready to change the subject, to protect Ess's sensitivities, when Ess says, 'Awful business. And yet isn't this reality now? Bombs, terrorism, fanaticism. This is simply global reality. There's no escaping it. If it doesn't get you here, it'll get you somewhere.'

'That's an interesting view.' Harry smiles a humble smile. 'You know there were bombs here? Right here in Leopold's. 13 July, 2011. I was home sick that day. I turned on the TV…' He waves a hand, as if clearing a pall of smoke. 'Don't listen to me. You guys make up your own minds. People come out here with so many fixed ideas, they already know what they're going to see. Bombs, temples, bombed temples. That's the danger. India'll pretty much let you see whatever you're expecting to see.'

An hour or so later we're all on our feet, shaking hands again. Harry and Ess exchange cards then Harry makes a mild but prolonged fuss when he realises that Ess has somehow managed to pay his bill without his noticing.

'I can't let you do this,' Harry murmurs, his hands clasped in a begging gesture.

'You can and you have.' Ess slaps him on the back. 'Don't give it another thought. We're far from hard up. Isn't that so, Mr Strauss?'

I nod, smile.

Still, Harry is oddly difficult to reassure. Outside on the pavement he lingers with stooped shoulders, dipped head, clasped and begging hands. 'You're sure I can't...?'

'Put it from your mind, Harry.' Ess winks at me. 'We're not on our uppers just yet.'

One day Ess came into The Hanged Man looking extremely pleased with himself. Unusually he'd called earlier to say that he had appointments all morning and I should work from home then come to meet him for lunch 'at the usual place' (guarding his words on the phone). As he swung down next to me under the horse-brasses he seemed ready to break into song.

'Look.' He held up a folded piece of paper. 'Do you know what this is?'

'I've no idea what that is.'

'It's what we've been waiting for.' When I looked no more enlightened, he said, 'It's the code, the access code. For the company account. For Tarik's fee.'

'Ah. His "sizeable sum".'

'Got it off Cantor this morning. Wee bastard put up quite a fight, I can tell you, I had to chase him round the Playpen to get it. But get it I did.'

'That's great.'

'Great? It's *incredible*, you little heathen. It's *momentous*.'

I nodded, smiled. Because what I knew and he didn't – what I knew because Martin Cantor had told me – was that Ess hadn't got anything. The code didn't work, the account didn't exist. Resolute hadn't given him a penny. We were going to India with the company's blessing, but not with its money.

3

Back at the hotel Ess says he thinks he will spend the afternoon resting in his room, and suggests I do the same. This time I don't fight him. My shoulders feel locked in an unbreakable hunch and I can barely ungrit my teeth long enough to say I'll meet him for dinner. As I head up the stairs – the needle-pain in my back still being infinitely preferable to riding up in the lift alone with the thin-grinning attendant – Ess lingers at the reception desk. I suffer no illusion about his 'resting'. No doubt he'll spend the afternoon chatting up as many of the staff members as will let him, pressing the flesh of the other guests, holding court in the dining room.

In my room on the third floor I shut the curtains, strip naked and lie spread-eagled on the bed. For a while I listen to the soft throb of the air-conditioning, the raucous gossip of the birds outside the window, the restless *click-click-click* of the needle in my back. Then I lie spread-eagled on the floor. I fall asleep and wake up surrounded by shadows. In the bathroom, as this morning, I can't work out how to make the intercom-like apparatus over the bath dispense hot water. My second cold shower of the day. My hair is turning to cardboard but I feel savagely alert. As I change into a shirt and jeans for dinner, I notice that the pain in my back has pretty much disappeared.

The Ess I meet on the roof terrace is a gloomy Ess indeed. We've had a setback, he tells me. Asha has called. Her current job – the one with the Spanish clergymen – has overrun and she won't be able to join us this evening after all. In fact she

31

won't be able to join us until tomorrow evening at the earliest. While he tells me this he moves his arms lightly, airily, but the disappointment bears down on him, compressing his eyelids and lips.

For Ess the news is a double blow. As much as he's keen to begin the next leg of our journey, I know he's been looking forward to seeing Asha again. Since his return from India last year, he's had a great deal to say about Asha Jarwal, about her professionalism, her fearlessness, her no-nonsense strangeness. Almost daily he has recalled for me his first meeting with her, at the office of the Adventurers tour operators, where (he insists) it was immediately evident that she was in charge, despite her being the company's youngest, and only female, employee. He recalls that when he approached her at the reception desk, in a clanging, whirring Colaba back street, she glanced up from the report she was jabbing into an old-fashioned desktop, silenced him with a raised finger and a brusque hiss – he acts it out for you, the finger, the hiss – jabbed into place the final characters of her report, printed it out of a choppy printer, frowningly reviewed it, smartly filed it in an adjacent cabinet and then turned and smiled at him with beaming courtesy, as if she had only that second seen him. 'Like the woman who raised her finger and hissed at me and the one who smiled at me were two completely different people,' he will say, admiringly. 'Pure Asha!'

I feel terrible for him. But at the same time I'm delighted. The news that we won't be venturing into the countryside at first light is indescribably wonderful. Nonetheless I work hard to keep a glum look on my face over dinner, throughout which Ess attempts crestfallen little bursts of conversation. Then we sit for a while with our coffees watching the sky darken and the lights of the city come out, a vast brilliant web growing quickly more complicated.

'Well,' he sighs, 'at least tomorrow we can have another stab at finding a nice gift for your Alice.'

'Yeah, *yeah*,' I agree enthusiastically. 'I hadn't thought of that.'

'Have you talked to her? Since we arrived?'

'We said maybe we'd Skype. About nine-ish. Allowing for the time difference.'

He squints at his watch. 'It's nearly nine now.'

'... Is it?'

'Go on, scoot. Speak words of love to your Darling.'

Alice and I met, very boringly, through friends.

To be precise, Alice met me through a friend, and I met her through a colleague. A few years ago there was a keen bean in admin called Guy who kept trying to organise work socials: after-hours drinks, weekend walks, all sorts of crap I wasn't interested in. I formed the habit of deleting Guy's all-staff emails as soon as they appeared in my inbox, but at last he wore me down and one Friday night I found myself with a bunch of the admin kids in the worst bar in Yeovil. Some of the girls had brought friends, and one of these friends was Alice. A peculiar effect of the bar – the lights, something at the molecular level – forced the two of us into a corner, where I remember we had a pleasant conversation, and where Alice remembers she took the piss out of me for three hours.

'You just took it,' she says, 'just stood there and took it. Hour after hour. Unbending. Unflinching. How could I fail to take pity on you? It was so *sweet*.'

'It wasn't *sweet*,' I try to tell her. 'I just didn't know what you were doing.'

'And all that time I was thinking you were *so* not my type. And that's true, isn't it? You are *so* not my type.'

For the last two months we've shared an attic flat in Hawks Rise. It's the same flat I started renting seven years ago, when I got a job at Resolute and realised I had a weekend to find somewhere to live. Alice tells me the place is far nicer than I deserve, and regularly scolds me for not making the most of it. And so for the last two months she's been making the most of it – putting in new blinds, putting down new floors, replacing the bed, replacing the cupboards. At present we're deadlocked over the couch. She wants a new one. I don't see much wrong with the one we've got. 'But it's a *ghost couch*,' she wails. 'You can't sit on it, you just fall right through it. You sit down and it's like there's nothing even there.'

She may be right. Alice is very clever. She's twenty-six, she has a PhD in Politics (Dr Alice Darling) and she teaches at Exeter University. She's taught there for five years on a knotted string of part-time, fixed-term contracts. Currently she lectures two mornings a week and says fairly often that if the university doesn't give her anything better soon she's going to lose her mind and 'just blow the fucking place up'.

Oh, and she's beautiful. Did I mention that? She's beautiful.

One night about a month ago Ess came to the Hawks Rise flat for dinner. It was the first, and to date only, time he and Alice met. He brought a bottle of wine, which he and Alice drank, and Alice made spaghetti Bolognese. I was horribly nervous, but Ess and Alice quickly settled into a favourite-uncle, favourite-niece sort of rhythm and sat talking warmly at the table, Ess surprisingly restrained, modest, moving his brows and smiling gradually as he spoke, Alice gamely listening and twisting the ends of her hair, the really blonde bits, the bits that are practically white. Afterwards she said she thought he was a remarkable man and she didn't know why I'd had to be such a gibbering wreck all night.

I was pleased; also irritated. Alice thought Ess was remarkable, but only because of how well he was doing, how bravely fighting his illness, how valiantly battling his demons. She'd never known him when he was *really* remarkable. Which, as far as I was concerned, was the whole point. She should have thought he was remarkable not because he was struggling to overcome a mental collapse but because he was *a remarkable man*.

Back in my room on the third floor, I keep my Skype date with Alice.

The software's unfamiliar – neither of us has used it before – but promptly at nine Alice's grinning contact photo appears in the Skype icon surrounded by aquatically pinging circles, impact rings. I tap the photo and all at once there she is.

'Hello, Darling!'

'Hello, Jug-head!' A reference to my ears, which are not fortunate. An equally likely greeting would be 'Hello, Baldie!' – a reference to my supposedly delusional belief that I'm going bald. Only it's not delusional. For at least six months my hairline has been thinning, withering, turning to feathers and soot. 'Good grief, I can see you! Your funny little face, your fizzy little eyes…'

'And I can…' Then I can't, her face smearing about in the screen. Sitting on the bed, my tablet laid across my raised knees, I wait until she's got herself good and comfortable on the ghost couch in our Hawks Rise flat. Finally the laptop sways to a standstill in her lap and there she is, again, grinning, clever, beautiful, looking as if she may cry.

'How are you, then? Is it shocking? Have you been *deeply* shocked?' She laughs. Alice's laughter is quite a thing, not at all the sound you'd expect to come out of her. It is a boom, a lusty and barrelling *ho ho ho*. She actually sits there and says, 'ho, ho, ho'. Like she's Father Christmas or something.

'I'm okay,' I say. 'It's...' But I've no idea what it is, so I just shrug and say, 'It's okay. How about you?'

'I'm fine. Just working.' Her appearance – chunky non-retro specs, hair tied up in a rubber band, porridge-coloured sweater – tells me she doesn't mean working as in rushing about campus, delivering lectures and leading seminars, but working as in sitting at her desk with her laptop and her papers and her books, as in *thinking*. This, I know, is what Alice considers to be her real work: her vocation, her calling.

'Anything interesting?'

'I could tell you, but you literally wouldn't understand the sounds I was making. It'd be like another language to you. Alien clicks and gutturals. Anyway, it's boring, let's not talk about it.' I know also that she doesn't mean this, that Alice doesn't for one second believe her work is boring, but I nod and smile anyway. 'I'll probably call it a day in a bit, go over and see Dan. Any messages, or...?'

'Tell him I'm drinking gallons of the water,' I say.

'Oh, no!'

'Gallons of it. Straight out of the tap. And I feel *amazing*.'

'He won't think that's funny. He'll just think you're a dick.'

When Alice's brother Daniel found out I was travelling to India he spent a lot of time on his computer researching the country, then a lot of time afterwards telling me that as long as I got the recommended shots I would probably be okay *as long as I didn't drink the water*. He printed out for me about ten pages of traveller's advice that all converged in the view that if I ate a leafy salad I was as good as dead. Even in the taxi to the airport I'd got his text: 'Have a nice time but do NOT drink the water.' Dan is seventeen and he goes to a boarding school in Exeter. He has MS and no one thinks he'll see twenty.

Obviously, I'm kidding about my drinking from the tap. Bottled water is my constant companion. And I'm actually less worried by the water than I am by mosquitoes – airborne hypodermics crammed full of malaria. But I've been brittled with repellent since the plane, and I take my pill twice a day. I have a net, too, though I've not used it yet.

Alice says, 'And how's the Grand Poobah?'

'Ess? He's having the time of his life. I've never seen him so happy.'

'Are you having the time of your life too?'

'I'm okay.' I should leave it at that. But instead I say, 'Maybe a bit worried about where everything's leading.'

'Oh really? Why? You're doing what you can. What else can you do?'

'Nothing.' I give a trembly sort of shrug. 'There's nothing else I can do.'

'And you don't know. It may be all right. Everything may just... turn out all right.'

'How is everything just going to turn out all right?'

'You don't know. Maybe you'll get there, and you'll meet this Tarik bloke, and he'll show you this machine of his, and... you know... it'll work.'

'I don't think that's going to happen.'

'But you don't *know*, do you?' Apart from the very first second after I told her about it ('Ess wants to go to India to buy an antigravity machine'), Alice has maintained an annoying agnosticism on the subject. I'm fairly sure she does it only because from the start I was so definite in my own view (that it's bollocks – a madman's dream, a psychotic's folly). So she wavers, she prevaricates. 'Who *does* know any more? These days it's not obvious what's possible. Maybe there was a time when everyone knew what was possible and what wasn't, but we bloody well don't now. Every other day there's some sparkly new gizmo, and we all stand round and go *Aaah*, and ten minutes later it's just one more fucking thing taking up room in your coat pocket.

Look at what we're doing now. This is videophone, yeah? This is science fiction. This is *Blade Runner*.'

'You pulled such a face…'

In the very first second after I told her about it, Alice crossed her eyes and stuck her tongue out – hilarious lunacy.

'Yes I did, but you know since then I've had time to *reflect*…'

Someone knocks on my door.

'… And I just think it's not clear any more, the line's blurred, the ground's shifted…'

The knock comes again.

'Someone's knocking on my door,' I say.

'Does that mean you have to go, or…?'

'That means I have to go.'

'I love you, Jug-head.'

'I love you too.'

In the hallway outside my room Ess is waiting. His gloom of half an hour ago has vanished. He's excited, animated, his eye crinkles beaming.

'We're going out,' he says. 'Harry called. Drinks at the Oberoi. Are you ready?'

Outside the hotel Ess hails a yellow-hooded cab and we tear away from the kerb straight into the worst traffic jam I've ever experienced. Several miles' worth of motionless vehicles thud their horns as if speaking to each other, as if drolly discussing the blockage ahead. I feel we must be only seconds from catastrophe – shattering windscreens, exploding engine blocks. Nonetheless our driver is calm. Squashed against me on the backseat, Ess peers out at it all cheerfully. I know what he's thinking: *We're putting an end to the wheel.* No more cars. No more traffic jams. No more road accidents. No more *roads...*

By the time we break free of the jam we've left behind the neon squiggles of the city centre and we're speeding through a district of quiet residential streets – spruce greenery, high walls – then without warning the cab swerves out on to a spectacular coastal road, the Arabian Sea colossally massed on one side, corporate height and glitter arrayed on the other. 'The Queen's Necklace,' Ess confides knowledgeably. 'Marine Drive. Playground of India's hyperrich.' His breath smells thickly of alcohol. He must have had a drink or two – or three, or four – on the roof terrace after I left to Skype Alice.

We leave the cab at the edge of a complex approach system and Ess leads the way into the ethereal enormousness of the Oberoi, the wide spaces serving no visible purpose, a dish of flawless white pebbles here, a freestanding screen of trickling glass there. The place is so luxurious it seems impossible that we're not going to get kicked out. But Ess goes recklessly striding on and somehow we pass unchecked to a dim bar high above the city, its windows encompassing the splintery sickle of the lighted district below.

'Raymond! Steven!' Harry lumbers towards us with open arms. He's dressed more smartly than he was this morning, in a tweedy brown suit and a checked shirt and bootlace tie, but just the same he looks as if he's been awake for about fifteen minutes. At least the specs he's wearing are just specs, wire-rimmed, prescription-lensed.

'Isn't this place something?' he says, once we're seated at a table with our drinks – his beer, Ess's whisky, my orange juice. 'I love it, but it scares the hell out of me. I can only muster the courage to bring myself up here like once every six months. So I thought while you fine fellows were in town...'

'Oh, it's magnificent,' Ess declares, somewhat boorishly, 'but Harry, you and I must be mindful of my young associate.' He presents me, with a flourish, as if I were a sideshow exhibit. 'Remember, this is Mr Strauss's first visit. His head must be spinning. If we keep swatting him from one extreme to another like this, he may end up feeling overwhelmed.'

Harry looks at me. 'Are you feeling overwhelmed, Steven?'

I have no idea what they're talking about, but I say anyway, 'It's a lot to take in.'

'We don't want him running away with the idea that's all there is to the place, do we?' Ess says. 'Inequitable extremes. Filthy poor and filthy rich.'

'What place are we talking about now?' Harry asks, all wide-eyed innocence in his clunky prescription lenses. 'Mumbai? Maharashtra? India?'

'Mumbai. I would say Mumbai, certainly.'

'Sure.' Harry sips his beer. 'Though I do think it's kind of like that.' He looks at Ess, then at me, then at Ess again. 'Extremes. Rich and poor. I think that's kind of the deal.'

'Harry!' Ess laughs. 'We need to educate this young man. It's our duty, is it not, as his elders and… well, as his elders at least.' He veers across the table towards Harry in a way that makes me wonder just how many drinks he had while I was talking to Alice. 'Today we took a stroll along the causeway, and for some time we were shadowed by the most adorable wee beggar girl. Nothing out of the ordinary, but you should have seen this young man's face! Oh, the pain, the torment! So you see, Harry, it's nothing less than our duty to *explain* to him…'

'Yes, sir,' Harry says, folding his arms. 'Uh, what are we explaining?'

'The complex reality at work here. Certainly to the naïve eye it may appear that the city shows intolerable economic extremes, but that's only the surface. It is, let's say, even a form of theatre.

The forlorn beggar girl trailing along the street makes for a heart-rending sight, and indeed the heart of many a tourist is rent, and many a guilty rupee ends up folded into that tear-stained little hand. But it's theatre, is it not? The beggar girl is an actress. She lives in a perfectly decent home on the outskirts of Mumbai and she works for an entrepreneur who drives her to the causeway each day, fits her into her costume, daubs on her adorable smuts, even sources her props. Dozens of them, these wee actresses, walking round with babies in their arms which at the end of the day they hand back with their earnings. Which our canny entrepreneurial friend, let's not doubt, eagerly adds to his Kalashnikov fund.' Ess sits back, pleased with the comprehensiveness of his analysis. 'It's not poverty, not poverty *as such*. It's a business. It's a trick.'

For some time Harry has been nodding, as if in vigorous agreement. Then he says, 'When I first came out here I thought that way. Now I just think, "Poor's poor". I think, "What the hell. Give money".'

Ess is speechless. Then he says, 'But that's *ludicrous*.'

'You're right.' Harry makes his open-armed surrender gesture again. 'It's a trick, an illusion. What did you say? It's theatre. Last time I checked, people pay for that, right? For entertainment and all?'

For a moment Ess looks appalled. Then he throws back his whisky and starts to laugh. Harry starts to laugh too, so I start to laugh too.

Ess drinks two more glasses of whisky then teeters off to the bathroom. Harry takes out his phone. I'm happy to see that it's a piece of shit: not quite the Neolithic axe head Ess makes do with, but a good five generations behind mine. Benignly reviewing its screen, he says, 'Wow. Your boss is *bombed*, isn't he?'

'He's on holiday.'

'I thought the two of you were here on business.'

'Bit of both. Some business, some pleasure.'

'I'm not judging. I can only imagine the kind of pressure he's under. You Resolute kids must be feeling it at the moment.'

'It's a bad time for us.'

'But you'll turn it around, right?' He pats my arm without actually touching it. 'You'll weather the storm. Hold on for the safe waters and blue skies.'

'No,' I say. 'We're all going to lose our jobs.'

Ess flounders back to the table and starts telling a long, rambling story that no one listens to. Harry Altman in his wavery prescriptions is wearing a look that makes me nervous. Then, at the nearest thing to a natural break in Ess's narrative, he strikes. Eyes wide, arms folded, he shifts fractionally forward in his chair and says quietly, 'You know, I hope you don't mind my asking, but the question that most interests me is why you gentlemen are out here at all.'

'Is that so?' Ess seems surprised.

'I am really most interested in that.'

'We told you,' I say. 'Some business…'

'Some pleasure, sure. Though it's the business part that I'm really interested in. You mentioned you were here to buy…'

'Fervently so,' Ess says. '*Perfervidly* here as buyers.'

'If you don't mind my asking, here to buy what?'

'Oh,' I say, 'oh…' Suddenly I'm leaning over the table, pressing down on it with the palms of both hands. I'm trying to hide Ess, to cover him, shield him. 'I'm not sure we…'

'Now, Mr Strauss.' Ess grips my shoulder. 'This is Harry we're talking to. I think we can deal plainly with our friend Harry, can we not?'

With a woozy hand on my shoulder he signals for me to sit back down in my chair. I sit back down in my chair. There's nothing I can do, nothing to prevent this from happening, to keep Ess from making a fool of himself, from revealing to this sanctimonious old bastard what a mad and broken soul he is. I cover the bottom half of my face with my hand. I want to cover the top half of it with my other hand, but manage not to do that.

Ess smiles, goggled with drunkenness. He looks as if he might slide out of his chair at any second. 'We're here, would you believe, to buy an antigravity machine.'

Now my free hand actually flies up to cover my eyes. At the last instant I redirect it and use the fingers to scratch, stroke, soothe my horribly burning temples.

Harry blinks. Then he says, 'Okay.'

'What say you to that, Harry? What say you... to that?'

'Sure. Antigravity's an interesting field. There are some great people working in it right now. There's that Russian fellow, Podkletnov, right? Of course there's always talk about NASA... And isn't there an outfit in Switzerland that's gotten close?'

'Ah, yes,' Ess says, swilling importantly in his chair, 'plenty of people have got *close* to it. The difference is we *have* it.'

Slowly Harry smiles. Lost in the straggles of his beard, the smile is hard to make out. It's nothing, hardly anything at all. But for some reason this smile ignites in me a brief flare of panic, as if the smile is not the only thing he is hiding, as if there is something else, something important, he is concealing about his sack-like person.

I became a builder, he had said. *Among, ah, other things.*

'Well I'll be damned,' he says mildly.

Some time after midnight Ess crashes into the backseat of another yellow-hooded cab at the edge of the Oberoi's forbidding access system.

'Well I think that was a *terrific* night, don't you?' he says.

'No,' I say, 'I don't.'
'And isn't Harry just… a *lovely* man?'
'No,' I say. 'No, no, no he isn't.'

4

Next morning there's no sign of Ess at breakfast. On the roof terrace I eat a bowl of cereal, drink two cups of coffee, uncomfortably eye the hotel's other guests, a largely European middle-aged crowd, airily muttering at their tables. I overhear talk of the Bangalore bombing – the perpetrators, the death toll – but I'm not really listening. Where's Ess?

At nine, when most of the guests have already flip-flopped back across the tiles, I head down to Ess's room on the sixth floor. It takes me a long time to find the room: I've seen it only once before, late on the night that we arrived. I tap lightly on the door; get no response; tap more heavily. I'm already starting to think I may have come to the wrong room when a cleaner comes by, grinning and nodding over his broom. Pointing at the door, he says, 'Your friend? You look for your friend?' I nod and the young cleaner shakes his head and leads me with elaborate courtesy to the other end of the floor and a door I immediately recognise as Ess's. I knock and the cleaner waits with me, grinning, nodding. After a while the grin fades, the nod ceases. The cleaner continues to wait. Then he looks at me with very clear, very adult, scornful eyes – eyes that contain unimaginable pressures – and he turns and walks away, the brushes of his broom softly hissing over the tiled hallway.

Finally the door opens a crack. I glimpse a bushy eye, sense heavy breath. The eye vanishes but the sense of the breath remains as I push past into Ess's room.

45

The curtains are shut but even so I can tell the room is a lot nicer than mine – bigger, sleeker, with a smartscreen on the wall and, I suppose, a shower that dispenses hot water. Ess is already back in the bed, the plush duvet pulled up round his neck.

'Just thought I'd see how you are,' I call across to him, not sure whether or not I want to approach the bed. 'Just a bit concerned when you didn't show at breakfast.'

'Tired,' he says eventually. 'Jetlag. Catching up with me.'

A likely story. He's hungover, pure and simple.

But what I say is, 'It was bound to get you sooner or later.'

He breathes, moves under the duvet, coarsely coughs.

'So, uh, do you think you'll rest for a while?'

Another cough then a grunt yes.

'That's probably best. Should I pop back in, say, round lunchtime?'

A reedy sigh then another grunt yes.

'Oh, yeah…' I take a step towards the bed. 'Something weird happened just now. There was this cleaner…' But I dismiss the thought, retreat from the bed. 'Doesn't matter. See you at lunchtime.'

Outside on the hallway I carefully draw the door shut after me.

Jetlag! A likely story. I know a hangover when I see one.

I should be laughing my head off. But I'm not. For some reason I'm not.

I don't know exactly when Ess became ill – I doubt anyone does, even Ess, even Ess's doctors, of whom he ended up having a lot.

Things reached crisis point last July, but there had been warning signs for months before that. The first faint glimmers had appeared much earlier, even years earlier. I think I saw the start of it about the time of the Skycoach deal.

The Skycoach deal was a deal that went very badly wrong in October 2011. By then Resolute was already in serious trouble; still, dark murmurs of *the Skycoach imbroglio* or *the Skycoach fiasco* or *the Skycoach fuck-up* circulate the company corridors to this day. Ess never talks about it. The whole thing made a deep impression on him.

The worst part of it was that the Skycoach deal was Ess from start to finish: he came up with it, he sweet-talked everyone else into going with it, he hopped across the channel twice a month to exchange air-kisses with the French manufacturers and otherwise sell the idea that Resolute was the only company in the world that could build the wings their latest, greatest Skycoach iteration required and demanded – no, *deserved*.

Ess was extremely good at this sort of thing. From Resolute's earliest days he'd been the charmer, the showbiz smoothie who tempted back more than one lost contract with his too-white teeth and his baby-blue eyes. Certainly his magic was strong at Resolute and while the Skycoach deal was entering its final draft he persuaded the board to invest heavily in machinery and personnel geared specifically to the construction of the Skycoach wings. After all, the new Skycoach was going to be a behemoth – the biggest, heaviest civil airliner in history, with a tip-to-tip wingspan exceeding 78 metres and requiring wing units far larger than any Resolute had ever made. In order to build units large enough and durable enough to withstand the stresses of the new megaliner, Ess argued for an entire new assembly line as well as a dedicated team of specialist engineers. His arguments succeeded, and the board gave him what he wanted. Resolute's total investment in the still-unsigned Skycoach deal came to a little over eight million pounds.

In October 2011, after almost two years of negotiations, Skycoach invited Ess to visit its head offices in Toulouse to sign the contract and toast the beginning of a new Anglo-French partnership. In celebratory mood, he asked me to go along with him. Until then I'd never accompanied him abroad; I'd carried his folders on one- and two-day jaunts across England, but in fact the majority of my work as his PA was managing his phones and email while he was off in Saudi Arabia or somewhere, schmoozing a sheik. So the trip to Toulouse was the first, and the only other, time Ess and I went abroad together.

I am not well travelled. My family didn't take foreign holidays while I was growing up, and until I was twenty the most exotic journey I'd made had been a ten-day walking tour of the Lake District that I undertook with four friends the summer after I left school. While I was at university I went to Greece for three days with a girlfriend. That's pretty much it. Late last year I went to New York with Alice, but when Ess and I flew out to Toulouse in 2011 I had spent less than a week of my twenty-odd years anywhere that wasn't England.

It was, therefore, a fairly incredible eight days (I don't count the ninth). No doubt my inexperience of foreign parts came into it, and no doubt the Skycoach people put on a good show, but still my enduring memory is of Ess and I drifting from one sunny pleasure dome to another, drinking strong coffee, tasting strong cheese, and never paying for anything. Each day we were escorted by an elegant company representative who spoke romantically about her own dream of one day owning a vineyard in the region. In similarly romantic terms Ess praised her employers for their commitment to working with small, detail-led outfits such as Resolute, for their eschewal of the growing corporate tendency to work only with megalithic consortia, the multinational monsters crowding everyone else out of the field.

On the evening of the eighth day, reclining on the balcony of his executive suite, Ess grew especially sombre and Caesar-like. In heroic silence he sat absorbing the city. He whirled the brandy in his glass, pursed his lips. Later, maybe somewhat drunk, he began to speak in the loose philosophical vein that always betokened his deepest contentment.

On the morning of the ninth day, the day of the signing, Ess and I met for breakfast in the hotel restaurant. We were still waiting for our eggs when Ess received a call. The news came at nightmarish speed. The signing was off. The deal was off. Skycoach had decided to go another way. To give the wing contract to a well-known Anglo-Australian-American consortium. To one of the monsters.

I took the scheduled flight back to Bristol that afternoon. For two further days Ess held on in Toulouse. I don't know what he did in that time, but I imagine he did everything he could think of to persuade the Skycoach high command to reconsider, to tempt back the lost contract, as he'd done so many times before. Well, this time he didn't do it. His magic failed him and he came back to Resolute with a calm, sculpted, gradual manner that said he would now take whatever he was required to take.

Which he did. The fallout from the collapsed deal was dreadful – the company lost its millions, defaulted on several major loans and had to sack another 500 people on top of the 300 new hires who were at once redirected to the job centre – but he took it, every day, for what must have been the worst year of his life. Predictably there were calls for his resignation. But Ess wouldn't resign. If he resigned he wouldn't be able to make everything all right again. Even then there was a touch of that mania.

And yes, the deal was madness, and yes, it was Ess's fault. But the board played its part too. It shouldn't have given him what he wanted. But the board had always given him what he wanted. Because until the Skycoach deal Ess had always been right.

And anyway, like I said, Resolute was already in trouble.

What I remember most strongly from that time was the look on Ess's face in the hotel restaurant in Toulouse, when he got the call saying that the deal was off. I remember how his eyes steadied and seemed to stare right into it: Resolute's lost millions, the scrapheap of new machinery, the vanished jobs, scuttled lives. Abruptly he did his nose-twitch thing – a scurrying bob of the tip. Then he did it again. Then again, then again. After he hung up he couldn't speak to me for several seconds while the mask of his face kept sucking down into his mouth, scraping and dragging helplessly over his upper teeth. Then it decelerated and stopped and I didn't see it again, the twitch, not like that, for another two years.

And I think: was it Skycoach that broke him, or was it the way he'd always been right – the way, until he took that call in Toulouse, he had never failed?

I walk down three flights of stairs – still unable to face the lift attendant, grinning on his stool – return to my room and for an hour or so try to make sense of the document Ess and I were working on yesterday morning, the Product Development Plan, or PDP. But it's hopeless. Whatever I may have said, the PDP isn't good – isn't good at all. It doesn't help that Ess won't give me any proper numbers; but really numbers are the least of our problems. Our greatest problem is that the whole thing's gibberish. Page after page of flinty babble, like a survivalist manifesto. Not that it matters. Ess thinks that on our triumphal return to Resolute we will be expected to present the PDP to the board. Well, we won't. The board won't be expecting to see a document of any kind.

I leave the hotel, moving quickly, determined not to encounter the cleaner who gave me that weird look outside Ess's room. On the stairs I pass a pair of hotel employees, young men in overalls, carrying armloads of sheets, leaning against the wall, talking. As I take the turn onto the next set of stairs they break out simultaneously in soft laughter.

Thinking I may as well have another go at finding a present for Alice, I head to the street bazaar Ess and I explored yesterday (*the causeway*, is it called?) and stumble along between the veiled stalls, pausing now and then to let the slow, dense drifts of tourists in front of me break up and twirl apart like ice floes. I realise the only way to look at the stuff for sale is to scan the contents of each stall while more or less continuing to move past it; pause for even a second and the handsome trader jolts to his feet, spreads his arms, and then there's an awkward interval while he beckons to you and you nod and smile and wave a hand no, no, and edge your way horribly out of his orbit.

I can't see anything I want to buy, anything I want to give Alice. Is there anything here she would like me to give her? I don't know. All I know is, for Alice, objects are never just objects. She takes things in terms of their aura, their affect, their invisible, unguessable halo. In the end it doesn't matter whether I give her a diamond ring or a lump of coal; it'll still be all: *How did you feel when you bought this?* And: *But what does it mean?*

Then I have a brilliant idea. I stumble to the nearest stall and buy the first thing I see – a piece of wood about the size of a matchbox, carved into the shape of an elephant. I ask the trader what price he wants and I pay it – I don't haggle. The trader doesn't seem to be offended. He just takes my money, folds my purchase into a brown paper bag ands hands it to me. And I stumble on my way, well satisfied.

Obviously the elephant isn't a present for Alice. It's a present for Daniel, her brother. And it doesn't matter what I give Daniel, because he's seventeen and male and whatever I give him he'll examine disdainfully before chucking it into a corner of his room and saying, 'Cheers,' then making some comment about my hair loss. So no, it doesn't matter what I give Daniel. Because the present for Daniel is really a present for Alice.

I'm still feeling fairly pleased with myself – thinking what a bizarre thing it is anyway, buying presents: you buy an object from one person, with money, then you give it to another person, for *nothing* – when a kid I've never seen before comes padding along next to me with the hot murmur, 'Hash, hash, hash…' When this happened yesterday, I freaked out somewhat. Today I smile, straighten my back, declare calmly and loudly, 'No thank you,' and stride away from the kid with blithe insouciance.

I feel so great about this that on my way back to the hotel I stop at a roadside cabin and buy a packet of cigarettes. Nodding to the doorman, who appears not to notice me but goes on talking with the group of men who stand round him at all times, more hotel employees or not, who can tell, I sit on the steps and smoke a celebratory cigarette. Arriving on the roof terrace for lunch, after nine flights of stairs, I smoke another one.

A little after twelve I take a cup of coffee and a plate of dal and rice down to Ess's room. My cautious knock is met with his smart: 'Come!'

Inside Ess is a different man. He's sitting up in bed, smiling broadly in his reading glasses, a book in his lap. When he sees the cup and the plate, he puts his book aside and rubs his hands together.

'Fabulous! Just what the doctor ordered. Do you think you could possibly open the curtains? I've been delaying the inevitable, but I think my poor peepers may finally be back up to snuff… Ah! That wasn't so bad. And could you fetch my briefcase? It's there. Yes, there. And my laptop, possibly? Just next to it. Yes, there.'

All at once feeling sick, I fetch his briefcase and laptop and place them next to him on the duvet while he gulps his coffee and stirs up his dal and rice. I stand there feeling sick.

'Going to do some work, are you?' I ask.

'I may have a wee potter. I'm sure I'm past the worst of it, the exhaustion, the jetlag, but best to play safe. I want to be in tip-top condition for Asha when she joins us.'

'That's if she's not delayed again.'

'Banish the thought from your mind.' He snorts. 'No, I'll just have another couple of hours in bed. Take it a bit easy, have a poke about, see what's new.'

'Oh yeah? Anything in particular?'

'Not really. Just check in, see what's afoot in the world.' With a fingernail he taps the edge of his laptop. He smiles broadly. 'Is that all right with you?'

'Hey? Oh, sure. That's fine. That's fine with me.'

'He'll look.'

'He *won't* look.'

This was Martin Cantor, a week ago, in the Playpen.

'He may be mad,' I said, 'but he's not *mental*. He's high functioning. He's not just going to forget about this place. He'll *look*.'

'I don't think he will. I think once you're out there he's going to be so caught up, he simply won't think of it.' Cantor leaned forward. 'And if he does, if he does look, if he sees what's happening, fine. Put him on the phone. I'll deal with it.'

Yeah, I thought, great: if Ess goes mooching online and sees what you're doing to Resolute, you're a voice on the phone. While I'm there, on the ground, in the flesh. Not quite the same... But I knew Cantor wasn't really a bad bloke. He wasn't malicious, didn't mean Ess any harm. He genuinely believed that what he was doing was the right thing to do, the best thing for Ess, for Resolute, for everyone. He'd told himself this and told himself this until he had no choice but to believe it. And he did. He genuinely did.

For weeks I'd been trying to play a similar trick on myself. So far I'd not managed it. At some point the story I kept telling myself always stalled, froze, or revealed itself as only one of many stories that could be woven out of the same set of facts. The fact of Ess, the fact of Ess's illness, of his delusion, and his colleagues' priorities...

'Let me give you a number.' Cantor now took my phone from me, slashed it open with a fingertip and started typing. 'Anything makes you uneasy, you call me on this number straight away. I don't want you imagining even for one second you're on your own out there with him. Anything makes you less than a million per cent easy, you call this number.'

But I wasn't listening. Something else had occurred to me. 'How are we going to pay for stuff?'

'What's that?' He tossed my phone back, making me fumble for it.

'Well, you're not giving him any money, are you? The code, the company account... it's all bullshit, isn't it?'

Cantor looked confused. Then he said, 'Ray's paying. Same as always. Didn't you know about this?' When it was clear I didn't, he went on, 'Ray always pays. For his trips and so on. He won't claim expenses. Hasn't done in years. I offered him a travel budget but he wouldn't have it. He said to me, "Martin, there's a reason why it's called *petty* cash." He's covering the trip out of his own pocket, the flights, the hotel, this guide person you're hiring, everything.' Leaning forward again, Cantor invited me into a smirking confidence. 'You know Ess doesn't take a salary, don't you? He just comes in and does whatever he does, basically, for free. Little arrangement he's had for years. Going back to the Skycoach thing. The Skycoach fuck-up.'

Cantor seemed to expect me to be amused by this. But I wasn't amused. I was appalled, aghast.

Seeing my expression, he went on, more coolly, 'I wouldn't worry about Ray. He's done all right for himself over the years.'

Of course he had. It was well and widely known that at an early point in Resolute's success Ess had, in what many understood as a gesture of flagrant corporate disloyalty, sold a significant number of his shares in the company. Well, he was a founder; the shares only existed because he – and three other guys – had caused them to exist; he could do what he wanted with them. The sale had anyway amassed him a stupendous profit, and it was well and widely known also that Ess had in short order speculated this profit into a still more stupendous personal fortune. Until the dark days of Skycoach, this profit, this fortune had been the thing about Ess that everyone at Resolute most enjoyed talking about. Round the coffee nooks and the copier cubbies you heard regular mumbles about 'Raymond Ess's millions' or 'Raymond Ess's billions' or 'Raymond Ess's gazillions'.

It was bollocks – obvious bollocks, as Ess was himself the first to point out. He didn't have gazillions, and he didn't have billions. There was, however, a real possibility that he had millions.

Cantor seemed to assume that I shared the general disdain for Ess's wealth – where it came from, how he got it – and his eyes as he spoke to me seemed to contain a certain icy inflection. I shrugged, tried to smile. I don't think I did a good job of any of this.

Later, as he was genially showing me out of his office, Cantor said, 'Help me out. Did I just never notice it before, or did Ray come back from India with a thing for classical music? Whenever I see him now he's humming classical music.'

'Oh,' I said, 'yeah. He's always liked his classical music.'

'Can't believe I never noticed that before.'

It wasn't true. Cantor was right: since his return to work, Ess had been striding about the place humming bits of Mozart, bits of Wagner. However, he didn't do this because he liked classical music; as far as I knew, Ess didn't particularly like any kind of music. He did it to fill his own ears, to block out all sound, to make sure he couldn't hear what people were saying about him as he passed them on the company corridors.

As soon as I can get away, I leave Ess's room, stamp down the three flights of stairs to my own room and sit on the bed frantically thinking.

Let me give you a number, Cantor said. *Anything makes you uneasy, you call me on this number straight away.* Am I uneasy? I am. But I'm not sure this is what he meant.

I open my tablet, try to get online. No luck. The hotel wifi connection, which behaved so beautifully while Alice and I Skyped last night, has vanished without a trace.

I leave my room, stamp down the three flights of stairs to the reception area and ask the man at the desk what's going on with the wifi. The man assures me that nothing is going on with the wifi. I tell him I couldn't find the connection, open my tablet to show him, open the wifi options pane, and sure enough there's the connection.

'That wasn't there before,' I say.

Lightly grizzled, middle-aged, the man asks if I've purchased today's passcode. I tell him I don't know what he's talking about: the guy who was here yesterday just gave me the code. The man offers apologies on behalf of his colleague and explains that the passcode changes every day. And is purchasable, for a small fee.

I'd argue the toss, but I'm panicking too much. With a burning-at-the-neck sensation that says I'm being ripped off,

I pay the fee, get the code. The second I move away from the desk the connection drops out.

As I step round the reception area, tablet held high, a step sideways, a step forward, as if learning the sequence of a dance, I suppose that if I'm having this much trouble getting online, Ess surely won't manage it at all. Then again, he's been here before. He knows the hotel, the staff, everyone here is his friend. No doubt the wifi connection is his friend too.

I'm outside again, standing on the steps with the turbaned doorman and his gang, by the time the connection reappears. The wifi icon swells; I open the internet and with a surge it rushes up, photos, headlines, polls, live feeds.

I sit on the steps. I root through my pockets, find my cigarettes, light one with a trembling hand. Then I summon the search box, type in 'Resolute Aviation' and hit GO.

When I last made this search – not quite two days ago, in an unsuspected well of wifi at Doha airport, while Ess was off somewhere, befriending tourist or business traveller – there was nothing to see, or nothing out of the ordinary. Not so now. It seems that matters have moved on. Because now there's all this:

RESOLUTE IN ADMINISTRATION.
RESOLUTE IN DISSOLUTION.
RESOLUTE GOES UNDER.
RESOLUTE GIVES WAY.
RESOLUTE BREATHES LAST.
RESOLUTE R.I.P.

5

I'm still sitting there when Harry comes by. Without looking up from the screen I watch him lumber towards the hotel, pause to check the nameplate on the gatepost, make to walk past me into the hotel then swerve back when he recognises me. For a few seconds we both pretend we haven't seen each other; I stare at my screen with a probably overdone look of intentness while he looms on the pavement, frowning up at the hotel, hands in pockets. Then he says, 'Steven! I didn't see you there!'

I glance up at him. 'Hello, Harry. What are you up to?'

'Wasn't I invited for lunch?'

'Were you?'

'Wasn't I?' He waits for me to help, but I don't. 'Raymond was kind of hammered last night. Maybe he doesn't remember.'

'Maybe he didn't invite you.'

Harry frowns at me. 'That's certainly another possibility.' Then he nods, somewhat formally, and makes again to walk past me. 'Is he inside?'

'He's in bed. He's not well.'

'That's too bad.' Harry stands with his hands in his pockets, frowning now down at the ground, now again up at the hotel. Then he brings his frown back level with me and says, 'I guess that means you're at a loose end? With Raymond indisposed.'

The reply that comes to mind is 'I wouldn't say that', with some self-important hefting of my *cute* tablet, but now the opportunity is there I find I don't actually want to brush Harry off. So what I say instead is, 'Looseish. Why'd you ask?'

59

'I thought I was invited for lunch. I've an empty belly and no one to eat with.' He mimes dejection, despair, with alarming physical fluency. 'Come on, soldier, quit your post. Join me for a bite.' He tips his head towards the street. 'What do you say?'

'I should hang on here. He's pretty ill.'

'He can't spare you for an hour?'

'We're expecting Asha...'

'I solemnly promise I will take you someplace *quite* interesting.'

'Why are we having this conversation? I've already eaten.'

'Come watch me eat. You won't be disappointed.'

'By watching you eat?'

'By where you'll do it.'

I hesitate. As it happens I've a good reason to go with Harry, which is the fact that for several minutes everything I've read about Resolute has been making me want to flee, to run away from Ess and the hotel, anywhere, with anyone. But that's not why I'm hesitating, not why I'm even thinking about doing this.

I'm still hesitating when it seems I'm also standing, shutting my tablet and slipping it into my bag, saying, 'Why not? I'm hungry again anyway.'

Then we have an even more bizarre conversation.

As we reach the causeway Harry says, 'So, Steven Strauss. What kind of man are you?' I look at him and he's grinning in a way that shows he knows exactly how bizarre this question is. I play along, sort of.

'I'm not sure how to answer that. Can you be more specific?'

'Are you married?'

'Nope. I have someone, but... I'm not married.'

'How about Raymond?'

'Married? He used to be. Not any more.'

'I'm sorry to hear that. Does he "have someone" too?'

'You'd have to ask him that.' The truth is I don't know. 'What about you, Harry? Are you married? Do you have someone?'

'Oh, no. No on both counts, sadly.' He laughs. The grin of bizarreness has sunk into his face. He seems unable to form an expression that doesn't contain some wicked trace of it. 'You guys have different voices, accents...?' he says.

'We're from different parts of the country. Uh, England.' It's true: Ess is from Yeovil, the rural south, while I'm from a large, ugly town in Lancashire, the urban north.

'And your names... you won't mind my saying you guys have some crazy names. I mean "Ess". Raymond *Ess*. How does a person end up with a name like "Raymond Ess"?'

'I don't know. You'd have to ask him.' At this point I decide I'm not above having a bit of fun with Harry. I say, 'It could be some ancient, ancestral English name. He could be descended from an earl or something.'

'Do you think so?' Harry aims for a tone of polite interest, but in his lensed eyes it's all there: *Magna Carta. Downton Abbey.*

'I wouldn't put it past him.' In fact I know it isn't the case. Ess is not descended from an earl, or anything like one. 'People have all sorts of crap in their background once you go looking for it. The question is: Why would you bother?'

'You don't think it's important? The background, the history...?'

'Why would I? What does it matter?'

'Good for you.' Harry nods vigorously. 'Who needs it, right? History's a pain in the ass. These days what even is it? It's Nazis versus zombies, it's cowboys versus aliens, it's entertainment, it's a movie.' Warming to his theme, he shakes one hand out of its pocket and raises it rhetorically. 'Not that I'm against that. Bring it on, I say. Let's be a species that lives without history. Let's put all that nonsense behind us, all those claims, those ties, those burdens… Let's be a species that watches movies and, you know, doesn't *give* a shit.'

'Harry,' I say, 'you're a nutty guy.' In fact I've taken in barely a word he was saying.

'Why thank you, kind sir.' He laughs, a short, shrill sound, like a sneeze.

As we walk along I find I don't mind Harry so much after all. His straggly, anoraky presence is both irritating and curiously lulling. His size makes you think he's going to be clumsy but it turns out his movements are confident, almost graceful. Despite his age – he must be at least seventy – he's full of stealth and speed; the lumbering walk and frowning, elderly pauses are a sort of act. But what sort of act?

The question engages me only briefly. If Harry is a problem, he's not a major one.

'So!' he says. 'You kids are buying an antigravity machine!'

'You'd have to ask the boss about that.'

'Did you mention something earlier about Asha…?'

I did. I recall the slip bitterly. But what the hell does any of it even matter?

(It does. It does matter. Obviously it matters.)

'Great lady,' he blusters on, 'model employee, but not what you'd call on open book. Can you believe she hasn't told me *one thing* about you guys? About you or your business here? Not in all this time. And so, I think understandably, over our fascinating conversation last night, my interest is more than a little piqued.'

'Again,' I say. 'You should take it up with the boss.'

'Sure.' Harry breathes loudly through his nose: more old-guy theatrics. Now I've noticed it I can't stop. 'You're very loyal to Raymond, aren't you, Steven?'

'Am I?'

'That's what strikes me about you.' The grin seems finally to have drained from his face. His mouth is serious, almost grim, in the wild twists of his beard. 'You are strikingly loyal to your boss. Why is that, do you think?'

'Oh, well, you know,' I say. 'We've a lot of history.'

We do. Part of it is this.

One Saturday morning four years ago I woke up to find myself lying in a hospital bed. Ess was sitting in a chair next to me. I couldn't get over the way he was dressed. More than anything else – the bed, the room, the medical clutter, monitors, breathing equipment – what astonished me was the sight of his jeans, his patterned jumper, his open-necked shirt. I'd never seen his weekend attire before, and it was incredibly exciting.

'Mr Strauss!' he said, seeing I was awake. 'How are you feeling?'

'Not sure,' I replied. Speaking was difficult. As if I were having to operate my lips and tongue by remote control.

'That's all right.' He looked tired. His eyelids were red, his cheeks gritty, glittery with stubble. There was also something subtly wrong with his hair. 'By any chance do you know what's happened to you?'

I didn't. My mind contained only images. Night sky, slumbrous cloud. Carious brick and haggard tarmac. A street of wheeling light, of scrambling levels of brilliance – takeaway neon, slot-machine spangle – suddenly rising, suddenly falling.

'It seems you've had an accident,' Ess said then, with an air of delirious forced jollity. 'Actually there's no *seems* about it, you've had an accident. You were struck by a car. Late last night. Do you remember that?'

Did I? There was something: a distant sensation of force, of massive displacement, glancing volume.

'You were in town late last night. You were crossing a road, a side street... Not that there's anything to worry about. I want to make that absolutely clear. Any minute now one of the quacks'll

63

come in and say the same thing. You're going to be rather sore, probably going to feel like you've been roughed up for a couple of days, headaches, bruises, that sort of caper. But nothing broken, thank goodness. Just a touch of, let's say, *joggling about*. A modicum of joggling about to your back, to give it its technical name, but no cause for concern whatsoever. You're going make what's called "a full recovery".'

I tried to nod, but this was difficult to do too. I wasn't in any pain; for now my main sensation was one of lightness. My whole body felt light, insubstantial, its separate parts independently fluttering and flickering.

'The important thing now is to get you well again. Take it from me, that's priority one. Any minute now your mum and dad are going to waltz in here with some corroborative quack, and don't worry, at that point I'll give you some peace. I only want to make sure you know that whatever it takes, however long it takes, we're all in this with you.'

Ess paused. While I waited I seemed to rise towards the ceiling, which was covered with thousands of shiny dark specks. But were the specks on the ceiling or inside my eyes?

'Naturally I'm referring to this, to the accident. But also to the other matter.'

I looked at him, his clenched and priestly face, his streaked eyelids, his sandpapery cheeks. An agonising thought occurred to me. Had he been sitting there *all night*?

'We're going to do everything we can. Resolute, the board, the entire company. Because we care about you, because we love you, and from now until you don't need us any more, this is priority one.'

*

I'm about to ask Harry if we're far from this interesting lunch venue he's promised me when he steps off the pavement and waves for me to follow him along a narrow, stone-walled alleyway. I hesitate, my feet teetering on broken stones, then follow.

After several worrying turns the alleyway opens out on to a large, surprisingly quiet and leafy square enclosed by high walls and dominated on one side by a construction site. The rest of it is scorched earth, bright clay, a dazzlingly complicated tree. At first the eerie hush of the place makes me think Harry and I must be here alone. Then I see we are not.

'What do you think?' he asks, with a sweep of his hand at the construction site. It's not immediately clear whether something is being put up or taken down, built or unbuilt.

'What am I looking at?'

'My pride and joy, my labour of love, my pet project and old-man's folly. Otherwise known as The Harry Altman School for Wayward Girls.' He laughs, then adds with a startled look, 'That's a joke. I mean it's going to be a school. The wayward girls thing, that's a joke. Let's have a look around.'

As we approach the site we pass groups of young men sitting quietly in the square, to whom Harry calls with a raised hand of greeting. The men look up at him, nod then look away. Harry stops to talk to one man in particular, the site foreman, or 'the redoubtable Rajeev'. Harry introduces us, and Rajeev nods and smiles to me pleasantly enough, and we shake hands, me stooping while he continues to sit with his friends. Harry asks Rajeev if he could be prevailed upon to find us some lunch, and Rajeev nods easily.

Harry and I pass on to the site. Up close, there's not a lot more to see than vague depths of foundations, bags of cement, piles of tubing. Still, Harry insists on directing my attention to various blocks of unoccupied air while saying stuff like, 'Here's the kitchen' and 'There's the nursery' and 'Over yonder, note the sanctuary of the staff room' until I have no choice but to take a step back, breathing noisily through my lips.

'Sorry, Harry. Don't know you're talking about. I can't see it.'

'Ah!' He is triumphant. 'Because it's not there! And what on earth can we do about that?' He rubs his face eagerly. 'I'll show you what.'

Harry now leads me to one of three prefabricated offices on the edge of the site. The office contains a couple of garden chairs and a card table with a laptop on it. The laptop is connected to an unfamiliar chunk of hardware – a sort of steely microscope.

'You know what this is?'

'No idea what that is.'

'Then allow me to show you.' He fiddles with the laptop then turns back to me grinning. 'Sit, sit. You'll want to see this.'

We sit in the garden chairs. For a while there's nothing to see. Then with an abrupt bony click the barrel of the microscope-looking thing descends and its tip starts darting about on its platform – extruding, fusing, hectically welding.

Twenty minutes later Harry goes to the microscope, which has retracted its barrel with a series of further bony clicks, and he takes something from the platform. The something is bright green, plastic, about the size of a paperback book. It is a slightly warm, stunningly detailed model of an American-suburb style junior school.

'3D printout.' Harry smiles. 'The architect, old pal of mine, Belgian guy, he sends an email. He sits in his office in Brussels and he sends like *a zip file*. And we hit a button here and we just print it right out. A sketch, a model, a working design in three dimensions.'

'It's fantastic,' I say, turning the model between my hands. It is.

'Soon it won't be just models we're getting this way. In a couple more years, it'll be the buildings. We'll hit a button and we'll print out the whole building. The whole street. The whole city.' He takes the model from me and examines it, his smile as he admires the thing obscurely melancholy, as if his own thought has unexpectedly saddened him. I feel I should comfort him, console him, though I don't do this.

We leave the office. Harry directs me to sit in another garden chair under the tree at the centre of the square, disappears into the site and returns a few minutes later with two plastic thimbles of undrinkably hot chai and a paper plate heaped with chutney sandwiches. As Harry settles into a chair next to me, I wonder what happened to the redoubtable Rajeev. Then I see him, sitting on the other side of the square exactly as we saw him last, cross-legged on the earth in a circle of friends.

I take one sip of the chai then set the little cup on the ground and don't touch it again. I pick up one of the sandwiches, notice its garish two-tone filling – pink and green – and at once return it to the plate. Meanwhile Harry eats with relish. He chews carefully but quickly, with avid method, as if trying to discover a free gift hidden in his food.

'What do you do here?' I ask him. 'You yourself?'

'I like to think I'm pretty hands-on. Though I guess my role is primarily, uh, financial.' He chuckles through his food. 'I know what you're thinking: privileged, bleeding-heart, do-good American asshole blowing his dough on never-gonna-happen public venture. Tossing his money into the black hole of Indian inefficiency. That's what you're thinking, right?'

'I'm not thinking anything.'

'I know how it looks. These guys, they know how it looks too. That's why they make it look this way.' He throws back the chai as if it's a shot of whisky. 'I come by here maybe twice a week. Every time I come, this is what I see. Guys sitting on the ground, no work, nothing happening. Then I take a look around. And because I know what I'm looking at, I know what I'm seeing. And generally what I'm seeing is two weeks' work. Achieved in two, three days.' He smiles. 'I just don't see it happen. They don't let me. And why should they? Why should they put themselves on the line like that for some fat old loudmouth who shows up waving his cheque-book and saying, "Hey guys, how about we build a school"? If anyone can take credit here, it's Rajeev. He's the one making this project work. He they trust. They see what he's trying to achieve.'

I look again at Rajeev, talking and laughing with his friends. From where I'm sitting, he doesn't appear to be trying to achieve very much.

I say, 'How does doing a day's work put anyone on a line?'

'What's a day's work?' Harry laughs. 'For these guys it's more than a day's work. It's an attempt on the future, an assay on the future. A project like this asks you to believe the world can be a better place in the future than it is now, and a lot of these guys aren't easy with believing that. They know the hazards of building in this city. They know better than anyone what happens when a thing you put up comes down again. So they're like "Don't give me that shit". You know? They're like "Don't give me that hope shit".'

On the other side of the square Rajeev and his friends climb to their feet and begin passing a football between them. For a while the young men only knock the ball loosely back and forth, then as others join them they form teams and re-engage in sharper tussles, running, tackling, shooting, their feet and the ball lost in an ankle-height cloud of dust.

It's only a matter of time before the ball comes my way. I've been nervous ever since it appeared, sure at any second it's going to smash into the back of my head, so I'm relieved when instead it comes trickling to my feet. The men pause to look at me, to see what I'll do. Their looks are expectant, without hostility. I stand and kick the ball to Rajeev. He lifts the ball onto his head and butts it back to me. I return it with a clap of my forehead and then I'm running, leaving the shade of the tree and sprinting out into the afternoon sunshine, into the figures of the game, accepting a pass, escaping a tackle.

It helps that I'm a fucking brilliant football player. But Rajeev and his friends are fairly decent too, by which I mean they're all better than I am. Only Harry is definitely worse than I am. He throws himself about, howls a lot, falls over a lot, soon develops a dangerous scaly redness and has to settle for shouting encouragement from his chair in the shade.

Rajeev is my team captain; he establishes this by pointing at me then holding his fist to his chest. I nod. Rajeev is my team captain.

We play for an hour or so. The other team wins, despite Rajeev scoring four goals. I score none, though I have one pretty near miss, a helter-skelter attempt, my shot making the keeper leap, though at the last instant he stabs the ball away with a fingertip. Players on both sides clap. I assume they're applauding the keeper then hands start beating my back. Grinning, Rajeev nods to me. Panting, grinning, the heat starting to get a grip on my head, I nod back. Rajeev is my captain.

'Something weird happened this morning,' I say to Harry, when we're both sitting under the tree again. I'm aware that I'm speaking to him as I used to speak to Ess – as if he were the fount of all wisdom. I don't like it but I can't seem to help myself.

'Oh yes?' Harry says.

'There was this cleaner. At the hotel. We talked for a bit then he wouldn't leave me alone. He just stood there. Then he gave me this look, like…'

'Did he assist you in any way?'

'Well, yeah, he…'

'He was waiting for a tip.'

'It wasn't anything like that. I was looking for a room, and…'

'Guy was waiting for a tip.'

'That's… not really *on*, is it?'

Harry spreads his arms. 'You know how much those guys are paid?'

'No, I know, but… it's not like that's *my* fault, is it? Christ.'

'Is it his fault?'

'No, obviously not, but still. *Christ*…' I'm about to elaborate when my phone rings. I dig it out of my pocket. Ess.

'Where are you?' he says. 'Never mind, I don't care. Get back here. Get back to the hotel. Right now.'

6

I settle the fare, ricochet out of the cab and scuttle up the steps, past the doorman, into the hotel reception area, where Ess is waiting for me. I'm expecting a tower of wrath, a column of flame, but in fact he seems pleased to see me. Beaming in a shiny white suit with a black pinstripe, the cravat and the red leather shoes back in place, all spirited arm movements and postural buoyancy, he's unrecognisable as the bed-ridden invalid I visited this afternoon. It's a couple of seconds at least before I notice there's a woman with him.

'Asha Jarwal,' Ess says, bowing to the woman, 'it is my great and somewhat belated pleasure to introduce Steven Strauss. Steven Strauss, Asha Jarwal.'

Asha Jarwal: our guide out of the city, into the countryside. She's here.

'Nice to meet you, Steven,' Asha says, offering me her hand.

'Delighted to make your acquaintance,' I mutter, taking it.

My first impression is that she's very glamorous, in a shapeless ornate white-and-gold trouser suit, with a tiny gold handbag, high white heels, numerous sparkly accessories and rather thick and dusky makeup. She could be any age – twenty, forty-five.

My second impression is that she's very serious. Under the makeup her face is grim, the mouth set and the eyes gravely electric, as if she's already annoyed with someone. Her hair is a spiral of lively sheen, but pinned back, elaborately constricted. It must hurt her, pull on her scalp, every time she turns her head.

71

Incongruously, on a strap round her neck she carries a large old-fashioned-looking camera – mechanical, manual, possibly predigital.

Ess says, 'I believe they're ready for us upstairs, so what say we head up for a spot of dinner, then repair to the conference room for a late last sort of a briefing?'

For the second night running, dinner on the roof terrace is a muted affair. Amid the urban sparkles Ess does his best, embarking on any number of funny stories and shared recollections, but neither Asha nor I quite takes up his rhythm and time and again the only other sound is the click of a fork on a plate. While Ess speaks, Asha with a preoccupied air tilts her head suavely from side to side. It takes me almost the whole meal to realise that the gesture doesn't mean she's disagreeing with him. But what does it mean?

The conference room turns out to be a small dining room on the ground floor with a dinner table and a flip chart in it. Asha takes from her tiny handbag a cube of paper which folds out into a map like a blown-up photograph of a French cheese. She flattens the map down onto the table and she and Ess begin discussing it, leaning together, shoulders almost touching, her lavish red nails stabbing one point after another. They both speak the name of the place I know we're going to, a word I've heard many times but never seen written down, a word that starts with a P and has two or maybe three syllables. I'm still trying to catch the word, to form a picture of it, when Asha says, 'Beyond this, we'll just have to see what we find on the ground.'

Ess nods. I nod too. I'm still nodding when I say, 'Wait. What was that?'

'I said we can't speak too confidently about the terrain until we've seen it.' She glances at Ess with a knowing smile. It's the first smile of hers I've seen yet.

'So you've not seen the terrain?' I try, quite hard, to assume a neutral expression, wide-eyed, high-shouldered. 'You've never been there?'

'That's correct. When would I have been there?' Again she glances at Ess for support, which he all too happily supplies.

'Well,' I say, rather less neutrally, 'I don't know, when *would* you have been there? You're guiding us to this place, might it not've been an idea to… find it?'

'I've located the place. I've considered every detail of Raymond's narrative, and I've located our destination precisely and without the least possibility of error.'

'But you've never been there.'

'No. I've never been there.' Asha glares at me across the little dinner table. The contained charge of her eyes.

Then Ess says, 'I don't think we have any reason to doubt that Asha knows where we're going. Didn't you hear what she said? She knows *the story*.'

The story of how Ess met Tarik Kundra.

Once upon a time there was a successful businessman named Raymond Ess. One year he took a break from work and travelled far and wide about India, visiting its cities and exploring its landscape. When the time came that he wished to travel still more broadly, in Mumbai he contacted a back street tour company named Adventurers whose representative Asha Jarwal (after raising a finger and hissing at him, jabbing out the final characters of a report she was writing, and turning back to him with an unforgettable smile) escorted him on a projected thirty-day trek into the polleny wilds.

The trek began well, proceeding over broad plains under blue skies. Then, a little after two o'clock in the afternoon of day eight, Ess and Asha found themselves imprisoned by an entirely unpredictable swathe of monsoon weather. The two were swept apart. By the time the rain ceased Ess had been driven out alone to the bleakest part of the plain.

For forty days and forty nights – well, two days and a night – he wandered the plain without glimpsing another human being. Soon his supply of food ran out. Then his water ran out. For most of the second day he walked practically on his knees, his lips blistered with thirst. At some point he lost consciousness.

When he awoke he was lying on scorched earth in bright sunlight. A young man in a blazing white kurta and fashionably blocky, black-framed spectacles was standing over him, head at an angle, hands in pockets. This was Tarik Kundra.

Some time later Ess perceived that the young man was carrying him. This wouldn't have been especially difficult (Ess was light, the young man strong) but still Ess sensed that his saviour had taken on in him a burden more than physical.

They came to a metallic cabin with the look of an abandoned electricity sub-station. It was surrounded by smaller, rougher wooden sheds. This lonely cluster of buildings at the centre of the plain was Tarik Kundra's home, his test site, his priest hole.

For three days Tarik nursed the sickly Ess, and during this time the men came to know each other well. Not that Tarik was eager, at first, to surrender his secrets. When Ess asked him why his quarters in the cabin were crammed with packets of dry food, industrial quantities of rice and beans, Tarik's flippant first reply was that he was holding tight for the apocalypse. Later, however, he explained the far stranger and sadder truth.

Tarik was a scientist – in his own words, a 'technologist' – and after graduating from an elite Indian university that he wouldn't name he worked for three years at an elite Indian company that he wouldn't name either. His work for the unnamed company involved him in researching new technologies; and yet, as he took pains to point out, when his breakthrough came, it had nothing to do with the work he'd performed in his contract. The breakthrough work was a hobby, until all at once it became something else.

That night Tarik showed Ess what his hobby had become: against the vast canvas of the black sky, he demonstrated his wonderful, impossible machine.

He pointed out further that in inventing the machine he had more or less signed his own death warrant. Before his employers could discover his invention, steal it from him and kill him, he had fled to this lost place on the plain. The cabin, the sheds and a rasping stretch of river a few hundred yards away had been his entire existence for almost a year. He expected it would remain so, now, until he died.

Ess begged to differ. He made it clear to Tarik that he was interested in his machine; that it was, indeed, exactly what he'd been looking for. Offers were made, and rejected. Suggestions met with accusations, assurances likewise. For many days and nights the two men talked, argued, drank. They each punched the other at least half a dozen times.

Finally Tarik was ready to trust him. Ess persuaded him of what in any other setting would have been self-evidently true: that he, Raymond Ess, was a man of power and means and Tarik could trust him when he said he would not only keep his location a secret, not only return and pay him handsomely for his machine, but also provide safe passage out of India so that Tarik could escape his enemies and begin a new life in any corner of the globe.

'Just you see,' Ess had told him. 'Sit tight and I'll be back here with the money for you one month from now. Maybe two.'

'Two months,' Tarik had said, confirming nothing, merely repeating the words.

At last the two new friends parted. Tarik pointed him in the direction of a nearby town and almost two months after he'd vanished in the monsoon Ess was reunited with Asha at a crowded and joyous Mumbai bus station.

Except it's not true. None of that happened.

Or *most of it* didn't happen. Until recently I've assumed that the story was cut whole from the cloth of Ess's insanity. Now I know that Asha Jarwal exists, is in some sense a real person, I'm having to make a few adjustments.

Okay. He hired a guide, travelled the wilds, got lost in a monsoon. Two months later he resurfaced at a bus station with an astonishing story. This much I can accept.

Or can I? In the dining room Asha announces with a brisk air of prearrangement that our car is due to arrive at any moment. I ask which car and she says the car that's going to take us out – out into the Mumbai night. Ess nods eagerly.

I try to cry off: I have my Skype call to Alice in fifteen minutes.

'We can wait,' Asha says. She regards me steadily. I look right back at her, look her a look that asks: *What are you up to? What are you doing, with this delicate man and his fanciful stories?* And: *What are you? Friend or foe?*

'Can't talk for long,' I tell Alice's face in the screen. 'The guide's here.'

'Oh yeah? What's she like?'

'She's doing my fucking head in, is what she's like. We're going out, apparently. It's all arranged. Because *Asha* says. Because *the guide* says.'

'Mmn. I suppose this means you're in business? So to speak.'

'We hit the road in the morning. "At first light", whenever the fuck that is.'

'And you're cool with this. Just taking it in stride.'

76

'I'm going off my nut.'

'Yeah, that's what I...' Her face bats kinetically in the screen. More shifting about on the ghost couch. 'All right, Jug-head. What's bugging you? Is it this Asha, or...?'

'It's the whole fucking thing. Tomorrow we go tearing off into the countryside... then what? We go round in circles with Ess scratching his head and mumbling, "It may have been here" and "Or maybe it was here"... until what? We run across some random hovel in the wilds and he says "Yes! This is the place! Now we must wait until my good friend Tarik returns from his travels." And we wait... and we wait...'

'Do you know how you should think about this situation?'

'Tell me how I should think about this situation.'

'What's the alternative?'

'How do you mean?'

'Just that. Can you imagine any way you might have told Ess no, any way you might have refused to go with him? Because whatever happened he was taking this trip. Would you have let him go on his own?'

'Obviously not.'

But the question and my answer both unnerve me. Why *am* I here? Because Ess asked me to come here with him? Or because Martin Cantor did?

'There you are then,' she says. 'Just make sure you watch your step with this Asha. We both know what you're like.'

'Do we?'

'Well, this Asha sounds quite full-on. And you can be... funny about that, can't you?'

'Can I?'

'Oh, come on. You remember how you were about... Marie, was it?'

'Asha's not anything like Marie. '

'Remember when you had to go back under her yoke? You hated it. What did I have to keep telling you? "She's not 'bossy', she's your boss." And with what relief you went back to Ess…'

'That's bollocks,' I say. And it is. Marie was my boss when I started at Resolute, in the pool of HR, and I didn't mind her at all. Just the same, I've never pretended that I wasn't happy when Ess chose me to replace his retiring former assistant (an utterly frightful old crow called Ginger, who loved him, rapturously and ravenously, and hated everyone else). Not that there was any sense of special preference in his choice: he just came into the office one day, did *eeny-meeny-mo* with his eyes, then nodded at me and said, 'You'll do.' Of course I was happy; Marie in HR was Marie in HR, but Ess was *Ess*. And yes, a couple of times last year, while Ess was ill and then later while he was away on sabbatical (exploring the Indian subcontinent – getting lost in monsoons, meeting inventors), I did briefly return to HR and the temporary line management of Marie.

And it was fine. Alice doesn't know what she's talking about. She can be going off only whatever I told her at the time, and I never told her that I didn't like working for Marie. I did like it. Or, well, I didn't mind it.

'That's absolute bollocks,' I say, because it is.

'Admit it. You get funny about women, don't you? You don't like it when women tell you what to do.'

I stare at her. Unmoored, adrift: I get what? I don't like what?

'I'm right, aren't I?' She sends her eyebrows up with her voice. 'There's no shame in it, not any more. You're just one of those blokes who get slightly twitchy when it's a bird calling the shots. I'm right though, aren't I?'

'No,' I say. 'You're not.'

I'm annoyed, and Alice can see that I am. She sighs, somewhat heavily; her eyes cast about for something to do with all the wideness that has ended up stranded in them. She was teasing me, winding me up, and we both know it, but somehow we're trapped on opposite sides of what this knowledge represents.

'Well,' she says, 'never mind. The main thing is I'm not worried about you. I've been thinking about it, and I've decided I'm not worried about you *at all*. You're a capable guy. You'll make sure everyone's fine, you'll look after Ess, keep an eye on him, keep your fizzy eye on him, and whatever comes along you'll deal with it.' Will I? This doesn't sound much like me. 'And anyway,' she's going on, 'I still reckon you're going to get there, meet this inventor chap, buy his machine and come back, oh, richer than Warren Buffet. Richer than Bill Gates!'

She laughs. *Ho ho ho.*

Yes, Alice still thinks a deal could happen. She doesn't know that we've come to India without any money – that Resolute gave us a dummy code for a bogus account and we don't have a company penny. Somehow that detail didn't quite reach her.

I tell myself I'm protecting her, but it's not true. I'm protecting myself.

While she thinks I might not lose my job, while she thinks I might come back from my business trip richer than Warren Buffet, richer than Bill Gates...

Still fairly surly, not yet committed to trying to recover the conversation, I say, 'I got Dan a present.'

'Lucky Dan. What did you get me?'

'It's an elephant. Wooden elephant about yay big.'

'Yeah, but what did you get me?'

'I've not, uh, as yet...'

'I'm winding you up. You don't need to get me anything.'

'I should probably get going. They're waiting for me.'

'Oh. All right.' She nods, blinks. And an expression comes into her face that I can't immediately interpret: a sort of barbed blank. 'Same time tomorrow, or...?'

'Not sure. Probably not tomorrow. I'll let you know.'

'You will? Because where you're going is… fairly remote, isn't it?'

'I'll think of something. Remember, I'm this capable, reliable guy…'

'Because this isn't the last time we'll speak, is it? While you're out there?'

'No, no.' Is it? I haven't the faintest idea.

'You know I'm really not bothered about a present, don't you? I was winding you up.'

'Yeah, obviously.'

She blinks at me. 'And I'm not worried about you. I'm not worried about you *one bit*.'

'I know. They're waiting for me…'

Eventually she says, 'I love you, Baldie.'

And I say, 'And I love you.'

I told Ess and Asha I would meet them back in the hotel reception area at ten past nine, but by the time I leave my room it's already half past. I imagine Ess, arms folded, narrow-lipped, tapping his foot on the pavement, while Asha down in the street holds the car with a look of calm vindication. Even so, I can't bring myself to take the lift and pelt down the three flights of stairs, swinging at the turns, passing blur-faced cleaners who seem to howl with maniacal laughter before I have even left their sight.

I spill out into the reception area, gasping, arms flailing, to find Ess and Asha sitting comfortably on one of the couches along the wall, murmuring and giggling over the pages of a glossy lifestyle magazine. I sit and we all wait another half an hour for our car.

Which turns out to be a stocky all-terrain vehicle with the Adventurers logo on both sides and one of Asha's colleagues, a smiling young man named Cass, doubling as driver for the night. As we join the traffic Ess, Asha and Cass start up a conversation full of hooting and unintelligible innuendo that is still in progress twenty minutes later when the Adventurers car halts on a street crowded with well-dressed young people and so brightly lit the night air seems made of clockwork – the moving parts of a million mosquitoes.

Asha leads us to a doorway visible at the end of which is the familiar flaming red hell. The doorman, shaven-headed and ear-ringed, refuses us entry. Asha begins arguing with him, with startling ferocity. Ess and I hold back, crookedly grin at each other, flinch from the whirring mosquitoes. Cass, having parked the car, strides up and joins the argument also. Asha and Cass look as if at any second they're going to attack the doorman, stab him to death and throw his body into the bay. Clearly, for them, our being refused entry to the club is no mere inconvenience: it's a slight, a smirching of their honour. At last the doorman falls into a nodding reverie then steps back and opens his arms, ushers us quickly into the club, as if this is what he's been saying all along.

Inside the doorway we pause by a desk at which Asha pays our admission fee – she doesn't appear to haggle – then pass on to the edge of a dance floor as frenetic as any of a thousand movie images of Ibiza in season. Over the deafening noise Asha establishes that we don't want to dance, that we want to drink, and leads us up a flimsy metal staircase into a bar saturated with red light and so busy, every seat occupied, we are forced to become one more group standing uncomfortably round a decorative pillar. Ess and Asha talk inaudibly, cooing into one another's ear like turtle doves, until Cass brings our drinks and the three of them resume or anyway seem to resume the stream of patter they began in the car. Ess indicates me a couple of times – a pointed finger, a sweeping hand – and Asha and Cass look at me and laugh while I pull a face, or shrug, or take a bow.

81

After a while I tune out and think about Alice. Why did I hurry our call to an end? Because I was already late, or because I was too busy being annoyed with her – annoyed with her remarks about Marie, with her not being more impressed by my having got Daniel a present? Playing back our conversation, with a silent inner crash I suddenly realise why she was wearing that weird blank expression. It was because she was trying not to cry. Because she already understood what it's taken me until now to absorb fully: that we may not have another chance to speak while I'm out here. The thought of not seeing her face, not hearing her voice, for who knows how long, drags appallingly in my guts.

I have quite an interesting conversation with Cass. He's a business student, working part-time for Adventurers, with enormously ambitious career plans ('If I can't afford to retire before my thirtieth birthday, I'll consider myself a failure'). He says that for a long time he felt strange coming to places like this, seeing his peers pretend to be American teenagers, imitating the lifestyle tics of the actors in their favourite cable shows; the clumsiness of the imitation, as much as the playact itself, made him despair. Then, he says, a couple of years ago, one evening he came to this self-same bar, and it was different. The Mumbai hipsters were doing exactly the things they'd been doing before, but their behavior was no longer an act. The imitation was so perfect it wasn't an imitation any more.

'That was maybe the happiest night of my life,' Cass says, folding his arms proudly, leaning against the pillar we're all standing round. 'For the first time I felt I could believe in my country, my generation. I thought, "In India, progress truly is possible."'

He's kidding, in some sense, though I don't know which. Nonetheless we both laugh.

Cass returns to the bar for more drinks. As soon as he leaves I notice that Harry has joined us, and is standing deep in conversation with Ess while Asha plays with the settings of her big antique camera. I stand pretending to take part in Ess and Harry's conversation, though I don't take in anything either of them says and notice only the peculiar demeanour that the bar seems to bring out in Harry: rapt, alerted, embattled, with raised eyebrows and gritted teeth, though lacking the old-man, interloper quality you'd expect to see there. At last it occurs to me that he's enjoying himself – that this seventy-odd year old guy is enjoying the bar more than I am.

Suddenly depressed, or disgusted, or something, I push away from the pillar, scramble through the crowd to a doorway leading out onto a metal balcony overlooking the city lights and the black bay. I light a cigarette, sip my orange juice, blink down at the huge greenish clouds rolling in off the water.

'It's pretty, isn't it?'

I look up. Asha has followed me onto the balcony, still handling her camera. When I don't reply she waves at the green clouds. 'Pollution. Nasty stuff. But so very picturesque. You should take a photo. Do you have a camera? Or do you use your phone? Go on, take a photo, so you may share this spectacle with friends and family back home.'

'I don't need to do that,' I say.

'Go on. A beautiful image for your loved ones in England.'

'No,' I say. *You don't like it when women tell you what to do*, Alice said. But she's wrong about that – of course she is. That would be so... that would make me so...

'Allow me.' Asha snaps the view with her museum piece and turns to me, smiling stiffly. 'There. I'll keep it for you, in case you change your mind.'

'I don't think I will.'

Now she waves at my cigarette, as she did at the green clouds. 'You can smoke inside. The ban isn't strictly enforced here. Also, I'm friendly with the owner.'

'That's good to know.' I attempt a conspiratorial grin: 'Actually, I'm smoking out here because I don't want my boss to see.'

'Would Ess disapprove?'

Ess. Not Ray or Raymond or Mr Ess. Ess. As if she knows who he is.

'Ooh, he'd go mad. He'd kill me.'

'Interesting. You would rather keep this from Ess than face his disapproval?'

My grin is curdling on my face. 'I don't really think it's a big deal.'

'Interesting.' She smiles again. In the dining room at the hotel she seemed distinctly middle-aged. Here on the balcony she looks about nineteen. 'I'll have to make a Note to Self. "Steven is a person who keeps secrets from his boss and thinks it is quote no big deal unquote." I'll have to remember that.'

'You do that,' I mutter, with fairly unmistakable hostility, and she laughs.

'We're going to be spending a considerable amount of time together over the next few days. The three of us, Ess, you and me. Don't you think we should be friends?'

I shrug over my cigarette. I take a last drag then flick the butt from the balcony.

'Yes,' she says, in an odd, vigorous undertone. 'Now you have it.'

For a while neither of us says anything. Asha shows no sign of leaving but returns to fiddling with her camera. I light another cigarette and start to regret having been so nasty to her. But what can I say? What subjects, what ground do we share?

'I was sorry to hear about the bombing,' I hear myself say. She doesn't look up. 'In Bangalore. I was sorry about that.'

'Why? Did you do it?' She laughs softly, still tuning her camera – clicking switches, spinning wheels. 'Don't be sorry, Steven. This is India. This is the country that explodes.'

PART TWO
The House of Saffron

7

At what I take to be first light I go up to Ess's room and tap on his door. Hearing a distant groan I enter to find the place in disarray, his suitcase open on the bed and Ess in the bathroom, barely covered by his dressing gown, a bottle of skin-care product in either hand, apparently unable to decide which is his and which the hotel's. 'Sorry,' he keeps saying, 'bad night.' At first I'm alarmed by his manic appearance – hair on end, face red and tendrilled – then he laughs, and the picture clears, and I relax. Ess's mania this morning is that of a man almost intolerably excited, not a man capsizing.

I try to help but it's soon clear I'm only making him worse. By eight o'clock he's neither showered nor packed. He tells me to go down and find Asha, apologise to her for his delay; when I ask if I should check out also, he agrees warmly, then grins and says, 'Look out for the farewell party!'

About ten minutes later I see what he means. The hallways are empty, silent, as I pad back down from Ess's room to my own; then, the second I step out with my shoulder bag and my suitcase, three porters appear from nowhere, jostling each other in their hurry to assist me. Two reach for my case while the third makes a grab for my bag; I have to keep veering away from them, saying, 'No thank you,' then 'No,' then 'I said no.' I start down the stairs, my case bumping over the runners, banging my legs. At each turn more people seem to be waiting for me. I dodge my way past. I think I see the lift attendant, thinly grinning, stepping in front of me. But I step aside and scuttle down and on, teeth gritted, dragging my case, looking at no one and shaking my head and saying, 'No. No. No.'

At last I break out onto the hotel steps. I gasp; I could burst into tears or howl with laughter. An Adventurers car – possibly the same one that ferried us about last night – is parked at the kerb and Asha is loading bottles of water into its boot. In jeans, a white vest and an open white shirt, she moves quickly, lightly. Her face, however, is grey and heavy, the brows clenched, the lips an underslept sneer. She looks as if she's furious with her dreams, furious with her own night's sleep.

But I don't quite read it in time and totter down the steps on watery legs, cackling, 'Nice try, you bastards! Oh, you *bastards*! Nice *try*!'

'What are you talking about?' She looks round dourly.

'They were piling in, *scrambling* in… every picture-hanger and flower-duster in the place… but did I give them a penny? I did not.'

'You must be proud of yourself.'

'As a matter of fact, I am.'

'Are you sure they weren't just saying goodbye? Wishing you a safe journey?'

'Do you think that's what they were doing?'

'No.' She gives a short bark of laughter, shuts the boot of the car and starts past me up the hotel steps.

'Where are you going?'

'To pay my good friend the manager for your water and your lunch.' She smiles, with dazzling insincerity. 'Would you like to come with me?'

'Uh, no.'

'I didn't think so.' And she turns and strides up the steps into the hotel.

*

Half an hour later Asha and I are sitting in the Adventurers car, not speaking, staring out our separate windows, when Ess emerges from the hotel. In a silk cravat, his red leather shoes and shop-new khakis, with expensive-looking wraparound sunglasses and a wide-brimmed hat, he looks like some dinner-party version of a big game hunter. Additionally he's crowded by the same three porters who tried to assist me earlier, now carrying his suitcase, satchel and various files and folders to the kerbside and grinning as he passes each a fold of notes. Asha climbs out to transfer Ess's clobber to the boot. I climb out also then have to stand there while he talks to the doorman, shakes his hand, then laughs and embraces him and tips him also and then tips each and every one of his deadbeat friends.

Finally Ess strides down the steps and sweeps towards Asha and me, waiting by the car. 'Sorry, sorry!' He shakes his head, despairing of himself. 'Happily I've good reason to believe we're primed for the off, so I don't see why...' He takes his phone from his pocket, shows us its silently flashing screen, mimes shooting himself through the head and sweeps off up the street, clamping his phone to his face with one hand and displaying all the fingers of the other in a way that means 'Five minutes'.

Asha packs the boot then shuts it again. She doesn't climb back into the car. I don't either and we stand, not speaking, watching Ess take his call at the other end of the street.

I'm about to say something when someone behind us says, 'Good morning.'

We turn. The someone behind us is Harry. In sandals, combat pants, a sort of utility belt, a smeared T-shirt and a canvas fishing hat. Buckled into a backpack that appears to be wearing him more than he it.

Harry smiles at us. Then he stops smiling. Behind his specs his eyes bulge.

'He told you, right?' He looks at Asha, then at me, then at Asha again. 'Raymond told you I'm tagging along?'

'What?' The idea isn't sinking in so much as standing wall-like in front of me.

'Didn't he mention it? I'm coming on the road with you guys.' Harry lets out a titter.

I glance at Asha. Her whole face is tensely closed. She looks furious – but then, she's looked like that all morning.

'No,' I say to Harry. 'No, he didn't mention it, actually.'

A little after ten o'clock, we leave the city.

Asha drives. Ess rocks along next to her in the passenger seat. In the back my knees and I share space with Harry and his backpack, which over the course of the morning seems to get bigger and more complicated, to elaborate itself, to threaten at any moment to become something else entirely – a biplane, a hovercraft.

The city unravels in fits. I keep thinking we've left it behind then another chunk of it rears up, glassy, blunt-edged, billowing with vast friezes of comely Indian youth advertising insurance deals and broadband packages. Later it's hotels with drained pools and Faliraki balconies isolated by brown dust and tobacco-tuft palm trees. Later still, the trestle tables and soft-drinks logos of a derelict market, hulks of abandoned farm machinery reclaimed by the earth. Then the last threads twist apart and we're speeding along a freeway above bleak wetlands, nothing in sight on either side but watered-down sunshine, nothing ahead or behind but traffic and road.

*

We've been travelling for maybe two hours when I glance round at Harry. All but his face is concealed by his polymorphous backpack. I say, 'You okay there?'

He doesn't reply or give any sign that he's heard me. Sitting straight-backed and gazing keenly ahead, he doesn't appear to be asleep. It's crossing my mind that he may be dead when I notice he's wearing his smartspecs again. No, Harry's not dead. He's just watching a movie.

'Harry?' I say more loudly. 'Hello? Anyone in there?'

'Hello, Steven.' Harry nods, though the fixed cast of his eyes tells me he's still doing whatever he's doing inside his smartspecs.

'So you decided to come along for the ride then, did you?'

'I was invited. Raymond invited me.'

I nod for a while. 'It's quite a commitment you're making here, time-wise, isn't it? Won't they miss you at the school for wayward girls?'

The corner of his mouth tugs down: he knows I'm messing with him. 'I think Rajeev can hold the fort.'

'What about the Adventurers guys? Can they spare you?'

'I'm sure everyone will get along just fine without me.' It seems he's said as much as he's going to, then he continues in an unfamiliar voice, 'It's true, I have a broad range of interests, of "concerns". And yet the defining quality of my concerns is that most of the time they don't need me any more than I need them.'

'*Fantastic.*' I fall silent, let him reconnect with the contained reality of his specs, then start up again, 'So you're having a nice time, Harry?'

'I'd say I'm having a nice time. Are you having a nice time, Steven?'

'Oh, I'm having a brilliant time, drinking it all in, the scenery, the spectacle of our immediate surroundings. I can't believe you're missing this.'

'Who says I'm missing it?'

'You're watching a movie. You're watching *Turner and Hooch*.'

He does his shrill, sneezy laugh. 'I'm not watching *Turner and Hooch*.'

'You're watching TV. You're watching *Happy Days*.'

'If you must know, I'm uploading video to *National Geographic*.'

'Video of what?'

'Of this. Of now. The spectacle of our immediate surroundings.'

This should be pretty interesting, I should want to ask lots of questions about it – but somehow it isn't, I don't. And after another moment I turn my face back to the screen of the window, with its high definition, its retina resolution of the streaming world.

We leave the freeway and push on through the streets of a brand-new town, white, still, uninhabited. Harry sits up in his seat, cranes about to catch as many elevations of as many buildings as he can: Indian construction, after all, is his thing, or is one of his things. We see men in hard hats and jumpsuits consulting clipboards and taking panoramic shots of the new buildings with their smartphones. A group of handsomely dressed young women stand in frowning conference next to a van with an outside-broadcast look to it.

Then the town retreats and we pass on through a series of much older conurbations, without tourist colours, with the more sombre, hackled textures of the resident life. Chicken wire and planks and bright paper, scraps of magazines, an endless photomontage. At first I'm struck by the ingenuity, the inexhaustibility of these accommodations, but after a while it all just starts to look aimless. Where does any of this lead – where is any of this going? Somewhere or nowhere, nowhere at all?

*

About one o'clock we break for lunch. Asha halts the car next to a group of boxy concrete buildings comprising a garage, a shop, and a locked and empty cafeteria. We take turns crossing the stony ground to the toilet, a single cubicle accessible by a separate door at the back of the cafeteria, locked also until Asha talks a key out of the unsmiling, flabby, middle-aged man installed at the shop counter, the only staff member we can find anywhere in the complex.

We eat in the car with the doors open. From the boot Asha brings Ess and me each a bottle of water and a sort of cake box whose flaps pluck apart to reveal the packed lunches prepared for us by her good friend the hotel manager: an apple, a banana, a chocolate bar in an illegible wrapper, a box of mango juice with a straw in its own sachet gummed to the side, and a tinfoil-wrapped block that turns out to be a stack of chutney sandwiches. I eat the banana and the chocolate bar, leave the apple (a great boil of brown in it), try the mango juice then leave that as well. The sandwiches I just stare at forlornly until Harry suggests a trade. His backpack is as well stocked as a picnic hamper, and in exchange for my chutney sandwiches he offers cubes of cheese, slices of ham, a bunch of grapes and a chicken leg. After some thought I decide to let him keep the grapes – I'm not *a thief* – and get stuck in to the rest.

After lunch there's a slightly nasty moment between Ess and me. Asha announces that she needs to give the car a final once-over and Ess, Harry and I troop back to the shop to wander its un-air-conditioned aisles and kill time while she works. I'm more or less asleep on my feet, shuffling along behind Harry, when Ess points at my face and, with a zigzagging motion of his fingertip, asks somewhat imperiously, 'What's all this?'

I yawn. 'What's all what?'

'You're red. Burnt to a frazzle. When did you manage that?'

'Must've been yesterday. When we were playing football.'

Ess flinches, incredulous. 'You played football?'

'Yesterday afternoon.' Was it? Yes: unbelievably it was only yesterday. 'With Harry and some guys at his school. While you were resting,' I add, in a queasy voice.

'Well, that's… And your back was all right, was it?'

'Oh, yeah.'

'You didn't have any pain?'

I yawn again. 'Didn't seem to be a problem.'

'Well. That's… Anyway, you're burnt. You need to wear a hat. Buy a hat.'

'From here?'

'They sell hats.' He points: a skinny, skew-whiff display stand hung with flops of nylon like decayed fruit. 'Buy a hat.'

'I'm not buying…'

'This isn't a discussion. Do it,' Ess spits at me – literally spits at me, lips sparking, eyes throbbing. And for a second I see it again, it blinks on in his cheek again: the graph-paper scar with its ghostly incised lines. Then he turns, his whole face a grey heavy beak, and he struts out of the shop and back across to the car.

The traffic briefly thickens, a braying mass of cattle trucks and tourist buses, and then drains from the road one vehicle at a time. Soon the Adventurers car is the only moving object visible in any direction. Outside the marks of human presence fade away, the remote huts and loose-staked plots, giving way to vertiginously open space, rough and stubbled distance. I try to make out the furthest thing to be seen: a smudgy skyline, like a chute of collapsed smoke. Hills? Mountains? Clouds? A monsoon?

Fairly patiently I wait for the towns to come back, the villages, the huts and plots. An hour later I'm still waiting. The emptiness extending from either side of the road, the scale of it, the eerie, scooped-out quality, the electromagnetic concavity, brings a trickle of terror. It's like hanging upside-down from monkey bars; it's like lying on your back, staring into the sky and imagining what would happen if at just that second the earth gave up its gravity and let you go, let you fall and fall and fall into the waiting blue.

It's something after five when we get our next break. The instant Asha stops the car, in what looks like the dusty middle of nowhere, Ess thrashes out of the vehicle and stumps away along the side of the road, his phone again clamped to his ear. Diplomatically Asha props open the car's bonnet and goes about repeating the checks she made less than three hours ago. Harry wanders off somewhere to relieve himself. I do the same and when I get back find myself hanging round Asha at the front of the car, peering over her shoulder, taking little steps towards her then little steps away.

'Nice hat,' Asha says, not taking her eyes off what I think is the oil gauge.

'No it's not.' It's not: a roundel of artificial fibre with a headband all itchy trusses and grips. 'I only got it because he went so mental.'

She glances at me, then back at the oil gauge. 'Who went mental?'

'He lost his rag with me in the shop.' I nod at Ess, unhappily hunched over his phone fifty or sixty feet away. I suppose I should be glad, at least, that he can get a signal out here.

'Ah,' Asha sighs. 'It is often the way with powerful men. They need a release, an outlet. I wouldn't take it personally.'

'Is it "often so" with Harry?'

She slams down the bonnet and turns to me with a banal look.

'I mean you work for Harry, don't you?' I say. 'Isn't he a powerful man too?'

'I don't work for Harry.'

'I thought you said…'

'I work for myself. No one else.'

'Yeah, but I thought you said…'

'Harry owns the company. He doesn't own me.'

'No. Obviously not.' I stand blowing through my lips for a while. Then I nod at Ess again and say, 'Who's he talking to?'

'I don't know.' She folds her arms. 'Do you?'

'How would I know that?'

'How would I?'

Now I fold my arms also. 'Is he talking to Tarik?'

'Does he do that?'

'What?'

She raises her chin. 'Does he communicate with Tarik Kundra?'

'I've no idea. That's why I asked you.'

'Maybe.' She shrugs slackly, somehow aggressively. 'Maybe you already know the answers to these questions, and only want to find out if I know them too.'

'That's not why I asked you.'

We're sort of grinning at each other. I'm not sure what's going on.

'Let me ask you a question.' Arms still folded, she leans back against the car. Then she tilts her head, narrows her eyes, as if taking aim at me, and says, 'Does Tarik Kundra exist? Is he a real person?'

Even before the sky changes colour I know I've lost track of time. It doesn't matter how often I tell myself to look at my watch: every time I look I see that hours have vanished, leaked from its face. As if time has gone the way of space and become its own immaculate featureless body, unintelligible, ungraspable.

Then the sky changes colour. A tinge of citric yellow seeps in at the skyline, then deep acidic lemon, then gross tangerine. Then the whole sky turns red. The car seems to putter along in silence, through wave after wave of turbulent red. There's nothing else to see. Then the red darkens and the day starts to become night.

Blue layers of shadow are softly vying at the windows when Harry takes off his specs, pinches the bridge of his nose, and says, 'Well, that's me out.'

'No more signal?' I ask.

'No more signal.'

We're going along in pitch darkness, and it's obviously time for me to step in. It's time for me to lean forward between the seats and say something along the lines of, 'Okay, guys, what say we pick this up in the morning? Asha, is there anywhere round here we could turn in for the night?' I've been expecting this moment or one like it for weeks, for as long as I've been signed up for this trip, so I've had plenty of time to prepare for it. But now it's here there's a problem. I keep telling my mouth to open. But my mouth keeps not opening.

We stop. With the engine still running Asha clicks on the dashboard light and sits studying the map lying massively open in her lap. Then she grunts, throws off her whistling seatbelt, shoulder-barges her door and without a word disappears into the road.

Ess, Harry and I look at the black space beyond her door. Faint wisps, specks, floating bits of thread seem to rear from the darkness, and I fear mosquitoes, drawn by the dashboard light. I want to ask Ess to reach across and shut her door but at the same time I don't want to speak to him, don't want to look at him.

Asha returns. She slams back into her seat in a way that makes no one feel like asking her anything. She starts driving again very much more quickly. We smash down into potholes and smash up out of them again, everything in the car slewing about. Still no one says anything. Ess puts a hand on her arm but she doesn't seem to notice. We hurtle along, slew about in the cratered night.

We pass a village, a wide rotating edge of densely packed shapes like dark silos or enormous canisters. At each rotation hot dots of light spark out then vanish along with their streaks of nubbled infrastructure, their field tones, forest tones. I search the sky round the place for the flying webs of telegraph wires, and see them – see one maybe – maybe none.

A couple of miles beyond the village Asha stops the car again. She storms out into the road again. She slams back into her seat and sits studying the map again. In the rear-view mirror she looks as if she has to keep reminding herself to breathe.

She starts driving again, very much more slowly. She turns the car off the road; the headlights pick out the startling waste in front of us, the gnarled trees, the ashen bushes. Slow as we're going, the car judders violently and continuously, sliding on pebbles, crashing into rocks. Asha grapples the wheel like she's trying to force its arms behind its back.

Then she cries out. A wordless screech that freezes me into my seat. Is she hurt? Has something struck her? Has someone attacked her?

The car turns again and the headlights wash across a series of luridly pitted surfaces that tessellate only gradually into a lonely cluster of buildings: a metallic cabin surrounded by wooden sheds. Then there's a movement, the drift of a figure – the white kurta, the fashion specs – and there he is, standing in front of the car, in the glaring headlights, the inventor, the recluse, Tarik Kundra.

8

Now I know what heat is.

Outside the storage shed in which Ess and I have spent the night, I stand in heat like an act of violence. I thought Mumbai was hot, but I know now that the city is two hundred square miles of accessible shade and air conditioning; that heat there is an idea, an imitation of heat. This, this attack, this onslaught – this is heat.

Narrowing my eyes, I make out shapes against the furnace-white sky: the dazzling metal of the cabin; the bleached wood of the other two storage sheds; the rickety latrine; the silhouetted Adventurers car, a propped heel the only sign of Asha slumped in the back; the busy encampment that Harry produced from his backpack and in which I assume he's still sleeping. There's something else, further out from the cluster of buildings even than Harry's nylon homestead, the only other deviation from the level of the plain, tidy foundations, oddly orderly ruins – but I've had enough and duck back into the shed.

In the space we somehow cleared last night, stacking and re-stacking boxes in total darkness, Ess is sitting up awake. For the first time I notice how we arranged the sleeping bags that Asha brought us from the car: not top-to-tail, like camping teens, but face-to-face, like a married couple. Showing no trace of our uncomfortable night's sleep, he now springs to his feet, slips on his sunglasses, picks up his hat as if handling a soft loaf and drops it over his head. He throws my hat at me and says, 'Now you see why I made you buy *that*.'

Outside, he stands as I did a moment ago, surveying the contents of the plain, then he claps his hands together and says, 'You know, I've a jolly thought.'

I don't want to hear it. Whatever is on his mind, I'm not ready for it. I'm not ready for any part of this situation. Until last night I was sure that Tarik Kundra didn't exist. But then until three days ago I was pretty sure that Asha Jarwal didn't exist either.

'I wonder if I can't arrange a little demonstration for us.' He peers at me over his sunglasses, eyes brimming, the vivid crinkles spilling. 'What say you to that? Little demonstration? Little demonstration of an antigravity machine?'

'Okay.' Somewhat manically I nod, smile. What else can I do?

'Not too bad a thought, is it? Not *too* bad.' He laughs, managing to read in my expression the delight he's looking for. 'Very well, Mr Strauss. Let's see what I can't sort out.' And he strides away, across the plain, towards Tarik's cabin.

From the shed I watch as he reaches the cabin and knocks smartly on the door. We both wait. Then he knocks again and we both wait again. Then the door opens and there's Tarik, a slight, neatly made man, late thirties or early forties, with light designerish stubble and a thick mop of curls in which I intuit the touslings of product. This is no wild man of the plain; this is a city boy, an urban pretty boy, all trust fund and vintage vinyl. He has no more business being out here, in this stippled waste, than the rest of us do.

What else? But it's hopeless. I don't know what I'm looking at, I have no way of making sense of Tarik Kundra because the great majority of me still refuses to believe that he exists, is a real person, a living fact I'm at some point going to have to think about and deal with. Though I can see him, right there in the doorway of his dazzly metal cabin, he's still essentially a figure in a story, a figment, a ghost.

Ess talks. Tarik nods. Then Tarik says something and steps back into his cabin and closes the door. Ess bows to the closed door, then turns and strides back to me, his face triumphant under the wide brim of his daft hat.

'A demonstration, did we say? Why then a demonstration we shall have!'

'He agreed to it?'

'He did. Tarik is eager to exhibit his wares. And so he shall, immediately after our repast this evening.' Ess grins as if he could burst with it. 'What say you to that?'

'That's fantastic.' I nod, I smile. I don't want to say or do anything else. I have an idea that if I don't say or do anything else, nothing else can happen. Only it's not true, and eventually I have to shrug and say, 'So… what do we do now?'

'What we do now,' Ess says with his bursting grin, 'is we see what Harry's got in for breakfast.'

When we shout his name Harry rolls about inside his tent for a bit then sticks his head out of a polythene porthole and wishes us a civil good morning. Ess asks if he has a morsel or two of anything to eat and a minute later Harry is sitting wide-eyed and cross-legged over a tiny space-age cooker and silvery packets of astronaut food that disgorge hot delicious hunks of egg, bacon, sausage. We're wolfing our way through all this when a timer goes somewhere and then Harry's passing round tin cups of hot coffee.

'Your rude health, my fine fellows,' Harry says, and we clash our cups together with a happy chain-gang dinging.

It's a nice sort of a moment, blokeish, bullish, but its spirit soon passes. Ess and Harry fall into discussing the geography of the plain and I fall into gloomily wondering what the hell we're doing here. Why are we here – I mean Ess and me? And why is *he* here – I mean Harry? I'm aware that I have not yet asked Ess any of the many questions I want to ask him about Harry Altman. For instance: Why did Ess not even mention Harry to me until we were already in India? Why did he not tell me that he had invited Harry to join us on our trip to the plain? What reason did he have for keeping those things from me? Has he entered into some dark compact with the American that he doesn't want me to know about? Or – darker yet – has the American some hold over him, some leverage, some force?

One further scenario presents itself: that Harry has his own designs on the machine. That he is a con man and he's been fooling us from the start, charming us with his frowns and titters, with his lumbering, shaggy amenability, only and precisely so we would lead him to Tarik Kundra's wondrous antigravity machine and give him opportunity to steal it as soon as he's made sure it works. Well, if that's true, Harry is in for a disappointment, because the wondrous machine is not going to work. Still (I would like to know), has *Ess* thought of any of this? Has he considered the possibility at all?

But it's pointless. If there is some ingenious way I could pry the two of them apart, get Ess alone and make him answer my questions, I don't know it.

Ess and Harry fall into discussing the climate; I fall into thinking about Alice. All at once I need to see her face, to hear her voice. Moreover, I'm certain she'll know what to do. If I can only somehow speak to her, I have no doubt she'll be able to tell me what to do.

And so, when we've eaten, I fit my hat more tightly over my head, squint towards the horizon and ask, 'How far away do we think that village we passed is?'

'Three, four miles. Maybe further.' Ess frowns. 'Why?'

'If we're kicking our heels until this demo, I thought maybe I could walk over there, look for a payphone, anything, really, any form of...'

'No need.' Harry smiles. 'We've got wifi.'

'No…' I say.

'Oh yeah. Tarik's got wifi. See for yourself. Have you got your phone?'

I do. I check it and there's a wifi connection. I hit 'select' and the internet twirls open in my screen like a paper flower.

'How the hell's he managed that?'

'He works in mysterious ways, his wonders to perform.'

I glance up at Ess, to check that he's joking. And he is, more or less.

Ess and Harry start talking again, and after a polite pause I scuttle back to the shed. Sitting on my sleeping bag, next to the dead-umbrella tangle of my mosquito net, I open my tablet, link it also to the magical wifi connection, and login to my email account.

Three messages. None, somewhat ominously, work related.

Again I think about contacting Martin Cantor – about checking in, sending an update. But the thought of tapping away at a message to him in the hot storage shed is unexpectedly repellent, shameful, even. I think: I'll do it later.

A message from Alice.

And a message from Daniel.

And a message from Michael – the elder and the bigger dick of my two dick older brothers. This one, for some reason, I open at once.

'hey steve! hope you're having fun out there with crazy ess!! how is the old nutjob? foaming at the mouth yet?? howling at the monsoon moon???'

There are no real surprises here. My brother Michael is well known for his trade in this sort of weak, jokey viciousness. My brother Peter is the same. I honestly don't know what's wrong with them. Mum says they suffer from 'an excess of high spirits', which isn't it at all. Dad doesn't say anything. Suggest to him that (at least) two of his three sons are unusually nasty pieces of work and he doesn't contradict you – he's not that sort of bloke – but he smiles, with deflecting creases of his mild, round, wax-white face.

Still, re-reading the email, I can't help myself.

'Oh, you dick,' I mutter softly, almost wonderingly. 'Oh, you *fucking* dick.'

Yes, that's right, Raymond Ess went mad, ha ha ha.

Is it funny? This is funny: I thought he had a cold. For about two weeks in March last year he came into work with red eyes and a blocked-sinus voice and a tendency to trail off in the middle of whatever he was saying then spend a long time blowing his nose. For about two weeks that was it: he just couldn't seem to stop blowing his nose.

Then he went off for a couple of weeks. I spent the time helping out back in HR – back under the mild auspices of Marie, who, as I've said, I didn't mind at all – and guessed he was taking it easy in bed with an extra blanket and a hot lemon drink.

Early in April he came back to work, but didn't seem better. If anything, he seemed quite a bit worse. His face looked as if it had been lightly peeled; his voice sounded trapped in his guts – hollowly resonating in his bowels. In his new, gaspy boom he began sentences that didn't trail off but rattled on and on along unmappable tracks, sentences that started off being about the day's meetings then went on to consider the nature of days, the nature of meetings, man and his improbable lot. He began talking about Eunice, his ex-wife, which he'd not done before, when she'd still been his wife.

He talked about the collapse of their marriage, which had largely taken place the year before, and which he'd barely mentioned to me – barely exhibited any sign of – at the time. He talked about the separation, the trial period, the effort made by both parties to salvage what of the union could be salvaged (nothing, it transpired). He defended Eunice vigorously. Whatever she'd done, she'd done with the best of reason. He understood exactly why she'd left him; he upheld her decision in every particular. To say that she'd left him was not strictly accurate, given that Eunice still lived with the girls in the house in Montacute while he for the last nine months had been renting a two-room flat in Yeovil, but I saw no need to point this out. He wouldn't have listened anyway. By then he was far too busy explaining Eunice's superb reasons for leaving him, chief among them the fact that he was not, nor had ever been, 'a spirited lover'.

'And that's true, you know,' he gasped and boomed, with a vibrating sort of nod, 'she's quite right to say it. Never a truer word spoken, as far as I'm concerned.'

It was about this time I realised there was something pretty seriously wrong with him. Ess had always enjoyed risqué conversation, but nothing like this, so personal, so private. Now he seemed unable to talk about anything else. If it wasn't man and his earthly destiny it was the paltriness of his amatory technique. If I tried to lead the conversation back to work matters he grew irritable and glared at me with his nose violently twitching until I shut up and let him get back to how crap he'd always been at cunnilingus or whatever.

'You have to tell someone,' Alice said, when I raised the subject with her one night.

'I'm telling you, aren't I?'

'You have to tell someone else.'

'Such as who?'

'Would there be any point talking to his wife?'

'Eunice?' Eunice Ess: I'd only ever seen her at the Resolute Christmas Dinner, high and hard and haughty on the stage next to Ess while he made his speech, like the painted wooden prow of a Viking longship. Once or twice I'd spoken to her, exchanged chill party pleasantries, held the tips of her long fingers; she'd seemed to me perfectly pleasant, with a nice unexpected raucous woof of a laugh, but obviously it was impossible – unthinkable – that I would talk to her, about Ess or anything else. 'No,' I said to Alice. 'Oh, no, no…'

'Does he have kids?'

'He does.' Esther and Krista. The owlish twin faces that haunted every surface of the Perfume Counter with their ribbons and bows, their enamelled fringes, their unearthly pallor. I'd never met Esther, but I'd met Krista. One day I walked into his office and she was there – some arrangement or other had fallen through – sitting curled in a chair at his desk, drawing in a large sketchbook. Visibly discomfited, Ess tried to introduce us, to make the odd situation less odd. He didn't succeed. And it wasn't really that the situation was weird; it was Krista who was weird. She refused to leave the room, refused to respond to either of us in any way, only worked continuously in her sketchbook, drawing something with sullen concentration. And then at the end of the day she uncurled her legs, sprang from her chair, ran round the desk to kiss Ess on the cheek, and said to us both with great gulps of passion, 'Thank you, thank you! I've had such a *lovely* day.'

The look on his face then, clenched, ridged, gritted – it was a look of terror. The holy terror of his daughter-love.

Krista was, I think, twenty-one at the time.

'I'm not talking to his kids,' I told Alice.

'Well then someone at work. Could you tell someone at Resolute?'

'Such as who? And tell them what? "Ess has gone a bit wonky now his divorce is final"?'

'Do you think that's what it is?'

'I don't know. Maybe. It could be that.'

I kept thinking he would get better, but he didn't. In the office he started reading aloud to me from the love letters Eunice had written him in the early days of their courtship: "'My dearest one,'" he intoned in his hollow boom, the paper trembling between his fingers, "'I have been thinking all night about what you said to me at the pavilion yesterday, and I have decided you are right. Mitch and Gwen are slow, dull, lapidary people, pleasant after their fashion but quite incapable of fineness of feeling…'"

Soon afterwards he contracted a private investigator to 'keep friendly tabs' – as he put it – on Eunice. A couple of times the man appeared at the Perfume Counter and then I had to sit excruciated while the two of them went through the photos he'd taken. Ess tried to involve me in these examinations, recommending the pictures on their artistic merits. 'You know, Bill here in his day was an absolutely exceptional wildlife photographer,' he told me. I looked at a few of the pictures (Eunice in a café, Eunice in her car, Eunice half-dressed in a bathroom window) and I could see what he meant. The private investigator clearly enjoyed his work as much as he did Ess's praises. A jaunty, jowly fellow, given to shrill bursts of decorative whistling – birdcalls and birdsong – he laid his glossy snaps across the desk as if preparing a complicated card trick.

I kept thinking it was just the divorce, kept thinking that Ess was having a funny turn, going through a funny phase, while he absorbed the reality of his divorce, and once he'd done that he would quickly rally and get back to normal. It wasn't true, and I knew it wasn't true. But while I could entertain the thought I could maintain my position of not having to do anything. While he was just having a turn, going through a phase, there was nothing to do anything about.

Except it wasn't just his divorce. It was also work, the company, the slow death of Resolute Aviation. For years his attitude towards Resolute's troubles had been whimsical, if not outright cavalier; only now it gained the brittleness, the clanging hardness of denial. After a genuinely terrifying episode in the office one morning – the quickening gasp, the gnawing twitch – I decided I would ask him no more direct questions about the company's future. Others were not so mindful (not so cowed, or cowardly), and Ess's meetings with the board soon became unminutable, unbearable. The questions Martin Cantor put to him during these meetings were not merely reasonable, but urgently legitimate; nonetheless for a while I hated the man, hated the way he pushed, the way he insisted, until Ess could do nothing but snap, snarl, scream and shout. More than anything else about those meetings, I remember Ess's pain. I don't know how the rest of them managed not to see it, the pain he was in, the twists of the agony.

It was in one of these meetings that he finally reached crisis point: that things came to their head. By this time (late July) there had already been any number of public and semi-public embarrassments, slanging matches spilling out into the corridors, gaining momentum in the car park. Ess had denounced Cantor, belittled him in front of colleagues, berated him in the presence of clients; yet all this had been tolerated. Whatever Ess threw at him Cantor blinked into it, with a mild boyish flush, then said no more than could defensibly be said. The crisis point, the breaking point, came in a meeting of the company's senior executives and their PAs (the likes of me – the mutes, the untouchables). It was a cool summer morning, the bickering in which Ess and Cantor were locked making its familiar pitter-patter, nothing apparently too serious, their wrangling over detail hardly worth paying attention to, when Ess rose to his feet, his face a grinning mask of baffled agony, and he said, not even very loudly, but quietly, tractably, almost endearingly:

'Shut up, you awful little cunt, before I fuck you like I never fucked my wife. Do you hear? Shut up before I fuck you, and I fuck you, like I never even fucked my wife.'

It wasn't a silence that followed this speech but a void, a gulf. Ess looked around the room with eager eyes; then he glanced down at the table, which he began thoughtfully to tap. When the board member sitting next to him stood, spoke into his ear, nodded towards the door, Ess moved away from the table and walked out with him, still not looking up.

I don't know why it wasn't me who stood, spoke into his ear, led him to safety. It just wasn't. I just sat there. And when I finally got up to leave the meeting, straightening my jacket, patting my files together, all the glances my way were sympathetic.

That afternoon I was called to a small conference room on the ground floor of the main office complex. I sat facing Martin Cantor, his sneering PA, and another woman who didn't at any point say anything and who typed at a laptop all the while I was in the room. This was, in fact, my first ever conversation with Cantor. I hated him; I trembled with an urge to knock him down, to tell him that Ess was right, he was a cunt and he should shut his cunt mouth. But Ess wasn't right. Cantor wasn't a cunt. And for the duration of the meeting I heard myself desperately, cravenly trying to ingratiate myself with Martin Cantor.

The next morning Ess didn't come in. I made a start on rearranging the office filing system. I kept thinking that I should give him a ring, though this was one of the things Cantor had specifically told me not to do ('I don't think we want to be bothering him right now with phone calls, emails, any of that. Anything that could be seen as our being, you know, not quite *sympathetic*'). Obviously, I should have called him anyway. I should have gone straight round to his two-room flat and done whatever he needed me to do. But I didn't. I didn't call, didn't go round.

By the end of the week I'd been drawn again into the fold of HR. I kept an eye on Ess's phone calls and email accounts, same as usual, but here too I had my instructions: anything of interest that came in I was to refer directly to Martin Cantor. Which I did, at first with visceral spikings of remorse, then soon robotically, unblinkingly.

And the next thing I knew Ess had taken six months leave and bought a plane ticket to India.

'A-ha! *There* you are!'

I'm still swearing over Michael's email when Ess comes striding back into the shed, crouches over his suitcase, unzips it and begins vigorously rummaging through. He says, 'I hope you brought your swimmers.'

'Why do you hope that?'

'Because you're going to need them. Come on. Look sharp.'

Harry, waiting outside with his toiletries bag, is at least slightly more helpful. 'We thought we'd have a look at the river.'

With our bags Ess, Harry and I leave the triangle of the storage sheds. We mill about, making false start after false start; I squint again at that odd collection of shapes, foundations or ruins, long, dark oblong hulks exposed to the sun, but fail to make any more sense of it. At last the plain starts to green and we find a slope that scutters and scabs its way down to a clutch of dry trees, a bit of grassy riverbank and a broad passage of almost motionless brown water.

Ess says, 'Last one in's a drain-snaker's glove.'

'This is a good idea, is it?' I look from Ess to Harry then back again.

'Swim in it.' Ess slaps my shoulder. 'Just, you know, try not to drink it.'

Very disconcertingly, Ess and Harry start to undress. There's nothing to do about this except pretend to become suddenly fascinated by the branches crisscrossing overhead (wires, tungsten filaments of shade; but shade, anyway). The next time I look round the two men are in their trunks – Ess's red and flared and goading as a matador's cape, Harry's a pinch of too-tight pea-green – hopping about at the edge of the water, putting a toe in, taking a toe out. In the end it's Harry who coughs ritually into each bunched fist, measures half a dozen paces back from the brink, then starts forward at a lumbering run, his belly a bagged dog trying to escape drowning in every direction it can think of, then leaps and vanishes with a smash into the water.

This before I can suggest we check the depth or make sure there's not a ziggurat of tin cans at the bottom or any of that boring stuff.

A moment later he resurfaces as if lifting a trapdoor of water, splashing, laughing, evidently having neither smashed his head open nor gashed his shins. His naked eyes are tiny, straining, comically vulnerable. His beard seems to have disappeared; then you see the gunpowder trails on his cheeks and neck, the smoky meniscus wobbling under his chin.

I teeter in after him and for half an hour or so tread the numb water. Ess, meanwhile, enters the river last and leaves it first. He wades out up to his waist, briskly scoops water over his chest and head then returns to the bank to loll in his sunglasses and snooze and dry off. Harry goes on swimming, loosely circling against the current.

Midday comes and goes. On the riverbank, in the wiry shade of the trees, we eat lunch – another bourgeois picnic from the wicker-lined deeps of Harry's backpack – then Ess drops off under his hat, Harry disappears with a stick along the river, and

I'm smoking a cigarette, fiddling with my tablet, emailing Alice to set up a Skype date for this evening, when a shadow thuds into the grass beside me and I see that Asha has joined us.

She yawns. 'Is there any food?'

I close my tablet and point at the remains of our picnic. 'Breakfast is served.'

'Hilarious,' she says, sorting through the picnic plates. 'You remember I drove for fifteen hours straight yesterday.'

Asha finds a chicken leg, holds it up to the light for a moment, as if looking for a maker's mark, then begins cautiously to eat it, using only the outermost planes of her teeth. And then, because he's on my mind, and because for the first time since we arrived he's not breathing benevolently down my neck, I say, 'So Harry, eh?'

'What about him?'

'Well... he's a *case*, isn't he?'

'I'm sure I wouldn't know.'

'Does he do this a lot? Tag along on your trips, that sort of thing?'

'I wouldn't say "a lot".'

'Why do you think he wanted to come along this time, then?'

'I've no idea.' And her face turns to me with a bland look that has a blazing line of fire right through it. 'Why do *you* think he did?'

'Christ, I've no idea either. I'm just talking...'

'No, please tell me. Clearly you have thoughts on the matter. Why do *you* think Harry chose to come on this trip? What maniacal purpose do you think cleared his diary? What unscrupulous motive do you suppose packed his bag?'

'I've no thoughts on the matter,' I say. 'I'm just making pleasant conversation.'

'Are you? I'm never sure about you.' She leans towards me, squints into my face. I hold in my smoke until she leans back, sniffs. 'Your eyes are weird.'

'So I hear.'

'Bits and pieces, whirling around.'

'My girlfriend says they look like something exploding.' Only Alice doesn't say this; I've just made it up. Why?

'Like a sandstorm, like a blizzard,' she says emphatically, as if telling me off. 'How the world must look through such eyes. It's a wonder you can see anything at all.'

We're sitting on the riverbank, the four of us, sitting or lying in the tungsten shade, Harry in the middle of a colourful and vaguely improving story from his Baltimore youth (a stolen car, a friend's drug-addict father), when I notice Tarik approaching. At the same time I notice that the sky behind him has, if not exactly darkened, dulled or cooled, lost its seething white-hotness. What time is it? Is it evening? Is it night?

Tarik marches past us to the edge of the water, kneels, removes his specs and lays them on the grass at his side, then sweeps three quick handfuls of water into his face, a fourth over his head, into his hair. Then he picks up his specs, stands and turns towards us, water streaming down his face, swirling over his lips, whorling in the stubble. He takes the hem of his kurta and begins using it carefully to clean the lenses of his specs.

For a while no one says anything. Tarik seems to have this effect. Last night, during our introductions, he greeted each of us with a curt nod that made clear he had no interest in hearing what any of us might have to say. I suppose a genius would probably come off like this, especially one living in perpetual fear of his being hunted down and killed by agents of his nefarious former employers. But then (I further suppose) so would a cheat, a con artist working an elaborate scam on a wealthy lunatic.

'Good evening, Tarik,' Ess now says, his cheer for once not carrying well – faltering, failing in the rivery air.

'Hey, Tarik,' Harry says, his elderly murmur for once elastic, assured.

Asha says nothing. Merely stares at him, as if at an image on a screen.

'Hey, Tarik,' I say, feeling I should say something; then, realising my intonation has trapped me into saying something else: 'How'd you get wifi out here? I mean it's great and everything… but how'd you do it?'

He looks at me. 'I steal it.' He finishes cleaning his specs, slots them back onto his face and says, 'Let's eat. And then, if you wish, I will demonstrate my machine.'

9

Under the cooling sky Tarik leads us towards his cabin. I'm
wondering if he's going to invite us in, serve us dinner in the
secret interior of that metalled shell; then I see the ground in
front of it is covered by a dusty carpet of flung-about rugs, an
informal arrangement of place settings. Asha drops onto one
of the rugs with a martial-arts-looking roll and sits inspecting
her feet. Ess, smiling at nothing, folds his legs into the rug next
to Asha's. Harry bobs downwards, as if to sit, then goes on
awkwardly standing. I go on standing too. For some reason, it's
weird to sit down. But now it's also weird to stand because Asha
and Ess are sitting down. Tarik ducks into his cabin, ducks out
again with bowls of curried beans and rice and bottles of water.
At this point abruptly it's not weird to sit down any more and I
sink into a rug and so does Harry.

Then for a while it's the Mumbai roof terrace all over again
– though minus the forks clicks, because Tarik doesn't have or
doesn't give us any forks. We eat with our fingers in an unevenly
shared silence. Finally Ess murmurs, 'Quite the feast, this, Tarik.'

Tarik looks at him. He adjusts his specs with odd, flickery
gestures, a stop-motion or slipping-pause-button stutteriness,
then says, 'It's rice and beans.'

'Yes, of course I realise that.' Ess attempts one of his razzamatazz
grins. 'But what beans! What rice!'

No one laughs. Tarik nods then looks down at his food. We
all carry on eating.

I keep glancing up at Tarik. And I return to the question I began considering earlier: What is he? Somehow the idea that he's a conman – a conman *as such* – doesn't quite fit. Surely if he were a conman *as such* he would have some of the swagger, the blithe flash of the high-stakes criminal. And Tarik doesn't have that, doesn't have that at all. He flickers, he stutters. He's like a nervy postgrad running late for a deadline.

Which leaves what? A fantasist, a crackpot? Some bedroom-dwelling fanboy long lost to the digiscapes of his franchise movies and the lasersights of his games? That is, a hyperindulged product of India's burgeoning middle class, a souring and a mangling of new-minted privileges, a messiah-complex tech junkie camping out in a wilderness bought and paid for with his parents' new-minted money? Sort of thing?

Or what? A lunatic – a simple lunatic? That stop-motion, slipping-pause-button way of his could be an indicator of lunacy, though a quiet, inward, somehow *not very interesting* lunacy. But then (I think) all we need out here is another madman.

There's something else: something I'm missing. But before I can track it down Tarik is standing, sliding his hands into his pockets, nodding at some point across the plain, saying blandly, 'I think we're ready for the demonstration.'

As the first dim swirls of evening start to show in the sky, we set off across the plain. It's soon clear that Tarik is leading us towards that collection of shapes I've seen during the day, those dark oblongs exposed to the sky, which turn out to be six huge concrete blocks arranged in a circle, their shorter ends pointing inwards and outwards, like the aftermath of a gigantic domino run, like a toppled Stonehenge. The blocks are strange, immediately but obscurely strange, and I get so interested in working out why that I miss the first few minutes of Tarik's commentary on what we're looking at.

I catch him referring to the place as his 'test site'. The blocks – he calls them 'casts' – are each belted with a rope and a wire. Leading us round the outside edge of the circle, round the outward faces of the six blocks, he shows us how each cast is tied by a rope that is in turn tied to a steel stake driven into the ground. Leading us through the gap between two casts, he then takes us round the inside edge of the circle, round the inward faces of the blocks, and shows us how each cast is tied by a wire that web-tremours its way into a machine mounted on a platform at the exact centre of the circle. Without taking his hands out of his pockets he indicates the machine and we all look at it. It resembles a very, very primitive cassette player.

'There it is,' Ess confirms, as if no one else has quite noticed the thing. He's excited, but mindfully doing his best to control himself – after all, he has, or believes he has, had this tour before.

'So,' I say to Tarik, who happens to be standing next to me, 'these blocks, these "casts", they're…?'

'They're blocks. They're casts.'

'Yeah…?'

'Swimming-pool casts. Casts of swimming pools.' He looks at me. Then goes on in the quick-fire monotone of someone who has just said exactly what they're saying now: 'I bought six identical swimming-pool skins, filled each with concrete and then stripped the skin away to produce six casts in precisely the same material of precisely the same dimensions. My reasons for doing so are technical and without significance to the layman.'

It sounds improbable, impossible. Then I look more closely and I see this is what's so strange about the blocks: the round corners, the ladder-shaped incisions that show they were moulded in swimming-pool skins and that render them coolly, surreally identical.

'How did they get here?' I ask.

'I brought them here.'

'How? From where?'

But Tarik is no longer talking to me, instead impatiently addressing the group: 'For the purposes of this demonstration, I have attached all six casts to a single machine. Each is attached by its own tether. There's no special reason why there are six. It isn't a limit or an optimum or any such thing. There could be fewer, there could be more. As many as you like. So long as each is attached by its own tether. In any case, here there are six.'

Not much of a public speaker, then – no oily hoaxer's patter. Which leaves crackpot, does it?

A crackpot who has somehow transported six unbelievably massive concrete blocks to the middle of the wilderness.

Which leaves crackpot plus trust fund, does it?

Or what?

Tarik says, 'I will now begin the demonstration.'

He walks to the platform; he reaches for the machine. Everything that's happening now is interesting, almost unbearably interesting. The evening clouds taking shape above us, the plain shadows extending around us, the air dimming, thickening with concealment, right in front of our eyes; all this is interesting. I smile (I can't help myself) and look about for the wires, the extra wires, the fishing-line supports; the platforms, the extra platforms, the camouflaged hydraulic rods and beds. Is it dark enough yet that there could be a crane somewhere – that there could be *six* cranes? I'm smiling, looking about, high and low, eager for a glimpse of the secret mechanism of the illusion to come.

My smiling look falls on Ess. The expression on his face is indescribable. Like a child who... like a saint who... But it's indescribable.

I look at Asha, standing next to him with her arms folded and chin raised, expectant, waiting to be convinced. I look at Harry, standing a little further away. There's nothing very remarkable about the expression on his face – a big boyish American grin – but somehow it reminds me, with a flash of distant panic, of all the questions I still have about Harry. Why is he here? What is he up to? Who, in fact, is he? He doesn't make sense, doesn't fit together. And there's the feeling I've had before, that there is something about Harry Harry is hiding, something important critically encoded by the specs and the beard, by the whole shaggy-dog demeanour, that there is a whole other man standing and grinning in the disguise of this other one's flesh...

I look at Tarik, his fingers trembling on the machine's control panel. I look at the six concrete blocks, huge, dark. And now I'm not just interested, I'm excited. I'm thrumming with excitement, with awful, stomach-churning hope and dread, wanting, wishing, willing the blocks to move, to rise, to lift from the earth in silent, miraculous flight...

Tarik throws the switch.

At first, nothing happens. Dark air swirls round six concrete hulks.

Then nothing happens. The heaving shadows, the soughing plain.

Then Tarik says, 'All right. Uh, sorry. We've got a fault.'

Still none of us can breathe. Then Ess says, 'A fault?'

'I thought this might happen.' Tarik's expression is grim. 'There was a chance. Eighty-twenty if not fifty-fifty. Maybe seventy-thirty. I was trying a shortcut, trying to avoid a complete fix, but... looks like I'll have to do a complete fix.'

'And that'll take...?' Ess is wrenching back his sleeve, groping for his watch.

'A few hours. I won't be able to run the demonstration now until morning. Or later. Some time tomorrow.'

The thrumming drains from me, a series of sharp, bitter shocks. A fault – a glitch – a delay – a postponement. Obviously. Well, obviously.

But the sudden drain-off has left a trace in me, a rough sediment that scores my guts, that rasps my skin. I'm hurt, suddenly. I'm in a peculiar sort of pain.

'Tomorrow.' Ess sags, crumples. In an instant he appears to shed about two-thirds of his body mass. He attempts a gesture – rising shoulders, spreading hands – but it fails to cohere. 'Oh, well. That's…'

Asha drifts towards him and places a hand on his elbow. The hand lingers; then she removes it and drifts away. At no point during this contact did either one of them look at the other. And this, I think, is fairly interesting too.

'Poor Ess!' says Alice.

I'm sitting in the storage shed with my tablet in my lap and my eyes moving rapidly between the screen and the open door. After the failed demonstration Tarik retreated to his cabin and Harry invited everyone else to join him for a nightcap at his camp. I made my usual excuses, scuttled back here to keep my nine o'clock Skype date, but I have a feeling that Ess won't be far behind, and I don't like the idea of his walking in on me when Alice and I are saying we love each other or whatever. From where I'm sitting I can't quite see Harry's camp, but I should at least have a good view of Ess before he makes it in through the door.

'Don't feel too sorry for him,' I say. 'He got over it in like a *minute*. Like a *minute* later he was carousing round the campfire, joking, singing… He's tougher than you think.'

'Is he?' Said as if it were I, not she, who underestimated Ess's resilience. 'And isn't it funny how he's been right about everything? He said you'd go to such and such a place and meet Tarik Kundra, and you go there, and there Tarik Kundra is...'

'There's a guy here called Tarik Kundra. Proves nothing.'

'You don't think he's an inventor then, or...?'

'I think he *thinks* he's an inventor. But if you're asking do I think he's invented this, this machine... no, I don't. Obviously I don't.' This comes out more abrasively than I intend. But I can't seem to help myself. The wound, the peculiar scorches in my guts.

Alice raises her eyebrows. 'Do you think he's lying?'

'Not *lying*... It's like half the time he's not here. And I don't mean the time he spends hiding in his cabin, I mean when he's standing right in front of you. It's like... he's low-def. Like he's missing some pixels. A few dots, a few specks...'

'You're making me feel sorry for him. Poor bloke! Poor Tarik!' She laughs: those booming *ho ho hos* (where do they come from – out of what barrels, what tunnels, what deep-girded chambers?). 'You'll look out for him though, won't you? '

'I'll what?'

'Make sure Ess doesn't run rings round him. Take poor Tarik for a ride.'

'Where's "poor Tarik" come from? What happened to "poor Ess"?' And – while we're talking about it – what happened to poor *Steven*?

'You said it yourself, Ess is tough. He probably doesn't realise how tough he is, or when he's being tough on other people. You've said enough times he's tough on you... Just don't let him be too tough on poor Tarik.'

'I literally don't know what we're talking about now.'

She laughs again: more Father Christmas booms. It strikes me, not for the first time, that it is *she* who is running rings round *me* – which admittedly she has opportunity to do quite a lot. In fact I mind this much less than she seems to think I do. Alice

121

is clever; it's just how she is. But the way she always swerves to puncture anything she says that could be construed as being even remotely clever (a sputter of trail dots, an artfully aimed obscenity, booming laughter) makes me wonder occasionally about the history of her cleverness, the history of its reception, of how people have taken it.

Certainly it can be unsettling – Alice's cleverness. When she's working, *thinking*, sitting at her desk with her laptop and all her papers and books, it's like another presence in the room, a weight on the air, a steely vibration or hum, a threading of migraine. Usually I can cope with it, but sometimes it builds up and up in my head like the bandwidth of a pylon and I just have to stop what I'm doing and get out of the flat and stay out until she's finished *thinking*. It's weird. Though the really weird bit is, when I come back she's always hugely apologetic. As if there's something wrong with her, when it's perfectly obvious that there's something wrong with me. *It's not your fault, it's my fault*, I want to say, on these occasions. Though I don't say it, haven't ever yet said it. I'm not entirely sure why.

Alice says, 'Let's talk about something else. Did you get Daniel's email?'

'I did.' That's right: I did, didn't I? I was going to open it, read it. But somehow this didn't happen – this hasn't happened. 'Yup, yep. Pleased to see that.'

'Anything you'd like me to pass along?'

'How do you mean?'

'I'm seeing him tomorrow, so if you want to reply in any sort, I could…'

'I can reply myself.'

'You can?'

'I'll send him an email.'

'I just thought if you were too busy, or…'

'I'm not too busy. I'll do it.'

'He'd appreciate that. I think he's got worked up over this Bangalore situation. The bombs, the… well, you've read his email, haven't you?'

'Yup, yep.' I nod mechanically.

'It just seems to have got to him. They're reporting it like mad over here. I imagine it's even worse where you are…'

'It's pretty bad.' I have no idea what it is. It's not just that I've not sought coverage of the Bangalore bombing – I've avoided it, sidestepped it, shut my ears to it.

'What freaked me out was that thing about shoes… Did you see that? About rescue workers finding people's shoes in the street. And finding people's feet in the shoes…'

'Disturbing.' Up and down, my head on its hinge.

'You just think: Why? Why would anyone do that? What could possibly justify doing such a thing?'

'People are mental.'

'No they're not. Well, yes they are. But at the same time no they're not. You know what I mean? That's the worst part of it. No. They're *not.*'

'I know exactly what you mean.'

'Do you?'

'I do.' I don't know what she means.

'Are you all right out there, Jug-head?'

'What? I'm fine.' The acid of ridiculous disappointment burns in my guts, and I'm terrified that I'm going to lose her. That when I come back from my business trip not richer than Warren Buffet, not richer than Bill Gates, she's going to leave me. That she's going to recoil in disgust from my poverty, my joblessness, my powerlessness, and leave me. 'What are you talking about? I'm great out here.' I attempt a smile. 'Time of my life.'

Then she says I love you and I say I love you too.

I go to the door, look towards Harry's camp and see no one there but Harry, sitting upright with a fixed expression: watching TV inside his specs. Then I scan further and I see Asha silently rolling inside the Adventurers car, making herself comfortable for the night, and then Ess, standing by one of the other sheds, his phone clamped to his face. I'm turning away when he makes a gesture, a slicing motion of the blade of his hand, and I pause, continue watching him. For a long time I try to hear what he's saying, but at this distance it's difficult, and I'm reluctant to go any closer, to let him see that I'm listening. Finally, for a moment, his voice rises, shrilly he utters the words, 'No, no. Fancy! Well, quite! Fancy! Well, yes, that's right...' then his voice drops again and he goes on speaking, quick, irate, busily snipping. His head and limbs seem dangerously impacted into his body. I wait for him to make another dramatic gesture, to raise his voice, to mime or shout some reference to the person he's talking to, but if anything he seems to grow calmer as I watch, a familiar Ess tactic, shrinking the argument he's having until the person he's arguing with (whoever, in this case, that may be) forgets they were ever arguing with him. I watch a little longer, then turn back into the shed.

I remember Daniel's email, and settling back down on my sleeping bag, I open it:

Steven,

I am writing to you because Al tells me you have bought me a gift, which I have to say strikes me as odd for a number of reasons. As far as I was aware, my sister is already sleeping with you, and therefore you have no need of recourse to such transparent and frankly vulgar strategy. Also, am I to understand that the said gift is an elephant? A wooden carving of an elephant? Allow me to apologise if at any point in our recent dealings I have given you to believe that I am nine years old. You fucking, fucking fraud.

Otherwise, have a care, you godless sister-grifter, and make sure you steer clear of any major cities while you're over there. Impatient as I am with the bombastic, hysterical and casually racist manner in which the British media has taken to reporting it, I don't mind telling you this Bangalore situation has put the shit up me. In a context wherein a retard such as yourself is blundering about with an ice-cream cone in one hand, a camera in the other and a note pinned to his chest saying, 'Infidel Dreg/Western Scum. Fire at Will'.

So fucking watch how you go, reply if you can be arsed, and, as always, if you make Al unhappy in any way I will hunt you down and kill you,

DD (Daniel Darling)

I should reply straight away: not even think about it, scrawl down the first thing that comes into my head and zap it back to him before I have chance to lose momentum. I open a 'reply' pane and stare at the cursor – that blinking, living paper-cut. Doesn't need to be special. Anything. The first thing that comes into my head.

Then it's not night any more but a moment of enormous orange stillness either just before sunset or just after sunrise and there's no one in view for hundreds of miles and I know this because I'm suspended in the air above the plain, not drifting or floating but sort of *hanging*, looking down at the cracked vast plain, the cabin, the sheds, the six huge inert blocks in their circle, looking about at the orange emptiness of the air, frozen cloud shapes, distant specks that whirl and twirl and slowly grow larger, become people, Tarik cleaning his specs, Asha taking a photo, Harry running and leaping with his wobbly belly, Ess arguing angrily on his phone, Alice settling in front of her laptop, they

125

and others, a hundred, a thousand, a million, all the population of the planet whirling and twirling round me, swooping at my face then spiralling upwards, and then without any sensation of falling or having fallen I'm down on the ground, walking over the plain, the whole population of the planet waltzing in the air above my head while I go along, picking up the shoes I find discarded everywhere on the dry-dead earth, hundreds, thousands, millions, picking up humanity's shoes and putting them away for safekeeping in my shoulder bag.

I wake into fiery darkness. I'm flapping round on top of my sleeping bag. Something long and thin and silky skitters away from my arm and I roll onto my back and grab at my elbow. Everything is sticking to me. I'm wet, drenched, drowned in my own sweat.

As I struggle to sit up, I realise my arm is suffused with a steady, ravenous stinging; on the back of my elbow a hot node beats with its own pulse. I twist my arm, try to turn it so I can see the back of my elbow, but the turn can't be made without further pain and anyway it's so dark in here I can't see a thing.

'Ess?' I call piteously into the darkness. 'I think something bad's happened. I think something really bad's happened to me.' But he doesn't reply, doesn't make a sound, doesn't give any sign that he's in the shed with me at all.

For a minute I try groping round for my tablet, for my phone, anything with a screen that can be lit up and used against the darkness, then panic gets the better of me and I climb upwards against the wall, rock to my feet and blunder about with my hands outstretched until I find the door, push it open and dive out into the lesser darkness of the plain.

What was I thinking? It's the middle of the night. The darkness outside is lesser, but it's still darkness; and my arm is no easier, no less painful, to turn. I can't see the back of my elbow and the node there bulks against my fingertips like a tumour, an alien growth.

A mosquito has bitten me. I have malaria. I have no future now but delirium then death.

The air is full of grief, full of an inconsolable keening. I assume it's me, my keening, then I realise it's not: the sound is coming from elsewhere. For a long time I don't care about the sound; then I stop trying to turn my arm, allow it to fall naturally against my side, though I keep my other hand pressed hard over the point of the elbow, as if trying to push the node back in, to force it to break up on the bone, and I look about for the source of the sound.

Now the lesser darkness is lesser still; against the grey sky the cabin and the sheds appear in phantasmal outline. I scuttle towards the cabin, but the sound grows no louder; I scuttle towards one of the other sheds, and the sound grows softly quieter. Then I scuttle towards the final shed and the sound becomes loud, rich with detail. In the same instant that I realise it's Ess making the sound, Ess crying, Ess keening, I plunge myself against the front of the shed, find the door handle, turn it, and fling the door open.

Inside the shed there's a small, yellow light; I can't see where it's coming from but it makes me think of candles, vases, a leaking wick under glassy sheen. Ess is lying on the floor in the yellow light. His face is tipped so that I can see only one ridged side of it.

'Get *out*,' he hisses. 'Get *out* of here.'

'Yes,' I say, 'sorry, fuck...'

I fling the door shut and reel backwards into the darkness. Nonetheless all I can see is the yellow light, the side of Ess's face, and Asha lying under him, her eyes alertly amused, softly chiding, and seeming to ask, *How does the world look to you now?*

10

'It's nothing,' says Harry. 'A fleabite, maybe. A *splinter…*'

'Are you sure?' I push my elbow closer to his face, almost hitting the end of his nose. 'Have a good look.'

'You've turned over in your sleep, hooked a splinter out of the wall…' He goes back to prodding our breakfast round the pan – two sausages, two eggs, two rashers of bacon. 'Sure, you'll want to keep on top of your antimalarials…'

'I had a double dose this morning. Two pills.'

'I don't recommend that. No sir. Keep on top of your regimen, because that's what you'd do anyway, but you've nothing to worry about there.'

He gives me a reassuring smile then returns his attention to the pan. And yes, I'm reassured, I'm grateful. But still for a moment I go on looking at him, wondering: *Who are you, Harry? What are you up to?*

'I just wish I could *see* it…' I'm about to start my whole futile arm-turning thing again when the shed furthest away from us clunks open and Ess steps out of it. In a state of fixed-smile dishevelment, pretending not to have seen us, he crosses to the latrine and carefully shuts its rickety door after him.

Harry hands me my plate. I take it and begin greedily eating without moving my eyes away from the shed Ess has just left.

'Didn't you gentlemen…' But I shake my head until Harry shuts up and joins me in staring at the shed.

We've both finished eating by the time the shed clunks again and Asha comes out. She walks straight up to us, drops herself down on the ground next to Harry's cooker and taking out a nail file asks if there's any more breakfast stuff because she doesn't know why but she's *starving*. She says this looking right at me, as if we share a delicious secret, which to my mind we don't.

'No problem,' Harry says, and goes on in a way that suggests the significance of Ess and Asha stepping out of the same shed passed him by completely, 'important we keep our strength up. Place like this, it'll wear you right down.'

'That's absolutely right.' Asha spins the twinkly file.

'And it's an important day, right? Take two of the big demonstration.' Harry chortles over his pan: his space-shuttle eggs, his zero-gravity sausages. 'That is, assuming Tarik's got his shit together. Man, at this rate those Swiss are going to leave his ass for dust.' He glances at us, expecting to be asked for clarification, but Asha is more interested in her nails and I'm having trouble looking up from my plate. He clarifies anyway, 'Those Swiss guys, they're making strides. I don't know that they're even so far behind Tarik with this one now. We're talking, like, any day...'

Then the latrine door clicks again and my head snaps up and I don't hear much else of what Harry is saying because I'm watching Ess, still with his fixed smile, still jolting along with his alone-in-the-world automaton carriage, walk to the cabin, knock, wait, then stand in uneasy conference with Tarik, who leans out the door at him in the manner of a suburbanite disturbed by police in the night for no proper reason. Then Tarik disappears and Ess comes veering towards us, holding his hands out and rubbing them together as if he's just washed them with a powerful disinfectant.

'Morning, morning,' he calls, already skirting Harry's camp, 'I believe we're looking at lunchtime for the demo, so, don't tell Tarik, but I thought I'd pop over to the village. Stretch the old legs. See you later, and for god's sake don't tell Tarik.'

'I'll come.' I stand quickly, knocking my empty plate, flipping it over in the dust. 'You don't mind, do you?'

'As you please.' He clearly minds very much, but there's nothing he can do about that now. I'm walking along next to him, and Harry and Asha are watching us. 'I only wonder,' he murmurs after a few more paces, 'if you're quite up to it.'

'Why wouldn't I be up to it?'

'Well it's quite a way, isn't it? How far did we say? Five miles, six? Might be a bit rough on the old back.' He nods confidentially.

'We said it was two miles. I'll be fine.'

'Will you.'

'It's been okay. "The old back". I think it might actually be getting better.'

'Do you?'

'I think it might.'

'Well.' He smiles, laughs, apparently despite himself. The stiff eye crinkles soften and flex. 'That *is* good news.'

Isn't it?

One Friday night four years ago I got myself knocked down by a car. There was damage to my back, a nebulous wedging or rippling of the flesh round my spine, a 'joggling about' that left no material injury but deeply baffled the pain receptors in my lumbar region, promising years of lost signals, ghostly sensations, the busy click of immaterial needles. A fairly mild course of physio was suggested and once a week for six weeks a cheerful guy called Dolan rearranged my limbs on a crash mat. I took some heavy-duty painkillers, then some less heavy-duty ones, then none at all on a regular basis. Occasionally I would feel something weird – gripping, contracting, clicking – but a couple of days of gulping over-the-counter aspirin soon smoothed everything out. And that was pretty much it.

Except, that is, for the matter of how I'd got myself knocked down in the first place.

I was still in the hospital when Ess started talking about it. He had several reasons to do this. One was his concern for my wellbeing. Another was his concern for the company. Both of these concerns related to the fact that the hospital's careful overnight examination of me had discovered, among other things, that my system was pumped full of narcotics. That, at the time of the accident, I'd been illegally intoxicated. I'd been smashed out of my head.

'We're not going to worry about this,' Ess said, leaning forward at my bedside (this was my second or third day in). 'I mean the legal dimension or what-have-you. This is not a dimension I individually or Resolute Aviation as a whole takes an interest in. And if we're not interested in it, we won't hear it said. And so it isn't said. It goes away.' He made a swiping gesture – a magician vanishing a small object. 'It's gone, it never existed.' His smile narrowed, came to rest on me with delicate purpose. 'Which, I'm happy to say, leaves only my other concern. Which is you. Which is you, Mr Strauss.'

At the time I didn't fully register what he was saying: that he, or the company, or at any rate someone, was going to suppress the hospital's report on me – to detain it, isolate it, bury it. Were such things possible? Did people like Ess, companies like Resolute, have the means to achieve them? It seemed fabulous, impossible. But this occurred to me only later. At the time I couldn't think about anything but the series of questions contained in Ess's narrow smile.

The answer to more or less all his questions was that I was smoking a lot of weed, among other things. You wouldn't have thought it then, and you certainly wouldn't think it now, but for about three years I was a full-on caner. Every day during that period – from within a couple of months of my move to Yeovil

132

until the Friday night I got myself knocked down by a car – I was at least a little bit mashed, and on many days I was very mashed indeed. I presented no drug culture for the reason I didn't have any: when I indulged I indulged alone, in the aerated isolation of the (pre-Alice) Hawks Rise flat.

Why? That's what Ess wanted to know too, and while I ended up saying a great deal to him on the subject I'm not sure I ever really gave him an answer, because I'm not sure I ever really had one. Why, during that period, did I get quite so fucked up? I don't know. But I knew I couldn't say that to Ess, not when he was taking such trouble over me, not when he looked at me with that narrow, delicate smile, and without exactly lying I tried to come up with stuff that would suffice, frowned and struggled to fit words like 'stress' and 'crisis' and 'depression' into sentences that made sense.

Entirely confidentially, he arranged some counseling sessions for me. Twice a month for almost a year I met a sweet-natured middle-aged lady called Janice in a small homely room at the top of a gappy flight of stairs at the Yeovil Drug and Alcohol Centre. Most of our sessions took place on work nights, and usually I arrived at the centre and strolled past the druggies and junkies, raggedly writhing in their plastic chairs, still in my work clothes, and sat down in the high bare room still crackling with my work energy, my office snap and whiplash. I don't know how to say it: Janice was impressed with me. I think I wasn't in the least what she was used to. She asked how I was and when I gave her some breezy anecdote about my working day she laughed automatically, nervously, shrilly. Quite a heavy lady, Janice was: lots of lumps of Janice to love.

She shouldn't have thought so well of me. Ess drove me to those sessions and sat in the car with his newspaper and when I came out he drove me home. He never asked how a session had gone. He never seemed annoyed when a session overran

133

(as they did increasingly, until we agreed to discontinue them altogether). And he never missed one. Two a month for almost a year. Not one.

It was Janice who suggested that I'd not had a problem with drugs so much as a problem with loneliness and despair, which seemed to me to be letting me off altogether too lightly, though this was more or less the same interpretation Alice took when we got round to talking about that part of my life. 'Is that right?' she asked, protectively circling one of my arms with both of hers. 'Do you think you were very lonely back then?'

'I suppose I was.'

'But you're not any more, are you, no? You're not lonely now, are you, no?'

'I'm not lonely any more.'

This answer seemed to satisfy her, because her next question was simply, 'Where did you get it from? The stuff?'

'There used to be a bloke in one of the other flats. He was actually called Randy. He sold the strongest skunk I'd ever come across. He called it "mind control". He was very helpful.' He was a drug dealer, was what he was.

'Mmn. It sounds like *Ess* was helpful. Do you think he felt guilty?'

'Why would he feel guilty?'

'Well there you'd been, right under his nose, off your gourd every day for what was it, a year? Longer? He must've felt bad about that.'

'I suppose so.' But I didn't. I didn't suppose that was why Ess had helped me.

Her final question was, 'What was it like? Being so stoned all the time?'

'It wasn't like anything. It was like… no edges, no corners. Just… floating.'

'Was it nice?'

'Some of the time it was nice.'

'And you just gave it up?'

'After I got knocked down by a car and shopped by my boss and ferried to and from counseling for a year, yeah, I just gave it up.'

'Just like that.'

'Just like that.'

Ess and I have been walking for at least an hour, barely speaking, only occasionally commenting on our surroundings, when we come in sight of the village, a thatched horizon with black trails of smoke coming out of it. The dust thickens, darkens, and starts to show the patterning of human industry – rows, furrows, raddled meshes. As we approach the road an incurious shepherd passes with his herd. We pause to watch the last of the cattle go by, their hind parts like unslung saddles rocking and sliding inside bloody sacks.

At the edge of the village we pause again to inspect a tall, skinny sort of pylon with a meteorological look to it. While we're standing there I decide that enough's enough and I start to say, 'Uh, last night…'

'Oh, no.' Ess smiles mildly up at the pylon. 'No. I don't think so, do you?'

We enter the village, briefly sharing the lane with a group of turbaned men trooping out to the fields with their hands full of slender, wand-like tools – antennaed rods, eyeleted sticks: hoes? rakes? – men who observe us with as little curiosity as the farmer we passed on the road. Then the lane empties and we go on between rather squat, solid circular huts each with a springy blonde thatch and frenetically textured walls, the painterly plastering on every side carrying rigid whirlpools of mud and hay and a taut clean tang of shit.

We pass workshops, something like a blacksmith's, something like an ironmonger's, a brackish roaring concrete building with kilns at the back of it. We pass huge steel-and-glass pods full of water. We pass a tamarind tree with an easel propped against it, except the easel isn't an easel but a flat metal box gripped in a tripod with cables snaking into it from every part of the village. We pass a stone well surrounded by ornately carved wooden pillars and brilliant chalk patterns etched in the dust: supernovae, chemical formulae…

At last we enter a courtyard with the bristling atmosphere of a marketplace, though it's not a marketplace. Veiled women stalk past us with a faintly indignant air. I expect Ess to try charming them, waving, calling out, but he doesn't do any of this. He walks along with a concentrated expression, lips pursed, eyes not narrowed but unnaturally still.

The courtyard is full of people eating, drinking, talking, sitting, standing. Absurdly I think for a moment that the place must be a sort of open-air café. Then I notice a strange absence, which is the absence of currency. No money is changing hands. No one is buying anything. No one is selling anything. For some reason I think of the roaring kilns. Then I notice a strange absence, which is the absence of Ess. Suddenly he's nowhere near me, he's gone. I look round and there's only the bristling life of the villagers with their tea and their bread, their voices, their laughter. My hand drifts to my elbow, its sore malarial node.

Then I see him. He's strolling towards me, talking earnestly with a kid of sixteen or so in a bright red T-shirt. I shoot my arms in a what-the-fuck gesture. Ess laughs.

'Laxman, allow me to introduce my impatient young associate.'

The kid grins at me, startlingly. His lips twang and reduce to a stealthy insect pulsing at either side of his mouth. His teeth are immaculate, but they glare out in a pale block of naked gum. All I can see when I look at him are grooves, notches, bulges of gum.

Laxman leads us to a corner of the courtyard, urges us to sit, then brings us dinged tin plates of roti, clenchy clay mugs of chai. Ess is halfway through a speech about the rustic charm of it all when Laxman, innocently, unpointedly, takes a phone from his pocket and slits its screen with his fingertip. I start to laugh and kick Ess's leg. I roll onto my back and I see them everywhere in the courtyard: turbaned men, veiled women, kids mounted on saffron laps, flicking, scrolling, pinching at touchscreens. Denizens of the Indian wilds, downloading movies and music, Skypeing friends in New York and Beijing.

'It was a mast!' I hoot, getting in a couple more good kicks at Ess's leg. 'That pylon thing, it was a mast!' I turn to Laxman. 'It's your mast, isn't it? We saw your wifi mast.'

'Did you?' Again he grins his ghastly grin. 'Which one?'

'Ha!' Ess says, and kicks my feet until I have to actually roll him over in the dust.

While we eat, Laxman tells us about his village (its factions, its rivalries, of which he speaks with a tolerant irony) then he gets up to leave. When he shakes our hands Ess tries to pass him some money. Laxman doesn't want it; but Ess insists. Their struggle becomes ludicrous. Ess keeps driving the notes at him; Laxman keeps driving them back. Then Laxman doesn't quite throw the notes down – they slip from his fingers and flutter to the ground. I pick them up and slide them into my pocket. Laxman bows to each of us, smiling with closed lips, then turns and heads away down a crowded lane.

If Ess is embarrassed he doesn't show it. He smiles, sighs, gazes contentedly round the courtyard.

After a while I say, 'Last night. I know you don't want to talk about it…'

'I do not,' he agrees.

'I just think I deserve to know what the situation is. Between you and Asha.'

For a moment he goes on smiling brightly and blandly round the courtyard, a sort of holding position. Then, without any change of expression, he starts to say, 'I honestly don't know. True, while I was here last… it was an exciting time, as I'm sure you can appreciate. Both of us were terribly excited. We were solving a mystery together, we were…' He is hating this; the strained dome of his forehead shows how much. 'I think perhaps we got rather carried away. There was a night, not long before I came home… but I can say in all honesty I had no thought there would be any recurrence of, any resumption of… Altogether I was quite as surprised by our rapprochement last night as you were.'

'I doubt that.' I consider rolling him over in the dust again, but don't. 'Do you see it going anywhere?'

'I'm by no means persuaded there is an "it". And no, I don't see "it" going anywhere, because at present my thoughts are not tending in that direction. Naturally I'm not opposed to the idea, Asha is… well, she's… all I mean is let's deal with one thing at a time, shall we? First things first.' He goes back to his survey of the courtyard.

It occurs to me that, while he's in a talkative mood, now may be a good time to ask Ess about Harry – about who Harry is, about what Harry is up to, or whether he's up to *anything* – but before I can find a way into the subject he says, 'Isn't it marvellous? All this? Gandhi said "the soul of India is its villages". Did you know that?'

'I didn't know that.'

'And to think, if Tarik had his way, we'd never even get to see it…'

'Why is that? Why doesn't he like us coming here?'

'*Oh*… Tarik has some funny ideas.' He laughs indulgently. 'Thinks there are spies round every corner, company eyes and ears the length and breadth of the continent, bounty hunters desperate to collect "the price on his head", who knows what else…'

'You think he's not right about that?'

'I think he's a touch overcautious. No one, no company on earth has the resources he seems to imagine his angry old bosses have.'

'Have you told him that?'

'Of course I have.' Ess beams readily – maybe half a second too readily. 'Told him till I was blue in the face. But would he listen?'

'Couldn't you… *make* him listen?'

'How do you propose I would do that?'

'I don't know, it just seems… you're saying the only thing keeping him out here is a mistake. The only reason he's hiding in that crappy cabin is some wild idea he's got about the power of his old company. If you could make him see that… well, he'd be free, wouldn't he? That's right, isn't it?'

'I suppose it is.' Ess beams. In this beam his teeth are forks, glinting spikes.

'He could do what he wanted, go where he liked. Free as a bird.'

'Yes, I suppose he could.' Ess beams his spiky beam. Then he frowns, somewhat flutteringly, and says in a rapid undertone, 'I'm just not sure we can describe Tarik's state of mind as being simply "mistaken". Believe me, I've told him these things, and he rebuffed my arguments with a vociferousness that suggested the issues went… rather deeper. Naturally I don't want to cast aspersions over our good friend, though when we consider what he's been through, what infernos he's passed through, we can hardly be surprised if along the way he's acquired… complications.' Ess sighs, twists a smile into the middle of his frown. 'You see, poor creature, he's formed a sort of delusion. Awful, I know. And yet in a case such as this, positively the worst thing you can do is try to force a chap to confront his delusion.

139

Far better to go along with the delusion, to tolerate it, to pet it even, and wait until it breaks up of its own accord. Altogether the best policy.'

I look at him. Then I start to nod. 'You really think that's best?'

'I really do.'

I sit nodding. 'Tarik's delusional. He has delusions about things.'

'When we consider what he's been through, the gauntlet, the defile of flame…'

'Do you think maybe he has delusions about other stuff?'

'What other stuff would that be?'

'Maybe this whole thing. Antigravity, his machine, the whole thing…'

'In what sense?'

'Well. Maybe it doesn't work.'

Ess laughs, not at all indulgently, a reproving hard bark. 'You're forgetting, dear boy, I've seen it. Evidence of my own eyes.'

'How do you know what you saw? How does anyone? If someone's made up their mind to fool you, to *deceive*…'

'If you're a complete idiot…'

'I'm not saying that. But if you *want* to believe, if you *want* it to be true…'

'If you're crazy, if you're a crazy person who's lost their mind.'

I sit back, away from him, showing him the palms of both hands.

After a while I take out my cigarettes, light up, begin gustily smoking. Ess watches me curiously: something he's not seen before. Then he says, 'Could I trouble you for one of those?' I hand him the pack and he lights up also. Absorbing the first sharp lungful, he waves his cigarette airily and says, 'Think about where we are. How logical is what you're suggesting?'

I don't say anything. Then I say, 'I don't follow.'

'If Tarik were taking us for a ride. Supposing what I saw the last time was an illusion, a rope trick. Now we're here, we've got access to the money, so why would he delay? Why keep the deception going when he could've simply extracted his fee and bumped us off the night we arrived? Couple of hired hands, he could've done it in two minutes. Clueless foreigners, remote location. Flip open a laptop, wave a knife in our faces while we transfer the funds, all that, then slit our throats and chuck our bodies in the river. Easy as pie.' He smiles at me, fairly gently. 'You see? It doesn't make sense.'

I don't say anything. Because now I finally see it, the thing I've been missing. Tarik is dangerous. Whatever else he is – criminal hoaxer, curdled nerd, all-out lunatic – he's a threat to us, to our actual *lives*.

As we re-cross the plain, my thoughts are all questions. What am I doing here? Why did I come here? Because Ess told me to? Because Martin Cantor told me to? How did I fail to see that this entire trip was not simply madness but *incredibly dangerous* madness? Who kept that from me? Who allowed any of this to happen?

It strikes me that the only decisive action I've taken since arriving in this country was my refusal to tip the staff of the hotel in Mumbai. I could cry, I could scream.

As we approach Tarik's cabin, several things start to happen. My elbow starts to pulse, my double dose of malaria pills starts to clank in my stomach, my back starts to click, click, click. Tarik comes out of his cabin and starts shouting at us about something. Hearing the noise, Harry and Asha start walking towards us from the direction of the river.

Tarik shouts at Ess, who for a while tries to speak calmly during Tarik's pauses for breath, then starts shouting also. Tarik gestures repeatedly and violently towards the village. With both hands Ess grips his head, as if trying to rip it open. They've been at it for some time before I realise they're speaking English.

While they argue Tarik's face keeps changing shape. It darkens, splinters, jags. It's the face of a dangerous man, the face of a violent lunatic, the face of a murderer. It can be the face of no other sort of man. How did I fail to see it? How did I contrive not to know?

Harry and Asha stand nearby, in bathing costumes, their arms draped with towels. They look on with expressions of amusement, and irresponsible unconcern. I could seize their wet shoulders, scream into their dripping faces: *Run!*

Still shouting, Tarik swivels away from Ess and begins to march towards his test site. Ess starts after him, but as a gap widens between them I see my chance. I scuttle to Ess's side and, almost fainting with terror, with the pain in my back, with the malaria in my veins, I grab his arm. 'We need to go,' I say.

'What?' he shouts, still striding after Tarik, who has stepped in between the blocks and disappeared from view. 'What are you talking about?'

'We need to leave. We need to get in the car...'

'What are you talking about?'

'We need to *leave*...' Gnashing with pain, frothing with malaria.

'We're not going anywhere. They only place we're going...'

'Jesus fucking Christ.' I throw myself in front of him. 'If we stay here...'

'What? If we stay here what? What's wrong with you?'

'What's wrong with me...'

Smoothly the sun changes its place in the sky. In the middle of the blazing afternoon we're standing in darkness. Ess looks past me and up. I turn and look up also and there are six blocks of concrete lightly anchored twenty or thirty feet above the surface of the plain.

11

Six blocks of concrete lightly anchored twenty or thirty feet above the surface of the plain.

In the air. Above the ground. Identical grey-black hulks with their straight lines, their corners and edges, moored in the white sea of the sky.

Tarik stands gazing up, surrounded by wires. His hands rest loosely on the platform in front of him, either side of the machine. He, the machine and the platform all look suddenly and obscenely exposed, though none of them seems to have noticed yet. Moving his head very slightly from side to side, he wears a faint contented smile. A man at leisure on a warm day, scanning the sky for any sign of a change in the weather.

Ess smiles, sighs, shakes his head, takes a couple of steps towards the blocks, arms open, as if planning to take them into one of his famously enveloping embraces. Then he stops, spins round, glares back at me with bared teeth. His eyes crushed to slits, his lips glittering, scaled, spittle-seared.

'*See?*' he hisses.

Harry drops his towel. There it goes, out of his arms, over his belly, down his legs, into the dust. His mouth falls open, his eyes widen with an elderly jitter. He puts his hands into his beard and starts winding up little bits of it, tying his fingers into its straggly coils, as if bracing himself for impact. He looks exactly, exactly like an American grandfather surprised by a TV film crew bringing heart-melting news during a family outing to the beach.

'Oh wow,' he says. 'Oh I mean *wow*.'

Asha laughs. She hooks her towel over her shoulders and just stands there, laughing.

I say, 'No.'

I look, I see. I wonder if I'm going to pass out. I wonder if I've already passed out – if I'm in fact not here at all, not standing in the middle of the plain in the middle of the blazing afternoon, but lying under a blanket on the backseat of the Adventurers car while Asha jolts over pot hole after pot hole in the headlong, mosquito-tumbled night, speeding to reach the nearest clinic, to save me from the lethal weir opened at my elbow, the death-white waters of malaria. Am I here? Or there? Or where am I? Lying on a bed in a hospital room, watching specks form and reform, configure and refigure on a blank field of ceiling?

'No,' I say.

After a while Ess turns away from me and starts walking towards the blocks.

Soon Asha steps past me and starts walking towards the blocks.

Harry steps past me and starts walking towards the blocks.

I look down. I lean forward, put my hands on my knees and stare at the ground.

The earth, dry, grey, particulate. The rippling and waving of this bare stretch of plain land, the torsions of the microterrain, its straining fault-lines, its stones in their sheared grids. Familiar and yet fascinating, banal and bizarre. What's more real than the earth? There it is, right under your feet.

I straighten, look up again, and there they are.

Six blocks of concrete airily anchored twenty or thirty feet above the surface of the plain.

Each of the airborne blocks is anchored at its outer end by the rope tied round its middle and descending to a loophole in a metal stake hammered into the ground. Each of these ropes now describes a taut diagonal line, but shows no suggestion of strain.

Similarly, each block is anchored at its inner end by the wire tied round its middle and descending to a port in the machine on the platform in front of Tarik. Similarly, each of these wires is taut but free from strain.

The ropes and the wires are roughly the same length, but not quite, and the longer you look the more clearly appear the subtle differences in elevation from block to block: a nosing-up here, a dipping-down there. And yet, you feel, smoothly, strongly, without strain, each block is seeking the level, as water does.

I start walking towards the blocks.

'What do we think?' Ess shouts, spinning at the edge of the test site, arms open, apparently surveying us each in turn for our opinion. 'Shall I do it?'

The blocks no longer seem identical. Up there, the way the light dives at them, hacks at them, peels the skin from their surfaces with its crazy little knives.

'Shall I, though? Who thinks I should do it?'

Texture like combed hair. Like charity-shop chiffon. Like adolescent acne. Like polystyrene packaging. Like pond scum. Like ancient bark. Like everything on and of the earth.

'No!' Asha shouts, laughing.
   'I really don't think…' Harry says.
   'Don't do it!' Asha laughs.
   'No, sorry, I'm going to do it,' Ess says.

Nor are the blocks quite motionless. They carry no force, exert no pressure, the perception of which itself rolls over and over in the stomach like vertigo. They look exactly as they did while they stood on the ground, possess the same dimensions and substance, except now they are weightless. The majesty, the terror of their weight is gone and they turn on their anchor-lines as the breaths and breezes of the plain dictate.

Ess, arms open, spinning at the edge of the test site.
   Then I see what he's going to do.

*

A block of concrete the length and breadth and depth of a backyard swimming pool.

Suspended above the hard pack of the plain by a wire the thickness of fishing line.

By a machine that works but shouldn't work, that may realise its mistake at any moment.

He's going to run underneath it.

A connection failing. A circuit silently blowing. An invisible fault twanging the length of the taut-drawn wire.

And then the return, the revenge of all that weight.

He runs under the block.

A bird blurred to shadow skimming a lake surface at night.

He runs out the other side. Spinning. Falling over. Hooting in the dust.

Then we're shouting, all of us, screaming out our lungs.

It happens then it's happened.

The world is not what it was – is no longer or never was.

Everything slides, everything spills. That terror.

The earth is fluid pouring away. The sky a huge gaudy reflection – slightly tinselly.

Then the earth is the earth and the sky is the sky and the world is just what it is now.

*

That shift, that accommodation.
Okay.

I run towards Ess. By the time I get there he's back on his feet.
He grabs my shoulders. I sort of grab his.
'Do you see?' he shouts into my face.
'I do. Jesus fucking Christ, I *do* see,' I shout into his.

Harry is jumping on the spot, his hands joined over his head
in a prizefighter's composite fist. His belly keeps elbowing for
more room over the waistband of his swimming trunks. His feet
kick at his towel under him. The towel flaps, snaps, catches on
his long toes.

'What do you see?' Ess shouts.
'What do I see? I see the end of the world is what I see.'
'Which is what?'
'No more cars.'
'No more car crashes.'
'No more buses.'
'No more bus stops.'
'No more traffic lights.'
'No more roundabouts.'
'No more roads.'
'No more motorways.'
'No more *roads*.'
'Which is before you even get to the money.'

*

Laughing, Asha falls to her kneels, rolls onto her side, laughing.

'No more what? Tell me.'
　'No more trains.'
　'No more railways stations.'
　'No more railway lines.'
　'No more ships.'
　'No more planes.'
　'No more docks.'
　'No more airports.'
　'No more bicycles.'
　'No more bicycle lanes.'
　'No more, no more *wheelchairs*...'
　'Which is before you even give a thought to the money.'

Harry bends, scrapes at the towel wrapped round his feet, working his arm like a mechanical claw in a tank full of fairground treats. He scrapes, misses. Scrapes, misses.

'You did this.'
　I grab Tarik's shoulders. He smiles, nods, pleased, embarrassed.
　'Yes,' he says.
　I grab the sides of his face.
　'How did you do this?'
　'Well, I...'
　'You're a genius. That's how you did it, Tarik.'
　I squeeze his face. His specs ride up, his lips turn to pink blubber.
　He tries to say something but the blubber can't get it out.
　'Oh, yeah. That's how you did it. You're a genius, Tarik.'

I want to kiss him, I want to fuck him, I want to bear all his babies.

Asha stops laughing. She sits up and starts taking photographs.

'You *did* this.'

   'I did. But I can't…'

   'Just you. Just you, Tarik…'

   'No, no.'

   'You mean your guys, your team…'

   'No, no.'

   'Who do you mean, Tarik?'

I let go of his face. He plucks at the frame of his specs and places them back in true on the bridge of his nose. He smiles at me and seems to say, 'My lever.'

   'Your what?'

   'My lever,' he seems to say again.

   'Your lever?'

   'My what?'

   'Your lever.'

   'No, no.' He laughs, amused, embarrassed. 'My Reva. My Reva. My wife.'

Like *my Alice*. Like *my Eunice*.

   'Oh,' I say. 'Oh *of course*.'

   'Yes. Of course.'

Harry scrapes at his towel, misses it.

   Then the air comes out of him and he flops forward like a punctured balloon. Slack and heavy, he rolls in the dust. Puckers of deflation on his belly and head.

Ess shouts. Because he shouts, I shout as well.
Tarik runs to Harry, crouches at the fallen man's side.
Because he runs and crouches, I run and crouch too.
Asha carries on taking photographs.

'Oh wow,' Harry says.

He's sitting up, his thick pale legs spraddled in front of him.
His face starkly red and blue. His hands shaking, with the lumpy
stitches of their veins.

'He needs water,' Tarik says.

'Oh boy. Just give me a minute here…'

'Do we have water?'

'I'll get some,' I say. 'No problem. I'll get some water.'

All our bottles are empty.

Before anyone can stop me I run back across the plain to the
Adventurers car and realise only when I get there that the car
is locked. The backseat full of water bottles in their high-stress
plastic wrap. I pull uselessly at the door anyway.

I start to run back towards the test site, back to get the car-
keys from Asha, then I stop running and stand for a second in
the tinfoil glare of Tarik's cabin.

I glance back towards the test site. The vast sailing black slabs.
I try the door to Tarik's cabin. It opens easily and I go inside.

Inside the cabin is mostly shelves – wood shelves on three sides,
aluminum brackets, floor to ceiling, huge cans and sacks of dry
food, huge containers of drinking water.

At one end a hammock, like a grubby net, and a heap of
threadbare rugs.

At the other end a workbench covered with bits of what look like broken telephones, fax machines, radios, cassette players, stereos.

A stack of circuit boards. A soldering iron in its neat nylon pouch.

A laptop standing open with its screensaver slideshow, looped cameraphone shots, a very fat woman smiling in various sunny locations.

A ribbed metal box, like a smallish toolbox.

A wall of cabinets, all locked.

A fridge with two unopened two-litre bottles of water in it.

I take one, close the fridge, and leave the cabin.

I start running back across the plain.

As I go I have an oblique sense of something else I saw in Tarik's cabin, something I saw and didn't see, something in the small toolbox, which in fact isn't a toolbox but a carry-case, which doesn't contain tools but something else, which in fact is a gun.

I'm still running when the blocks begin to lower out of the sky. I stop to watch them. Behind a rustling curtain of heat haze the black slabs smoothly descend. As they touch back down on the plain a skirt of pale dust furls out round them then spreads and thins and then disappears altogether.

Harry is still sitting on the ground where I left him. The wide burn marks in his bald head, the weeping blisters, the ruts and scuffs.

Asha is sitting next to him, her bag spread on her knee, her camera dangling from its strap round her neck. Ess and Tarik are nowhere in sight.

Asha takes the bottle from me and passes it to Harry. We both watch him drink.

'Man, do I feel a fool,' he says.

'We need to get you out of this sun,' Asha says.

'Oh, there's no call for that...'

'You need rest, you need shade...'

'I don't think I do. No sir.'

He gets to his feet like water somehow running uphill.

'Where's Tarik?' he asks.

Where's Ess?

Ess and Tarik are standing inside the circle of re-earthed blocks, a short distance from the machine on its platform. Harry, Asha and I enter the circle and move along between the blocks, their eerie dust-sprayed surfaces, their otherworldly pocked sides.

Ess grins at us, salutes.

'All things considered, I'd say that went rather well, wouldn't you?'

'Have you tried it on a human being?' I ask Tarik.

'On a person? No, no.'

'You need to try it on a person.'

'No, no.'

'Yes, yes.'

Ess and Tarik are talking. Harry and Asha are talking.

I wander over to the machine on its platform.

The machine is hooked up to a box of ports. The ground is covered with loops of wire. So in fact it's incredibly easy.

I pull all the wires out of the port box.

I take a fresh loop of wire and plug it into the port box. I tie the wire round my waist.

I look at the machine. It has only one switch. So in fact it's incredibly easy.

'Shall I do it? Who thinks I should do it?'

No one has time to stop me. Would they stop me, if they had time?

I throw the switch.

And I swim up in the air, catch on my line and turn and turn and turn in the white sea of the sky.

12

They bring me down a changed man.

It turns out the soft landing of the blocks was misleading. After a while of Tarik waving up at me and pointing down at the machine, of Asha taking my photograph, of Ess shouting through cupped hands, 'Try to crumple,' Tarik presses the switch and I slam down towards the ground. I land feet-first with a splintering impact that surely breaks both my ankles. I say, 'Ow.'

'Light as a feather!' Ess cries, and mimes my descent with fluttering fingers.

I wait for myself to keel over with my broken ankles. But I don't keel over. My ankles are not broken. I'm not in pain, not even dizzy. Only the ground, the earth, rushing against the soles of my feet.

'What was it like?' Ess asks.

'What was it *like*?' I free myself from the wire, stagger round a bit, start to laugh.

But they bring me down a changed man.

I stagger about in circles until my feet feel normal, or normalish, then get off to a limping start across the plain.

'Where are you going?' Ess shouts.

'Call of nature,' I shout back. Which, I suppose, is one way of putting it. One way of describing the urgency that now possesses my mind and body.

We've no money.

The machine works and we've no money.

As I limp across the plain I try to remember what else Ess said was part of the deal: 'safe passage out of India'. What's that? A passport? A visa? Papers – sort of thing? I'm pretty sure Ess explained all this to me in some detail. But at the time I wasn't listening.

I open the rickety door to the latrine, scuttle inside and drag the door shut after me. I stand in the reek with one hand looped in the bit of string that passes for the door handle while with my other hand I revolve the innards of my phone for Martin Cantor's number, the number he gave me for use in the event of unease, then hit 'Call'.

The phone rings, rings. The reek fumes round me.

Rings, rings. The torpid jets, the lazy furnace of the latrine.

Then the ring fillips and an automated voice reconnects me to voicemail.

'Martin? Hi, this is Steven, Steven Strauss? Uh, call me back. I don't know what else to say. I'm not in trouble or anything, but uh, we need the money. The money? The account? For Mr Kundra's fee? We need the bogus account to be uh, not bogus. We need it to be a real account with, with real money in it. I don't think he's tried it yet, I mean Ess, so it's all right, I don't think he… What I mean is we need to make a deal out here and I'm pretty sure he still *doesn't know* and so we need the money really as soon as you can manage that. I mean it works. It *works* and we need to *buy* it and we need *the money*… so call me back. Okay. Uh, thanks. Bye.'

The mood of general celebration lasts at least halfway into dinner, which is again rice and beans, again taken on a scramble of rugs under the plain's water-bright stars. With Asha more or less sitting on his knee, Ess makes a long and hilarious and heartfelt speech;

we all laugh and fall about and clear the corners of our eyes with the heels of our palms. Then he raises his cup – 'in honour of the genius of our dear friend, a benefactor of humanity and a guardian of the very earth, Tarik Kundra' – and we all go crawling over the rugs to join our cups to his in a clashy toast. Tarik sits with his sketched-on smile. Ess tries to get him to make a speech as well, but Tarik crumples the idea up in a twisting hand and throws it playfully over his shoulder. We all laugh some more.

Every few seconds, I check my phone. No reply from Martin Cantor yet.

After the toast, the mood drops. It may be no more than everyone realising how tired they are, how pummeled by adrenaline, by the racing chemistry of the day. Ess and Asha fold into their own quiet conversation, Tarik excuses himself and drifts away into his cabin, and Harry and I are left alone on our side of the rugs.

I watch Harry eat, drink, peer across the plain, smile over his thoughts. After a while I realise I'm not sure what I'm looking at. His face is like an optical illusion – a rabbit, a duck; the pouchy bags and random straggles of a well-meaning innocent; the spiked brows and lizard eyes of another sort of man altogether. Harry Altman: who is he again? What kind of man is he? All along I've felt it, something about Harry that he's hiding. Now, whatever it is, the concealed truth of Harry Altman seems close to the surface, close to the spec rims and the beard ends, as if at any moment it might burst into visibility.

At last he sees me looking at him. 'Great day,' he says.

'You think so?'

'I do indeed.' He laughs. 'Today we witnessed a miracle. A grandeur that will cover the earth. I'd say that makes the day pretty great.' Then he shakes his head and says, 'I just wish I knew how he did it.'

'Yoga,' I say.

'Huh? Oh, no. You think I mean: How did Tarik make the blocks go up? No, what I mean is: How did Raymond persuade Tarik to make a deal? That's the interesting question.'

'Is it?'

'Boy, I'd like to know what Raymond offered him. For the machine, the plans, the rights, the whole shooting match... I mean, what can that be worth?'

'You're asking the wrong guy.'

'I'm not asking anyone. I'm just saying. The thoroughness of the transformation, the *totalness* of it... what's that got to be worth? Billions? Billions of billions? The scale of this thing, you need new numbers. You need a new math.' He laughs one of his bullshit laughs. 'What do I know? I just hope Raymond's got deep pockets, is all I'm saying.'

'Or what?'

'Excuse me?'

'Or what? If he doesn't have deep pockets?'

'Or nothing.' Harry does his arms-open-in-surrender thing. 'It's no concern of mine.'

What is he? CIA? Corporate spy? Horned devil, avenging angel?

'You've got pretty deep pockets yourself, wouldn't you say, Harry?'

'Excuse me?'

'With your "concerns". Your tour company, your school. "The Harry Altman School for Wayward Girls". Must be a nice little pile you've got put away somewhere.'

'I've got money.' An earnest blink – so-what, so-kill-me.

'Must be a fortune.'

'I wouldn't say "fortune".' He snorts. 'I've got what you may call 'software money', but I'm not rich. Sure, it's relative, say in *Indian* terms... but not so much in American terms. In American terms, in my field, my ex-field, I'm pretty close to average. You work your window, your five to ten years, you make your "nice little pile", and you clear the hell out. Guys in my profession, my ex-profession, I could tell you about, not even guys who worked on like *Skype*... Wow. I mean "Wow". No, I'm par for the course. I only perhaps in my hubris like to think it's what I do with my "nice little pile" that's not quite so par for the course.'

He says this as if expecting a round of applause or something. I stare at him. Harry sits nodding to himself.

Then he says, 'Is it funny I still think about things like that in American terms?'

'No,' I say. 'It's not funny.'

'No,' he says, 'I guess not.'

'Why are you here, Harry?'

'Excuse me?'

'Why are you here?'

'I'm having a lovely time exploring the countryside and meeting new people. Why are you here?' His voice is steady. I'm shocked by how little shocked he appears by the conversation we're having.

'I'm here because it's my job to be here. Why are you here?'

'Raymond asked if I would care to join him on an adventure, and I said I would.' His tone is now one of exhausted reasonableness. 'As a guy who for the majority of his life has failed to make a high enough priority of going on adventures, who opened a tour company and called it "Adventurers" without ever having been on an adventure, I decided this time I would go on an adventure. That's why I'm here.'

'Do you feel like you've had an adventure?'

'I surely do, yes sir.'

'Then you don't have much reason to hang round any more.'

'I wouldn't say I'm "hanging round"...'

'Whatever you've got in mind, it's not going to work.'

'Why do you think I have anything in mind?'

159

'Because you don't make sense, Harry. You don't fit together.'

'I'm sorry to hear that.' With slow effort, Harry gathers up his brows – all their tired quills and points. 'I don't know what's going on with you right now, Steven, but I have to tell you you're seeing things that aren't there. You seem to think... when all that happened is I saw Raymond's expedition on our books, an enigmatic proposition if ever there was one, I took an interest, I made contact... and Raymond and I became friends.' Slowly the brows relax, spread their broken fans. 'Is that so hard to believe?'

'You've had your adventure, Harry. Time to move on.'

He sighs. Then in the straggle mass of his beard his lips palpably harden and he says, 'You know what, I'm not sure I'm done adventuring.'

'If I were you, I'd be thinking seriously about moving on.'

'Yeah well you're not me,' he says, and looks away from me across the plain.

I try to think of something else to say, but I can't. I'm sick with the sense Harry was ready for everything I had to say, deeply prepared for it. I sit with my arms round my knees, all my joints locked to keep them from shaking. Then I look away from Harry and out across the plain too.

'It works,' I tell Alice later, in the storage shed.

'Fantastic.' In the screen she nods, curls her lip.

'Uh, yeah, it is.'

'I agree.' She nods again.

'It's going to change the world.'

'No doubt.'

'Once you start thinking about it, it's like your head's going to explode.'

'That's probably because you've just started thinking about it.'

'While you...'

'I'm pretty used to the idea. I've been giving it credence.'

I nod. She has. Somehow there's nothing else to say on the matter.

I say, 'The only problem is, we don't have any money.'

'No?'

'We didn't bring any money.'

'You didn't tell me that.'

'No.'

'Well then you're going to be busy.'

'Yeah.' I blink at her in the skin of glass. 'How about you? Are you... well?'

'I'm fine.'

She's annoyed with me for some reason, I'm annoyed with her for being annoyed with me, so we bring the conversation to an early close.

We end on a bumpy note. I say, 'I love you.'

'Yeah,' she says. 'Yeah.'

I wait. Then I say, 'And do you love me?'

And she says, 'Yeah, yeah.'

Then I'm staring at the blank screen, thinking about New York.

Which isn't fair, because for most of the three days Alice and I spent in New York last year we were very happy. Staying in an apartment that belonged to a friend of Alice's (one of the stunningly useful contacts she'd made on the conference circuit), buying groceries at a local store that had the atmosphere of a second-hand bookshop and eating our homemade sandwiches on a bench in Madison Square Park, we enjoyed all the romance of a New York winter without feeling, as I'd feared we would, that the city was continually mining us – drilling our cells, chiseling our platelets – for money. We walked often, took cabs sparingly, spent a lot of time standing at the brink of crowded sidewalks with our arms round each other and our faces tipped up into the chasm of the skyscraper sky, pretending to see which of us could catch a snowflake on their tongue first, when in reality there were no snowflakes, it wasn't even snowing.

On our last night we decided to splash out. I booked a table at a restaurant on East 16th Street, put on the suit that had so far only gathered wrinkles in my suitcase, and took a cab across the flatiron with Alice in shiny dark eye makeup and another of the molten black dresses that she seems to have an endless supply of. We ate fish with roasted vegetables followed by a banana tart that we picked apart with two forks. Alice drank two glasses of the house white and began a happy-sad monologue about Daniel, about some dreadful thing he'd said to her the other day, some wicked prank he played on her when he was ten, about the impact of his most recent *lurch* – as she called them – the cerebral lapse or winnowing that made her hesitate to take the trip at all, though it was more than a year since Daniel had lurched and he'd now recovered to the point that he was up and bombing about in his chair again and doing a first-rate job of pissing everyone off.

Then she looked at me with her wine-sleepy eyes, and smiled her sad-happy smile, and said, 'But why am I telling you this? You've no idea what I'm talking about.'

'Don't I?' I said. 'Why don't I?'

'How could you? The way you live... no friends, never see your family, never see anyone, really, except me... no ties, no commitments, no attachments... you just sort of breeze along, don't you? Breeze along in a nice little soap bubble. Don't you?'

'No,' I said.

'Oh come on, you *do*.'

'No,' I said.

And then, for the first time in the two years since we'd met, it was impossible for us to speak to each other. For a while Alice tried gamely to talk a way into my 'sulk' or my 'grump' or my 'slouch', but she couldn't do it; I literally couldn't let her do it.

Staring at the dessert dish, the two forks whimsically crossed, I felt as if I'd turned to stone. I couldn't raise my eyes to look at her, couldn't open my mouth to speak to her. All I would really have had to do was smile – relinquish the tiniest, most rueful corner of a smile – and she would have burst out laughing (*ho ho ho*) and I would have too and the entire mass of the thing would have collapsed, dematerialised. But I couldn't do it. I started to become slightly afraid that I'd never be able to do anything again and would have to stay where I was the for the rest of my life, an odd and amusing exhibit kept in place by the restaurant's tolerant owners.

Somehow we managed to pay, find a cab and get back to our borrowed apartment. Alice stormed round the bathroom and made up a bed for herself on the couch in front of the attractive, iron-barred, exposed-brick fireplace. Remotely I experienced all this as violence, as a sort of violence that was happening to both of us, though I could do nothing about it. I tumbled over on the bed, a razed statue, a lopped-off gothic gargoyle.

Lying there, with genuine interest I wondered what was wrong with me. What was wrong with me? Was it that I resented Alice's insinuation that the life of a person who has a terminally ill brother is somehow more substantial, more ponderous, more profound, than the life of a person who doesn't? Or was it that I resented the fact that she was right, that my life was a soap bubble in a breeze, worthless, weightless?

About two o'clock in the morning I crashed down into her on the couch. I pressed my nose into her hair and told her I was sorry. She told me I'd better be.

In the storage shed I'm still staring at the blank screen when I realise why Alice is annoyed with me. She's annoyed with me because I didn't reply to Daniel's email. Because I said that I would reply to it, that I wouldn't forget, and I did forget, and I didn't reply to it. Because I am a liar, a fool, a dick, and no one should trust me to do anything ever.

I check my phone. Still nothing from Martin Cantor.

I left my message seven hours ago. I've been patient, respectful of the man and his status. But this is ridiculous.

I call the number again, get shunted to voicemail again, leave another message:

'Hi, Martin? Steven Strauss. Sorry to bother you again. Sorry also if I sounded like a madman on that other message, I think I'd been too long in the sun! Anyway, I'd just be really grateful if you could find the time to give me a quick call back. Hope everything's all right there with you. Okay. Hope to hear from you soon. Bye bye.'

I cancel the call and I'm ready to scream with it – the frustration, the fear. I swear, loudly and foully, at the gritty clutter of the storage shed.

I need to find Ess. I need to tell him that we've no money. I need to tell him Harry isn't to be trusted, that the old bastard is up to something. I need to find Ess and look him in the face and tell him pretty much that the whole deal is slipping away from us.

And then, if he wants to kill me, that's no business of mine.

But by the time I step outside again the only person left in view is Tarik, collecting up the rugs on which we ate dinner. As I walk towards him I notice the angry bounce of his bend as he reaches for a rug's edge, the furious swipe of his hand as he catches the edge and starts tussling the rug into a roll. He's in a rage, probably in no mood for a conversation. I should leave him alone, go back to the shed. But I need to find Ess and so I

164

pause a few steps away from Tarik then carefully ask, 'Where'd everybody go?'

'Excellent question,' he says, hefting the rug as if attempting to injure it.

I notice a patch of green light inside Harry's camp. That accounts for the old bastard, at least. But: 'Where's Ess?' And, for that matter: 'Where's Asha?'

'Where are they?' Tarik steps towards me, allowing the rug to topple behind him, and stabs a finger into the darkness. 'Exactly where I ask them not to go. And so they go.'

'They went to the village?'

'Where's the harm, yes? I just need to lighten up, yes?' Returning to the toppled rug, he makes a guttural sound of disgust. 'Where's the *harm*...'

Ess and Asha have gone to the village. Crashingly I realise that's why Ess wanted to go to there today – why with that concentrated expression he went seeking a helpful local such as Laxman. He was scouting for a place, a boarding house, a spare room, where he and Asha could spend the night without the prospect of another interruption.

For a moment I stand appalled, amazed (*the crafty fucker!*), then I shake my arms and legs as if warming up for vigorous exercise and say to Tarik, 'Let me give you a hand...' and start pulling at another of the rugs.

He gives me a furious look but doesn't try to stop me helping, and between us we gather up the rest of the rugs and haul them one at a time over the single step into the cabin then across the floor to their corner next to his hammock. We're fitting the last two into the heap when we both seem to become aware that I've entered the cabin. Tarik steps away from me and instinctively goes to stand by the workbench, on which his machine now rests. At some point he must have gone to retrieve it from the

165

test site. I stay on the other side of the room, but wave at the machine and say, 'It's fantastic. Your invention.'

'Thank you.' A flicker, a stutter of a smile.

I should go, but now I've seen it I can't take my eyes off Tarik's machine. The jagged black plastic case, cut and soldered together from this and that; the insulation-tape joins; the French plait of wires. I need to say something, but all I can think of is, 'Was it difficult?'

'That rather depends on what you mean.' He raises his chin. 'If you mean was this one difficult to make, yes, it was exceedingly difficult to make. If you mean will it be difficult to copy, no. I imagine with your resources you will have no difficulty replicating the device. You will find the key elements may be easily and cheaply synthesised into a chip. After that, I expect your greatest challenges will involve questions of marketing. The design, the body, the form factor. The brand. The logo. The price. Once those questions are dealt with, I'm sure you and your colleagues will become extremely rich.'

'And you,' I say. 'You'll become rich too.'

The smile that stutters on then off again looks like the most authentic bit of a smile I've yet seen out of him. It is incredibly sad.

'Won't that be nice,' he says.

I look at the workbench, notice that the toolbox that isn't a toolbox has gone, maybe never existed, that the laptop is still cycling its slideshow of a very fat woman smiling against different backgrounds of sun-spattered trees. I wave at the laptop and say, 'Is that…?'

He glances at the screen. 'Reva. My wife.'

'She looks…' I have no idea why I started this sentence. She looks what? She looks fat. She looks enormous. 'She looks… happy.'

He goes on staring at the laptop. 'That day she was happy. She was always happy in Cubbon Park.'

'Do you… still see her?'

Tarik doesn't look up at me straight away. When he does, there's no expression on his face, none at all. 'Good night, Mr Strauss.'

Back at the storage shed I check my phone. Still nothing from Martin Cantor.

I search my phone book for Resolute's main number. Okay then: if the cunt's lying low in his office, I'll get one of the girls on reception to put a call through and smoke him out. What is it – Tuesday? Wednesday? Two, three in the afternoon? Chances are I'll get either Becca or Manda, both old mates, so…

'You have dialled an incorrect number. Please hang up and try again.'

I haven't dialled any number. I just hit 'Call' on the number that's always been there.

'You have dialled an incorrect number. Please hang up and try again.'

It takes me a while to get there, but I get there.

Resolute is gone. No more now than an empty space, a vacant property, without even ringing phones.

13

As soon as there's light enough to see by next morning, I go up to the test site. I walk a full circle round the first of the blocks I come to, then using the rope knot on its outward end as a handhold, and then as a foothold, I climb on top of it. Sitting on the rough concrete, I check that I have a complete view of the surrounding area then open my shoulder bag and take out my water bottle and my cigarettes.

After about an hour Harry emerges from his camp. I watch as he goes to the latrine, rolls in the dust in what I eventually realise is a sort of morning exercise regime, then goes to Tarik's cabin and knocks on the door. Tarik opens the door, he and Harry briefly talk, then they go into the cabin together. I watch, I wait, I smoke a cigarette.

I'm still staring at the cabin door when out of a corner of my eye I register movement, and I see them: Ess and Asha, returning from the village. While they're still hardly more than specks negotiating the whorls of the plain, I can tell all is not well between them. They move at different paces, with different rhythms, and as soon as they reach the edge of Tarik's compound Asha speeds ahead, strides up to the Adventurers car and slams herself into it. Ess changes direction and veers down towards the river.

I leave it for as long as I can. (After all, he's going to kill me.) Then I slither down the side of the block and start in his direction.

'We need to talk.'

'Oh yes?' He's kneeling on the riverbank, shirtless, lifting cupped handfuls of water into his hair, over his head. He turns and sits and smiles at me with a coursing face.

I'm standing and he's sitting. Nervously I sit too, then realise too late I'm sitting too far away. But what am I supposed to do? Slide towards him on my arse? I stay where I am, blink at the sluggish brown river, try to think of a way of saying what I have to say. He waits with a pleasant, unsurprised air. Then I say, 'We've no money.'

'No,' he says.

'The account Cantor gave you, it's bullshit. Resolute didn't give us any money. They just wanted you out of the way while they dissolved the company.'

'Yes, I know,' he says.

I stare at him. His face coursing down, staying exactly where it is. 'You know?'

'Oh yes.' He flattens his hair with both hands. 'I assume you've been "following the drama" online? There's been some scrappy stuff, I can tell you. Quite scratchy stuff.'

'They thought you'd make trouble,' I say. 'They...'

'Where I take it "they" refers to Martin Cantor?'

'... Yes.'

'Who asked you if you would be so good as to take the old man off on his jaunt while the big boys do the serious work of breaking up his company?'

'... Something like that.'

'I suppose he said he'd look after you? Once the dust settles?'

'Actually, no.' It's true. Cantor made me no promises. 'I'm so sorry, Ess.'

'I know. I knew it was going to be hard for you, hard to believe... especially with my recent escapades. But I also knew that, once you saw it, you'd be with me.'

'I *am*,' I say, earnestly, passionately, 'I *am* with you. I'm just so… so…'

'Well. Enough of that.'

'But we're here, and the machine works, and we've no money…'

'Yes, yes. Not the end of the world, is it?'

I stare at him. His face isn't coursing down any more but I still can't get a fix on it.

He says, 'As it happens, we have something rather more valuable then money. At least as far as Tarik's concerned.' He waits. Then he says, 'You see, we have his wife.'

'What?' I'm sitting down but all at once I can't get my balance. 'We have his *what*?'

'Good lord, that sounds dreadful, doesn't it? Forgive me, Mr Strauss, but I haven't been completely open with you. I haven't told you quite everything I might.'

And then he tells me the story.

Once upon a time there was a boy called Tarik who lived in a village on the outskirts of a great city. He lived in a house with his father, mother and two brothers. The family lived in a house and not a hut because Tarik's father was the wealthiest man in the village, a merchant and landowner wealthier even than the village headman, who lived in a house too.

He was an anxious child, Tarik was. It seemed the anxiety was there before he was; anxiety that he lived in a house with brick walls and a slate roof while the other kids at school lived in huts of wood, clay and thatch; anxiety that these same children and his brothers too enjoyed in their bodies a litheness of movement he could find nowhere in his, a spangling jitter whose presence in wrists and ankles made even the poorest of his classmates solemn and gorgeous while he, lacking it, trembled like a sickly dog. He hated school, the dirt, the crush, the constant reminder in the press of flesh on his at all times that he was defective, missing a crucial part that others possessed so naturally they were not even aware of it.

In his corner of the crowded classroom he did everything he could not to be present – to withdraw, to vanish. Sometimes he tried to vanish into the teacher's shrill, violent voice; sometimes into the surface of the slate he balanced on his knees, the cracks, the jags, the zagging grain; sometimes into the work the class was set, the grammar tests, the sums. But he soon discovered there was nowhere he could vanish to, nowhere at all.

One day after school the teacher walked home with him. The teacher's silence left no room for doubt that he'd done something dreadful, though he didn't know what. As they walked, he grew certain that the moment he'd always feared had finally arrived: the moment when his defect was revealed, when he was reviled and cast out.

Arriving at the house, the teacher spoke quietly to one of Tarik's brothers, who went inside then returned with their father.

'There is a grave problem with young Tarik here,' the teacher said to his father.

'Is that so?' His father's easy smile told Tarik at once that his father was prepared to beat him: to pound out of him whatever sin was in him.

The teacher passed Tarik's father his slate – the one on which he'd completed the afternoon's sums. 'It would appear that he's a genius.'

'Oh yes?' Tarik's father's face looked suddenly jolted, shocked, shivered.

'It would appear so. Which creates for us the grave problem of what to do with him.'

The grave problem became the daily task and battle of Tarik's father for the next ten years. He determined to make the problem the village's problem – 'our gift, our burden' – and engaged in frequent lengthy meetings with the headman, meetings for which Tarik was always required to be present, at least at the beginnings and ends of them, freshly scrubbed in his best shirt and spectacles, with his slate in his hand, like a prop. While the meetings were in progress Tarik was allowed to sit in the kitchen and work on the tasks he'd been set by his very expensive private tutor from the city.

One humid afternoon Tarik was sitting in the headman's kitchen, struggling with a task, when the headman's daughter came into the room. She was tiny, dark, beautiful. She didn't go to school, because she was the headman's daughter. Her name was Reva.

Without speaking, she leant over the table and stared at his slate. She nodded then looked at him in a weird way: the eyes luminous, questioning, slightly bulging.

'You can't do it, can you?' she said.

'I can do it,' he said.

'You can't do it. And it's *easy*.'

She was right. He couldn't do it. And she picked up his chalk and solved it and she made it look easy. He was twenty. She was sixteen.

'How did you do that?' he asked.

'How did I do what? I don't do anything, I'm not here, I don't exist.' He saw then that the bulging of her eyes was not a look but something she couldn't help, an imperfection that was also part of her beauty. He saw also that she was about ten times as clever as he was. This was a part of her beauty too.

He studied in the city. During the week he slept on a cot in his uncle's flat and at weekends he returned to the village to pay his respects to the headman and the headman's daughter. By the time he was twenty-five he'd still obtained no solid evidence that Reva's interest in him extended to anything more than the tasks

173

he brought her – the homework he more or less brought her to do for him. Then, one afternoon, he obtained solid evidence. Twenty-one, glistening with intelligence and her new womanly fullness, she put down the chalk and picked up his hand. She looked at him with her bulging eyes.

'There is a grave problem with young Tarik here,' she said.

'There is,' he agreed, and put his other hand over hers, and two years later with the blessing of both fathers they were married.

After he completed his studies Tarik took a prestigious job at a prestigious company in the city – an electronics company with a reputation for innovation. Tarik and Reva moved into a flat in the city's fashionable downtown. They were happy. Tarik gained the respect of his colleagues, was admiringly addressed in the lab as 'the boy wonder', was assigned important roles on fascinating projects. Reva made friends, went modestly shopping, and continued at home to more or less do Tarik's work for him.

They'd been living this prosperous life for almost a year when Tarik began to notice a change in Reva. She grew quiet, irritable. She approached the tasks he brought her no longer as a ravishing pleasure but an annoyance, an inconvenience, while at the same time she seemed to have nothing else to do. She went out less and less often with her friends. Less and less often she presented him with the fruits of her modest shopping sprees.

He came home from work one day and found her crying. She told him that she hated the city, hated city people, hated her city friends and wanted to go back to the village. In the village, she said, she was beautiful. But here she was ugly. Here, she said, she was fat.

'You're what?' He had literally no idea what she was talking about.

'You've seen the women here. They're sticks, they're wisps. And I'm...'

'You're beautiful,' he said.

'Village beautiful. Here I'm a potbellied pig.'

'Here you're beautiful. Everywhere you're beautiful. You're everywhere beautiful.'

But it did no good. She stayed in the flat, refused to see her friends – who, she said, were all having 'gym parties' and would only 'snigger into their sweatpants' if she were to go 'waddling in'. At least she was able to laugh about it, for a while. Then she wasn't able to laugh about it. She became prickly, spiky, all the time. She cried. She told him she was too tired to do his work, or else she threw the papers away from her and told him to do his own fucking job. And she grew fat. By the time they'd been living in the city two years her village beauty had gone, her womanly fullness receded behind a veil of intricate flab. She seemed wreathed with it, ornamented with it, as if for a terrible wedding.

Tarik's work suffered – because, for the first time, it was truly his own. It turned out the village teacher had overestimated him, and he was a very bright fellow, but not a genius. His work for the company was excellent but no longer astonishing. Among his colleagues disappointment set in. The 'boy wonder' tag detached, dissolved. The assignments grew less fascinating. At home his wife grew sadder and fatter and in the lab he sat desperately working on small-time projects for spare-change money.

One evening he came home to find her staring into space. She'd fallen down on the bedroom floor and couldn't get up. The rubber ring, the perverse flotation device of her own fat had defeated all her efforts. She'd been there for six hours and had filthied herself.

That weekend he built a chair for her. She wouldn't get into it, screamed at him, wept. Then one day the following week he came home and she'd started to use it.

Six years, eight years. Tarik had painful little successes at work, painful little failures. Reva grew lighter, grew heavier. But they

175

lived no moment that was not pulled between these poles, these gravities.

Then all at once she was happy again. She was still fat, but happy, full of energy. When he came through the door he noticed everywhere signs of deliveries during the day: boxes, polystyrene packing blocks, sheets of bubble-wrap that combusted under his feet like gunfire. She told him she was working on 'a project' of her own. Cheerfully she presented him with her online purchases – not the saris or jeans or shoes of her earlier sprees but a soldering iron, a welding kit, a pack of circuit-boards.

One Friday afternoon several months later she called him at work and told him in a voice breathless with urgency that he had to come home right away. He vaulted up the nine flights to their flat, his heart in his mouth. She was waiting for him, in the sitting room, in her chair. She asked if he was ready. He said, 'Ready for what?' He noticed the modification she'd made to her chair, a ragged bit of circuit with a trailing wire and switch in it attached to the armrest, only when she depressed her right thumb into the switch.

The next thing he saw was that two things had happened to her face. It had changed its position in the room, and it was laughing. It was the most frightening thing he'd ever seen.

The next thing he saw was that her chair had risen three feet above the floor.

'How did you do that?' Because she was laughing, he started to laugh too.

'How did I do what?' She laughed harder, slapped the arms of her chair.

Grandly she invited his examinations. He took the mop and swept it back and forth under the chair. He waved an arm under the chair, then both arms. He climbed up into the chair and sat in her lap. She picked lazily at his head, subjected it to her usual search for dandruff, and told him with luminous, lantern-like eyes, 'Now I'm beautiful.'

'Yes,' Tarik said. He had no idea what she meant.

She showed him her schematics for the miraculous chair modification and he was still puzzling over them when she fell asleep. In her chair he floated her to the bedroom and rolled her gently out onto the mattress and pulled the sheet up to her chin. Then he went back to the schematics and to the sticking, snagging nag of his idea.

In fact it took him almost another year, working from Reva's schematics after hours in the lab, to reconstruct her circuit and build a prototype. At last, though, he grasped it – he understood what she'd done. While this work was not a secret, exactly, he didn't discuss it with Reva, who seemed never to consider that there was anything especially to be done with her invention. She didn't even use it much, and ascended in her chair only on days when getting round the flat was a particular chore. For her, the invention seemed to have been a point to prove, and now it was proven she had no further interest in it.

One Wednesday morning Tarik asked his colleagues in the lab if he could show them something. They smirkingly gathered round a heap of bricks, tied up in a rope and a wire, with a soldered black plastic box on top of it. With an effort of premeditated showmanship, not really successful, Tarik asked one of the researchers to hold the other end of the rope. The researcher took the rope, Tarik threw the switch on the plastic box, and the whole stack wavered up into the air. Fairly abruptly the researcher was flying a kite made out of bricks.

Tarik's colleagues responded to the demonstration with various grades of disbelief, euphoria and acclaim. The one who had flown the brick kite clutched his face on either side and roared, 'You did this? You *did* this?'

'I did,' Tarik said. 'I did this, yes.'

The researchers then inspected his prototype for themselves. They became serious, sober, eyeing Tarik warily. The supervisor kept going out to make phone calls. One of the researchers, a man Tarik had known for years, at one point took a hard hold of his upper arm and seemed about to say something, then didn't say anything.

Tarik started to freak out. He said he was suddenly feeling ill, overcome, and had to go home. The supervisor said he thought that was a bad idea, but Tarik packed up his prototype and left the lab. On his way out of the main entrance he was stopped by security. He opened his bag and spilled the prototype onto the floor. For good measure he trampled it a bit, pretending woozily to be attempting to pick it back up. The guard was so astonished by this performance Tarik was able to get away. He ran home and told Reva everything.

While he spoke her face barely moved. When he tried to explain why he had tried to steal her invention, to pass it off as his own, she seemed bored. When he tried to explain that the company would now very likely try to steal the invention off both of them, that the company would very likely do anything and everything in its power to make the invention its own, to get rid of them, to dispose of them, and they were now in terrible danger and had to leave, at once, she seemed merely annoyed, as if by a fly trapped in the curtains. He told her he would go to the bank, withdraw all the money they had, and they would leave the city. He wanted to tell her he was sorry, to weep and beg for forgiveness, but couldn't quite bring himself to do it. As he slunk from her unmoving, unremarking sight, he vowed he would do it when he came back from the bank.

And when he came back from the bank Reva, and her chair, were gone.

*

'So he came here.' On the riverbank Ess circles a hand in the air – the river, the trees, the plain. 'Tarik fled the city alone and here he has remained, watching the skyline for company agents, pining for his beloved and waiting to die.'

'Fucking hell,' I say.

'Fucking hell indeed. That's exactly what I said, though of course I said no such thing but rather "A-ha!" or "Now wait a minute!" When Tarik told me this story, I made him a promise. I vowed that I would purpose every iota of my shall we call it influence, dedicate every penny of my as it were capital, to recovering his Reva. To finding her and bringing her to him, to reuniting them, husband and wife, before expediting their swift transit out of India. This essentially was our agreement.'

'Okay.' I nod. I seem to be sliding about in the middle of some catastrophe.

'And, I'm delighted to say,' Ess says, 'thanks to a certain tireless associate of mine, my promise is almost kept. Reva is found, and en route, and due to join us any day.'

'She's coming here?'

'In the care of my indefatigable associate, yes. Reva is coming here.'

'Your tireless, uh, your indefatigable…?'

'To whom else would I entrust so solemn a task? Fancy Bill. You remember Fancy Bill, don't you? Of course you do. Fancy Bill Fancy.' Then Ess does an extraordinary thing. He purses his lips and releases a stunning salvo of highly decorative whistling. Suddenly, shockingly, the air by the river is full of the song of larks and nightingales. And then I remember, I know who he means: Bill – 'Bill here' – Bill Fancy, the wildlife photographer turned private investigator, the whistling detective whom Ess briefly contracted to keep tabs of a friendly sort on his ex-wife. The cheerful chubby cheeks, the cardsharp way he had of laying

179

out his photos – Eunice in a café, in her car, in a bathroom window.

'Have no doubt, my boy, Fancy Bill has been busy in our behalf. I don't pretend that his services have come cheaply, but then neither did he, to his undying credit, and his quest has unavoidably incurred expenses. But yes, he's done it. Ticklish sort of a business, tax returns, paper trails, I shan't bore, but the long and the short is he managed to track Tarik's missus to a cousin of a cousin – possibly of a cousin – working as a housemaid in a hotel in Goa. Seems she's been staying illicitly in this hotel, tucked away in a basement room or some such, in the care of this distant relative of hers. Fancy Bill reports that, uh, shall we say, Reva has attained a certain condition of physical fullness. Nonetheless, where there's a will, where there's a well-meaning penny, sometimes the mountain can indeed be induced to, to… no, I abjure that remark, don't know what's wrong with me. Overexcited, I apologise.'

He laughs, waves the hand again. 'Still, you get the idea. Even now Reva, under the careful stewardship of my Fancy Bill Fancy, is making her way to this very spot. They'll arrive any day. And then the lovers shall kiss, the papers change hands, the friends fondly part, and all shall be well.' He laughs again. 'I'm sorry I had to keep all this from you. But I understood you had your quite sensible doubts. So I edited somewhat, trusting the moment would come when I could open with you. Such as now.'

'Okay.' I nod. Reva has been staying in a basement room in a hotel in Goa. She's got very fat. Bill Fancy is by some means bringing her to the plain. All right. This sounds all right. Then I say, 'The company's gone, Ess. Resolute's gone.'

'The company hasn't gone. The company is precisely where it always was.' He taps the side of his head. 'Every name. Every address, every telephone number. Not quite every but a good few of the birthdays.' He pulls his shirt on over his head, making me aware for the first time in a while that he's been topless, and rubs his hands together. In his scrubbed face the graph-paper scar sheds a strong, pink, latticed light. 'I thought that might be something else we could do together. Once we're back in Blighty and we've registered the patent and whatnot. We'll take what's in here' – the head tap again – 'and put it to use. Every name, every address. None of your email, your phone. We'll go door to door. Everyone Resolute ever employed, every machinist, every cleaner, every manager, even the poor swine who got laid about by that Skycoach mess, every last one. A job if they want it. Sky-high pay and princely conditions in the world's first company to manufacture and mass-market antigravity technologies.' He stands, stands over me. He seems about to put his hand on top of my head. Then he puts his hand on top of my head. 'What say you? When everything's signed. We'll go knocking on doors.'

'Okay,' I say. But I can't shake off the sense of catastrophe.

He takes his hand from my head. 'We can look forward to a busy few days. Lots of comings and goings. I daresay I could stomach a bite or two of breakfast.'

Ess is preparing to leave when I ask him something else. He frowns, thinks about it, then answers. And then I know what I need to know.

I sit on the riverbank. Ess has gone looking for breakfast. I should go too. But I can't stand up, can't free myself from invisibly clashing waves of disaster.

Well, he didn't kill me. Only I almost – *almost* – wish he had.

I blink at the river for a bit, the trapped sludge, the wheeling foam. Then I sway to my feet and begin climbing the scoop of the bank towards the level above.

There's a kid standing in front of me, a teenager in a brilliantly red T-shirt. I cry out in surprise. The kid grins. His immaculate teeth in their promontory of gum.

'Laxman? Shit! Laxman! What are you doing here?'

'Ha! What are *you* doing here?'

'Laxman!'

'What are you what are *you* doing here?'

Laughing, he turns, all the red billow of his T-shirt, and sprints away, past the trees, their skinny shadows, away into the light of the plain.

Ess is preparing to leave when I ask him, 'Have you heard of a place called Cubbon Park?'

He frowns, thinks about it, then answers, 'Cubbon Park. That's Bangalore, isn't it?'

And then I know what I need to know.

14

Back at camp Ess is sitting with Harry, having breakfast. As I near them both men wave to me. Drily I wave back. I can't talk to Harry, and I can't talk to Ess while he's sitting with Harry. Also, I realise, this means I can't join them for breakfast. This is bad news. I'm hungry, starving, and the air is thick with the crispy-bit sizzle of the Altman frying pan. I nod a dry nod and move on doggedly towards the Adventurers car.

Asha is still in there – bundled in her own arms in the front seat and glaring out the windscreen, full of a rage that makes her slam of the door go on resounding all round her. I knock lightly on the passenger window until she glances at me and then drops a hand onto the dashboard. With a wasp-like whine the window lowers a mean half-inch.

'Yes? What?' Two rapid stabs. In the mood she's in she'll use words, and anything else she can get hold of, as weapons. This is what gusts at me through the tiny gap in the window: her readiness, her eagerness to use weapons.

'Two requests,' I say. 'Request one. Do you have any food?'

'You want food?' As if the thought disgusts her.

'Yes, yes please.'

'Your friends have food.' She indicates Ess and Harry with the same gesture she would use to hurl a rock at them. 'Ask your friends for food.'

'Ah, well, that's slightly tricky.' I open up for her a smile crenellated with not-worth-asking-about awkwardness.

'It isn't tricky.' She hurls another invisible rock. 'Ask. I've no food for you.'

'You must have the odd bit.' I feel my smile hardening up, clamping together of its own accord. 'In the boot, is it? Don't trouble yourself, I'm sure I can manage.'

I swipe back from the window and start round the car towards the boot, her voice carrying after me: 'Don't you *touch*...'

We arrive at the boot at roughly the same time. I bounce the lid and it pops free. She tries to grab it but I push it up out of her way. The boot is lined with the white cake box-like lunchboxes and I claw one open, dig out a handful of sandwiches and bite into it – bite into two or three four-day-old chutney sandwiches all at once.

'Oh!' she cries. 'This is excellent! Please, thieve on! Give me the excuse I've been dying for!'

'What?' I ask, through my mouthful of stale sandwiches. 'I'm not thieving, Christ, if you're so *bothered*...' I reach into my pocket for the fold of notes Ess tried to pass to Laxman in the village yesterday.

'You!' Asha suddenly roars. She moves her hands in a manner that suggests she's only just holding herself back from hitting me. 'You people are vile!'

'Okay.' I hold up my free palm while I chew, try to slow the situation down. 'Leave me out of it, okay?'

'Leave you out of it!'

'Just leave me right out of it. Whatever's going on between you two...'

'You people think you own everything, don't you? You think everything is yours, you think everything is already yours.'

'What the...' I struggle to swallow, 'what *the fuck* is that supposed to mean?'

'Even us. You think you own even us. Or you wouldn't do what you do.'

'I just think when a grown man and a...'

'How can you live with what you do?'

'What *the fuck* are you talking about? I haven't fucking *done* anything...'

Then Asha's restraint shatters, blows apart in near-visible fragments, and she takes hold of my throat and twists it in a way that makes me immediately and extremely compliant. She seems to want me to lie down on the ground, so I lie down on the ground. Her face looms above mine with a thoughtful expression.

'You take a woman, and you haven't done anything? You hold a woman in terror of her life, and you haven't done anything? You do this for your business, for your profit, and you haven't done anything? Then tell me please, when have you done a thing?'

The white lunchboxes seem to be tumbling about me in the dust. In my hand is still a wedge of chutney sandwiches with a large bite taken out of them.

'I haven't done that,' I somehow say. 'No one's done that.'

'I *know*,' she whispers. 'I know everything everyone has done. I know everyone's business and I know it is *vile*.'

'I don't know what he's told you...'

'You know exactly what he's told me. And I know what he's told you. Oh, I can just imagine the conversations you had about the "treasures" he claimed on his travels round India, the rich plunder he took, the foolish girls, foolish women...'

'He didn't tell me—' I try to say, but Asha isn't interested.

'Don't talk to me like I'm a fool. I know what I am to him. He walks into my house one day and he talks and talks and he laughs and laughs and he reaches for me and I let him. Why shouldn't I? He's such a powerful man, and we all love a powerful man, don't we? All us girls love a powerful man. I was his release, his outlet. Just like you, Steven.'

'That's…' I start to say, but I don't know what that is.

'Wake up, little boy!' She laughs, with rattling bitterness. 'You really believe that? You're just like him. You think he's "a powerful man" to me? You don't know anything about me. You see an Indian woman, and you think slums, you think wicked daddy, drinker husband, bruises all over her body. Well, think again. Do you know how many degrees I have? Three. Count them.' But she does it for me, counting them out on stabbing fingers. 'BA, MA, PhD. All my brothers do, and all my sisters do too. Yes, because our daddy is a rich daddy, and our mummy is a rich mummy. And we work, all of us, because we are not ashamed to work. Your Raymond Ess, what is he to me? He's like you. He comes to me with his excitement, his bright eyes, his big smile… why, he's a dear little boy.'

I stare up at her, say nothing.

'You see?' She laughs again, with the same bitter rattle. 'I know that man, and I know he's made a fool of me, but I know also the greater fool is Raymond Ess. Because now I *know* him. Better than you, his little suck-up lapdog friend, or whatever you are, know him. Better by far than he'll ever know himself. Shall I tell you what he is? Let me enlighten you, little ass-kiss boy. He's a lie. That man is a lie inside a lie inside a lie inside a lie.' She releases me, sits up, pushes her hands through her hair. 'You said "two requests".'

'Uh… Yeah.' I feel concussed, annihilated.

'What's "request two"?'

'Request two? Uh, uh, your camera.'

'What about my camera?' She takes a clip from her pocket and starts feeding her hair into it, roughly, as if disposing of a body.

'I was going to ask you for it.'

'Why were you going to do that?'

'Yesterday. During the demo. You were taking lots of photos.'

'So you were going to ask for my camera. Demand my camera. Take my camera from me, by force if necessary.'

'That was the general idea.'

'The poop-dog shit-nose kiss-ass and his general ideas.' Her hair dealt with, she lifts suddenly onto her feet like something being erected on a stand and strides out of my field of vision. Before she strides back into it I hear her saying, 'Do you know what makes me sick? You people think you own everything, you think everything is already yours. That's very sad, but it isn't what makes me sick. No, what makes me sick is: we just let you.'

Something smashes into the dust next to my head. I flinch, I whimper, I actually do that. Then I look and I see the something is Asha's camera, its lens smashed, its exposed archaic film turning brown, turning black in the morning sun.

At last I sit up. Asha has gone, slammed herself back into the car. I turn and see, fifty or so feet away, Ess and Harry sitting in Harry's camp, staring at me. Ess waves encouragingly. Tentatively I wave back.

Then I drop the handful of sandwiches I'm still somehow clutching, shake it off my fingers into the dust next to Asha's camera, gather up as many of the white lunchboxes as I can carry and start walking at speed with them towards the test site.

As I pass Harry's camp, head down, one or other of the sitting men seems to beckon to me. I don't look up. I don't reply.

The rest of the day I spend sitting on my block.

Water bottle, lunchbox; cigarettes, matches; tablet, phone. All this and a complete view of the surrounding area. What more could I need?

The more I could need, I soon realise, is shade. The heat is torrential, the concrete on every side of me glaring, blinding. But I've forgotten my hat, left it in the storage shed, so I take off my T-shirt and hang it over my head and shoulders. Nonetheless I feel my lower back and forearms and kneecaps starting to burn.

After this the miseries heap up. I watch Ess break off his conversation with Harry, take some papers from his satchel – unidentifiable at this distance, but no doubt a fistful of waivers, releases, prepared for Mr Tarik Kundra's signature – and brandish them over to the cabin, into which he disappears for so long I begin to realise that something else I could need up here is a toilet. Eventually I stand, my T-shirt swaying round my head, cross to the opposite end of the block and take a piss off it. I'm expecting a virile arc terminating with a patter in the distant dust, but in fact my piss just drops straight down the side of the block in a reeking black stream. By the time I get back to my lookout post I have no way of telling whether Ess is still in the cabin trying to talk Tarik into an early signing or he's come out and disappeared into another segment of my, it turns out, far from complete view.

The stale taste of the sandwiches, packed round my teeth, becomes impossible to ignore. I raise my water bottle, swig, find it empty. I check my cigarettes. One left.

I open my tablet and scroll through my emails. Nothing new. I'm not really hoping for anything, from Martin Cantor or anyone else. Why would I? I'm on my own out here.

I select the message from Michael ('hey steve!') and delete it, pointlessly but also euphorically. Then I find the message from Daniel Darling ('*Steven, I am writing to you because Al tells me you have bought me a gift*'), hit the 'Reply' option and begin, slowly, painfully, with stinging elbows and kneecaps, as if etching into the same concrete I'm sitting on:

Darling Daniel!
    Imagine my pleasure at receiving your kind and wise words! …

'Steven? Hey Steven!'

Pain in my throat where Asha's fingers went in. Pain in my head where Ess's story – Tarik, Reva, the machine, 'Now I'm beautiful' – went in. What else?

I claw the shirt from my face and sit up. I'm stranded on an iceberg of concrete in a numb blue sky. The voice is coming from under the edge somewhere and I already know it's Harry's. I slither over the concrete like a snake and look down at him anyway.

'What do you want?'

'I want you to come down from there. Sure, you needed some space… but time for you to come down. Let's go, kid. Let's get you down from there.'

'*Fuck* off,' I say.

He blinks up at this somewhat grimly. Then he asks, 'Have you got cigarettes?'

'Yeah,' I say.

'I don't think you've got many.' He jerks his head back. 'You come on down from there, I'll buy you a pack of cigarettes.'

'Where from? The village? It's a… fucking *yonk* away.'

'Not the village. I'll show you where. You come on down.'

In fact I don't have any cigarettes: I smoked my last one while chipping out my email to Daniel. Probably I don't need any more, hadn't planned to get any more, but now Harry is going on about it the idea is there, the taste, the snagging-hook sensation in the roof of my mouth, so I think fuck it and pull my T-shirt back on and slide down the side of the block.

Evening on the plain. Harry Altman in his wheezy combats.

'How are you doing?' he asks as we start away. 'Still dying of malaria?'

I move my fingers to the point of my elbow but find no trace of its node, its lobe, its poisonous flesh-tag. The skin is completely smooth. Bemused, I mutter, 'Don't think so.'

'Just beat up, then? That looked like some scrap you kids got in to.'

'I'm okay.' I raise my head and my spine unslots like the sections of a telescope. 'I mean, it was totally uncalled for. But I'm okay.'

'Tempers are fraying,' Harry says, as if this is deep truth indeed, which obviously it's not. 'People are not themselves.' He sighs. 'I'm sure Asha didn't mean you any harm.'

'That's what you think.'

'You don't think people are getting raggedy?'

'I think she's a lunatic, is what I think. I think you've employed a fucking *psycho*.'

Working his face a bit, Harry searches his repertoire of chuckles then comes out with his wise-old-geezer chuckle – his seen-it-all, done-it-all, nothing-new-under-the-sun chuckle. 'Where I used to work we had a name for situations like this. Like when a team was getting close to deadline, a project not working out, everyone going nuts and turning on each other, sharpening sticks, daubing their faces with mud… We called it "the volt room". We'd say, "Don't even talk to those guys. They're in the volt room. Those guys, they're all locked up in the volt room." That's where we are now, kid. All locked up together in the volt room.'

The edges of the evening sky remind me of a gas flame. We pass some dry, splintery trees like the collapsed remains of a firebombed building – of a *shop*.

But really it's a dream. The sky and the air and the great level of the plain. I breathe deeply, draw it up, take in the dream as far as I can take it into my body.

Harry says, 'I was listening to you gentlemen yesterday: "No more buses. No more trains". And yeah, I guess that's what we're looking at. But did you also think how what we're looking at is no more bus conductors? No more train drivers? No more ticket inspectors? And of course so on and so on and so forth and so forth?'

'Yeah,' I say, faintly smiling, looking at the sky and the air and the plain, 'I did think about that, and I decided I don't *give* a shit.'

We come to a tiny wooden shack surrounded by packing cases and metal buckets and glass jars and other bits of debris. Harry seems to think we're going to go into this shack. I'm not going into this shack. If I go into this shack I'm going to die in it. Nothing more certain.

'Here we are,' Harry announces, but I start to drag back, then stop. He stops also. 'Cigarette heaven.'

'I don't think so,' I say.

'Come on. Buy you a pack of cigarettes.'

'I don't really need cigarettes.'

'No?' He lumbers up to me, squints into my face. 'When did you last drink?'

'How do you mean?'

'Water, tea, anything. When'd you last drink anything?'

'I don't know.'

'Look at you. You're dehydrated. Dry as a bone.' He slaps my shoulder, Ess-style. 'Come on. Cigarettes and tea. Believe me, you need it. Nice hot tea.'

A cup of tea. Do I need it? Then I think about it and I realise that my mouth is a bone and my tongue is a smaller bone and I think fuck it and I go with Harry into the shack.

The room inside is lit by a kerosene lamp standing on one end of a longish table that acts as a counter and divides the front of the room from a smaller, darker area at the back. In this back area an old man is sitting in a chair, hunched forward, reading or praying, and when we come into the shack he stands and moves with a shuffling elliptical grace to face us over the counter. The lamp on the table in front of him illuminates every horror-film splinter and sliver of his upsidedown grin.

Harry tells him what we're looking for and the man retreats shouting into the back area then returns with a cardboard box that he sets down on the counter and urges Harry to examine. Harry passes the invitation to me and I look in the box, which contains packets of utterly unfamiliar brands of cigarette – logos like alien hieroglyphs, colours like a parallel universe. Finally I choose a packet. Harry tries to pay but the man shoos us away from the counter, comes round to our side with a chair in either hand. He puts the chairs down and waves for us to sit. We sit and the man retreats again into the shack's back area.

A few minutes later the man returns, monitoring the progress of a boy – no doubt the person he was shouting at earlier. The boy is about nineteen, tall and athletic, wearing a full Manchester Utd football strip and carrying a tea tray. He's holding the tray out to us before I notice his disfigurement: a wild white flower of discoloration covering almost the entire left side of his face. Harry, with courteous thanks, takes his cup of tea. Silently I take mine and the boy and the man retreat together to the other side of the counter.

I sip my tea and Harry sips his and as he does his face flickers and reveals his true intention in bringing me to this shack in the middle of nowhere, which is his intention to kill me, to have me killed, and the old man and the disfigured boy are the killers, or maybe just normal desperate people seduced by his American dollars to the point that they will kill. And this is the point we're all at now, we're all together in the execution chamber, locked up in the volt room, and there is only this one long looping moment while Harry sips his tea and I sip mine before the man and the boy come forward and one of them pins me to the chair and the other grips my head and slits my throat with a sudden knife and Harry sits there with his cup in his hand watching me bleed and croak and die. I sip my tea. Harry sips his.

Then Harry says, 'Let's get out of here, shall we?'

15

We leave the shack. It's almost night, almost too dark to see.

'We need to talk,' Harry says.

I nod hazily. This seems about right.

He lumbers towards one of the packing cases lying next to the shack, tests it with his foot, a light kick then a heavier one, presumably checking for stability and for any inhabitants that might come crawling out at an inopportune moment, and apparently satisfied he sits. I stand, arms folded. He picks up another, smaller case, shakes it about then sets it down again and pats its surface. I go on standing for a while then sit on the smaller packing case.

'I guess you're aware I've been talking to Tarik today. A lot of guy stuff, just chewing the fat. But also we got on to other subjects. You can see how that would happen.'

Again I nod.

'One way and another we got on to the subject of Tarik's, ah, arrangement with you gentlemen. And then, you know, the subject of his wife and so on and so forth.'

'Reva,' I say.

'Reva. Yes.' Harry sniffs. 'That's a sad story, isn't it? Tarik, Reva... I mean I don't know if what Tarik told me is exactly the same as what he told you guys, but I'm assuming it's broadly the same. In summary.'

'I don't know,' I say. 'I don't know what he told you.' I shrug. 'I wasn't there.'

'That the machine is his wife's invention and he took it to his company and tried to pass it off as his. He also said Reva was, ah, not impressed by his choices and left him. That the company got all up in his face and he had to hightail it out of there and recluse himself.'

I nod, shake my head: essentially perform Asha's mysterious head waggle.

'I assume that's broadly the same?'

I raise my elbows in a non-committal way.

'Steven. *Steven...*' In the near night it's easy to see how human he is. The bagged eyes, the twisting beard straggles, the lips constantly working to contain their spittle. Maybe I just mean how old he is. But now he draws the loose sack of his face into something more purposeful and he says, 'I'm a respectful guy, a respecter of persons and choices and maybe not always was but ever more shall be. And yet let me tell you I do believe this is a time for you to talk on a level with me. Yes sir. I do believe this is that time.'

'I don't know what you want from me, Harry.'

'I want to establish some common ground here. Can we do that?' His expression is pained but wistful – the expression of a man withstanding the buffets of rich experience. 'Believe me, I know how hard it is. I get that instinct to hold back, to break away, to put some distance between yourself and everything around you, people, places, backgrounds, histories, all of it, everything that wants to tie you down and tell you who you are. Because we don't want to be who they tell us we are, we want to be who we say we are. And it's hard. Hard to cross that gulf of difference between our lives, our persons and choices... oh, sure. I know all about that.'

'I've no idea what you're talking about,' I say.

'No,' Harry says. 'Well, how could you.'

He falls into a silent argument with himself. While this goes on I grow aware of things moving about in the trees nearby, nighttime shapes crashing from branch to dark branch. Then Harry says, 'Right now I'm trying to take the charitable view and allow that there must be factors, *knowledges…*' He smiles at me, wanly, but also with a new sort of focus. 'I'm a respectful guy, Steven, but I'm also a curious guy. If I get an itch, I have to scratch it. And that's what happened when I heard Tarik's story. Don't misunderstand, I was moved, I was in some sense *wounded* by that pitiful story. But also it made me itch. So, you know, I started to look into some stuff.' From a pocket of his combats he takes a stubby plastic podule and from the podule he takes his smartspecs, folded, dormant. 'Nothing too serious. You know how this shit is. You open it up and you go swimming. Like exercise only without the actual exercise element. I don't know that I was truly expecting to find anything. But, well, I did. I have to tell you I found something.'

He doesn't have to say anything else. I already know what he's going to tell me.

Reva has not been staying in a basement room in a hotel in Goa, or anywhere else. She is not by any means being brought to the plain, by Bill Fancy or by anyone else.

Because she's dead.

'I'm happy to share with you what I found, Steven. And I'm sharing this with you because I'm assuming this is something you guys didn't already know. That when you made this arrangement with Tarik, and you agreed it would be a fair and symmetrical transaction for you guys to take the machine and its schematics and its rights and what all in exchange for Tarik's wife. In exchange for the safe return of his wife, his wife who left him of her own as far as I can tell *will*, and who not only has never shown any indication of wanting to be returned to him, like, ah, laundry, but who also has gone to some trouble to make sure he is not able to find her, to locate her, by any electronic means or so forth.'

She's dead. Reva's dead.

'I want you to look at something.' Harry waves the smartspecs at me. 'With these.'

At last I nod. He opens the specs, they glow and boot up, he mutters a command to them – detaching them from his aura, his aegis – and he passes them to me. Somewhat awkwardly, I put them on. Then it's weird: I can still feel the edge of the packing case under me, still hear the night shapes crashing about in the trees, but I'm somewhere else. Another space, another world. Light as substance, as landscape.

Harry mutters another command and an image forms in front of me, a photograph, a portrait hanging on a wall of light. I recognise it at once from the slideshow on the laptop in Tarik's cabin: Reva smiling in Cubbon Park. Harry says, 'You've seen this? I… like I say, I'm an itchy guy. I captured this from Tarik's screen while we were talking. Tidied it up, put it to work.' In the world of the smartspecs Harry's disembodied voice is like the voice of god. I feel nothing unnatural about this. He continues, 'There's some nice stuff these days, face recognition and so forth, and to cut a long one short I fed the image you're looking at into a brainy little gewgaw and what came clunking out the other end was… this.'

Next to the image of Reva another one appears. It's a photograph of a woman. The woman is lying on an ashen background. The woman is large, heavy; her sides spread into the surrounding ash. The area round her face is blurred, crosshatched, buffeted by motion. Nonetheless it's clear that the woman is dead.

'She's dead,' I say. My voice is oddly flat, isolated, unresonant, in the brilliant world of light. 'Reva's dead.'

'Yes,' Harry says. 'It would appear so. Reva's dead.'

'In Bangalore. The bombing.'

Harry doesn't say anything.

'We didn't know,' I say. 'Ess didn't know. When he made the deal he didn't know.'

Harry doesn't say anything.

'There's some bloke,' I say, 'some associate of Ess's who says he's got her, says he's found her and he's bringing her here. Ess doesn't know. He's paying this bloke, this private investigator guy…'

Harry says, 'Reva didn't die in Bangalore.'

'In the bombing,' I say. Then: 'What?'

'Reva didn't die in Bangalore. She died in Kolkata.' Harry mutters again and the two photos in front of me peel themselves off into nothing and a jouncing mosaic of images takes their place. Heaps of rubble, vortices of destruction. Crowds, ambulances. Some of the images are video or even live feeds and show rescue workers crowded round weeping faces, a man gesturing violently while others hold him, a woman kneeling, screaming, her face distorted into a funnel of grief. Another pane shows on a fade-in fade-out loop a gallery of figures laid against a background of ash. These figures don't move. These figures are stillness itself.

'She died in a building collapse in Kolkata.'

'She… what?' I tear off the smartspecs and reel back into the world. The night, the shack, the packing case, the crashing trees. Harry next to me looks as if he's been woken from a deep sleep.

'She died in Kolkata last week. There was a building collapse. An office block on the outskirts. Usual story, ignored regulations, paid-off officials. Two hundred and twenty-six dead and counting. Not a headline-grabber like a bombing, but…'

'You know this how?'

'Like I said, I used the picture, I ran the software…'

'But you didn't find her name?'

'I did not find her name. But like I said, the software was able to link Reva's picture to the picture you saw, from a gallery showing those people killed in the collapse who've not yet been identified...'

'Why would Reva be in Kolkata? In where did you say, an office block?'

'I don't know that I have that information. I only...'

'Nah,' I'm saying. I'm shoving the smartspecs into Harry's hands, I'm standing up from the packing case, I'm saying, 'Nah. No way.'

'"No way"?' Harry is aghast. 'This is evidence.'

'This isn't evidence, this isn't anything. This is pictures. This is blurs... This is blurs in a story about a building. You're a *builder*, Harry. You're reading the blurs in a story about a building and you're a *builder*. This is gadgets, and gizmos, and *software*, and you're, you're...' I rock from side to side on my feet. And with something like genuine anguish I say, 'Why couldn't you have just told me she died in Bangalore? I was ready for that. I was ready to believe that.'

Sitting on his case, Harry looks utterly deflated. But still he goes on in a low, skittish, muddled voice, 'You believe what you like, Steven, that's your right and I'm... all I'm saying is I can't keep this to myself. I'm sharing it with you now so you gentlemen have a chance to keep some dignity. In the morning I'm taking this to Tarik and I'm showing it to him and I'm giving you guys until then to make your excuses and leave before Tarik finds out you've been promising to bring him a wife who's been dead for two weeks.' He blinks up at me with his human face.

'Do what you want.' I start away from him, calling back, 'You show whatever you want to whoever you want. It doesn't matter. It's not true.'

'I think Tarik should be the judge of that.'

'Show him. Show him your "facial recognition" software. Show him your blurs and your bullshit algorithm. It's *nothing*. You know it is and I know it is.'

'Nonetheless, I think…'

'Tarik should be the judge. Show him.'

'Don't let the money screw with you, Steven.'

'It's not *the money* that's screwing with me, it's…'

'Don't let the money get inside your head.' He blinks up at me with that face of his. 'You know what money is? Take it from someone who knows. It's piss. It's shit. A better piss and a better shit. You know what I mean? It's… superior plumbing. That's all. Take it from me, Steven.'

'Thanks. I'll bear that in mind. You fucking fat old *prick*.'

'We don't have to speak this way to each other, Steven.'

'I'll speak to you any fucking way I please.'

'In which case I stand by my former statement.'

'Stand by it.'

'You've got until morning. To leave. To walk away.'

'We're not leaving. We're not walking away,' I say, leaving, walking away.

For a while in the dark all I can make out is a need, which is the need to speak to Alice.

I need to see her face, to hear her voice. I need to ask her what I need to do, so I can do it.

I scuttle along over the plain with my need but not much direction. I look for the trees I saw earlier, the ones that resembled a firebombed shop, but I can't see them. I look back, or what I think is back, to see if Harry is coming after me. I can't see him either.

In the blinded dark I look forward again, or what I think is forward again, and resume my scuttling.

Harry. Fucking Harry. The fucking fat old *prick*.

Don't let the money get inside your head, he said. *It's piss. It's shit.* Meaning what? Something like: first to last money is bound to the tides of the body, to the currents and slipstreams of the body, and can't be diverted into higher channels. Well – so what? That's the problem with people like Harry, or with the people Harry seems to be like: they're always wanting to divert stuff into higher channels. But there aren't any higher channels. There's your body, and there's money, and there's the protection that money does or doesn't buy it. And that's all.

The fucking fat old...

I glance up and against the blue-black sky I make out distantly the black-black hulks of the test site and redirect my scuttling towards them.

Then I make out something else, which is a figure standing in front of me, which is Tarik's figure. Then I make out something else, which is that Tarik's figure is performing an action, which is the action of pointing a gun at me.

I am a person who a gun is pointed at. This is interesting. This is a person of a sort I've not been before.

Obviously I'm an idiot, a fool, a dick, but fortunately my reflexes are wiser than I am and know exactly what to do. My arms fly up from my sides, projecting my empty palms into the air, and my mouth calls out hootingly, 'Tarik, Tarik! It's me, it's Steven! You know it's me, don't you, Tarik? Tarik, you know it's Steven, don't you?'

'Steven,' Tarik calls back, without tone. He lowers the gun. His head dips.

I am a person who a gun has been pointed at. This is true now forever.

Slowly I walk towards Tarik. His head is dipped, his face hidden, but for now I'm not especially interested in Tarik's face. I'm interested in the gun, and give it my full attention. It's lowered, pointing down, a somewhat ugly tool, catching no gleam off the immense prism of the plain twilight. Not like a prop in a movie but like something you'd shape metal with, cut down trees with.

'Hey, Tarik.' Without my having consciously done anything to it, my voice is calm, soothing. 'What's this?'

At last Tarik looks up and I see his face. The eyes, the lips, the nostrils are all jitter, all stutter. He's an image embedded in white noise. He looks as if he could disappear at any second.

'Tarik? What's this now?'

'Forgive me,' he murmurs.

'It's okay...'

'I could have shot you.' He holds the gun away from himself, still pointing it at the ground, as if struggling to repulse a disgusting animal. 'How can you forgive me?'

'Hey, it's okay, you didn't mean it...'

'I could have killed you.' For an instant his eyes and lips seize up, clench in the teeth of their static; then they tick free and recommence their squirming, their writhing. 'Everything is very dangerous now.'

'No...' I say, no idea what either of us is talking about.

'The ones who want me dead are close now.'

'What? No...'

'I saw them.' With the hand not keeping the gun gripped in its posture of submission, he waves at the darkness, the plain. 'I saw their faces... watching... *spying*...'

'You didn't see anyone...' In fact I'm guessing he did see someone – Laxman, gofering for Ess or mucking about – but I'm also guessing this isn't the time to get into all that. 'There's no one else out here.'

'They've come to kill me. Do you think I should let them?' Tarik braces himself as if to hurl the gun away, to fling it into the darkness, then doesn't. The gun sags in his hand again. Again his head drops. 'Why shouldn't they kill me?'

Carefully, keeping my eyes on the gun, I take Tarik by the shoulders. I say his name until he looks up at me and then I say,

'I don't know who you think is here, but you're wrong. There's no one here. It's just us. No one here wants to kill you.'

'Yes,' Tarik seems to say.

'Yes,' I agree. 'That's right. You see? No one here wants to kill you.'

'No, no. *Yes*,' Tarik seems to say.

'Yes what? I don't...'

'No,' Tarik says. '*Ess.*'

'What? Ess doesn't want to...'

'He brought them to me. Led them to me.' The eyes, the lips, chafing between frames.

'Oh, now, come on, Ess has his faults, but I don't believe he...'

'He led them here. He showed them the way. Trotting here, there and everywhere, head high, voice loud: "Look at me! Follow me!"'

'Ess likes attention. Obviously he shouldn't have gone to the village when you asked him not to. But I really don't think he'd *mean*...'

Tarik gives a small laugh. 'I know he didn't *mean* to do it. He just didn't care enough to make sure he didn't do it by accident.'

'I don't think that's...'

'Why should he? No, he should bring them. They should come, they should kill me. I should thank them, welcome them.' He turns away from me, towards the huge blank of the night, and opens his arms. 'Do you hear?' he shouts. 'I *thank* you! I *welcome* you!'

'Tarik,' I say, 'I think this is enough now, don't you?'

'Gentlemen of the outer dark!' he shouts. 'Tarik Kundra *welcomes* you!'

'Enough. Enough now.'

'*Welcomes* you!' For a while he stands like that, arms spread, gun dangling. Then he lets down his arms and turns to me.

On his face there is a terrible look. A look emptied out by guilt, by ravenous shame. Pared eyelids, peeled lips. Most terrible of all, his certainty that he is being watched, and at all times. Eyes in the trees, in the rocks, the clouds.

'Hey, Tarik?' I say, when I can say anything. 'We should get back, don't you think? We should get back to the others.'

Exhausted, he finally nods. We start to walk in the direction of the cabin. I keep thinking I'm going to say something else, to touch him, put an arm round his shoulders, then I remember the gun and I don't do any of that and just keep walking.

It's almost nine o'clock by the time we reach the circle of storage sheds and Tarik, slumped, shoulderless, trailing the gun after him now like an invisible dog pulling at its joke-shop lead, drifts across to the cabin and goes quietly in. A faint glow under nylon tells me Harry is in his camp somewhere; a yellow smear in the windscreen of the Adventurers car tells me Asha is in there somewhere. I'm wondering where Ess is when suddenly I see him, standing next to one of the sheds, his phone clamped to his face.

One minute to nine. On another plane of the world, in the Hawks Rise flat, Alice is arranging herself on the ghost couch, settling her legs, straightening her back, flicking her head from side to side to free it of the blonde visor of her hair as she switches on her laptop. The Skype software warbles and pings its circles.

As I walk towards him I can hear Ess speaking into his phone: 'I don't pay… no, no… I don't *pay*… I don't *pay* you…' Speaking, no doubt, to Bill Fancy, the whistling detective, as he has been all along. On the pavement outside the hotel. By the road in the scooped-out wilds. Next to the storage shed at twilight.

I stop in front of him. 'Ess,' I say.

He ignores me.

'Ess, we need to talk.'

He ignores me.

'We need to talk, Ess. We need to talk right now.' I wave both arms in his face (signalling distress from a ship at sea). He blinks at me.

'Right now, Ess. *Right fucking now.*' He flicks a hand at me as if I'm a fly.

I try to take the phone from him. I have no idea what I'll do with it if I get it – crush it under my foot, hurl it across the plain, as Tarik almost did, but couldn't quite, his gun – but I don't get anywhere near it. He swirls violently away, still talking into his phone, now holding up the palm of a hand to me in a warding gesture. I'm not a fly any more but a bad spirit, a possession to be vanquished, exorcised.

I consider my options. I consider trying to wrestle him to the ground. Then I look at my watch and it's two minutes past nine and I turn away from him and run across the plain to the storage shed I've been sleeping in and I go inside and slam the door after me.

Five past nine.

I open my tablet, open the Skype software, put a call through to Alice. Her grinning contact photo appears inside the pinging circles.

I check the wifi connection, which has been unfailingly strong and sharp, and see a blinking dot in the dead tiers of the icon. The Skype circles ping and ping. I drop to my knees in the layered stink of my sleeping bag. Ping and ping, ping and ping.

Ten past nine. Is this what dying is like – this purity of agony, this pure experience of injustice?

Then she's there. ' – *hell*—'

'Alice? Is that you? Can you hear me?'

Then she's not there. The flat surface of a black virtual cube.

' – *ball*—'

'Can you hear me, Alice? Can you hear me, Darling?'

'Hello, Baldie.'

My sensation of triumph at the suddenly immaculate image of her face in the screen is at once qualified. Something is wrong, or several somethings are wrong. For one thing, she is not at home, not at the flat, not on the couch. She is outside somewhere, surrounded by the blowy ether of being outside somewhere; just past her head I can see brickwork, the frozen sickles of a bit of tree. For another thing, her face is full of a look of surly and ironic preoccupation that I've never seen before. Even when she's working, *thinking*, Alice doesn't look like this. She looks like she's planning a boring murder – like her thoughts are all blood and death and she can barely stay awake.

'Alice? Are you okay? Can you hear me?'

'Yeah, I can hear you. Can you hear me?'

'Yeah, I can hear you…'

'That's good.' An extraordinary spectacle befalls the screen. I think the image is breaking up again, then I realise she's yawning.

'Where are you? What's going on?'

'Where am I? Oh. I'm at the hospital with Daniel.'

She yawns again. I watch it – the huge expansion, the cataclysmic contortion – as every kelvin of warmth gulps purposefully out of my body.

'What? Why?'

'Why? Oh. He's, you know, had another one. He's had a stroke.'

'What?'

'He's had another stroke, yeah.' For now this is all I can notice: that she's saying *stroke*. He's had a stroke. Not *he's lurched, he's had a lurch, he's had one of his lurches*. He's had a stroke.

'Oh my god, Alice…'

'It was yesterday. Not long after we spoke. I got a call from the school. It was that one I've never got on with, you know, "Sierra"? She was all "We've had a slight setback here at school today" and I was like "What do you mean, a slight setback?" and somehow it took me ten minutes to work out that he was in the hospital. Which, as you can see, is where I am now. I think it's a sort of smokers' area, which is lovely when you think about it. But it's all right. No smokers around at present.'

'Just me,' I say for some reason.

'Yeah,' she says, so banally I'm relieved by the certainty she hasn't heard me, hasn't taken in my idiocy, then she says, 'Just you.'

'How is he?'

'Oh. Well it's really bad. All the talk here is of "massive neural impact" and "catastrophic damage". The nub of it is his brain's fucked.'

I didn't think I could be colder, but I'm colder. 'No...'

'Oh yeah.' She nods with horrible earnestness. 'Gone. He's fucked. He's going to die. That's the nub of it.'

'No, Darling...'

'They keep telling us "he's on the pathway". That's what they say now, when your brain's fucked and you're going to die. They say you're "on the pathway". And I want to tell them, "This one was always on the pathway. This little bastard was born on the pathway". I don't say anything, though.'

'Alice...' I don't know what to say. 'I don't know what to say...'

'No one does. Dad's here, he's up there now, staring at a bit of wall he seems to have taken a particular fancy to. Mum's on her way, apparently. I keep getting calls about all the many interesting nuances of delay and disruption to her flights. Last I heard she was at some terminal in the Arab Emirates looking for someone to make a bullet-pointed formal complaint to. But for now it's just Dad and me. "Sierra", she was here before, she said she saw it happen. She said he was sitting there, bullshitting with his mates, and then he just crumpled up. Sort of folded up in his chair. "Like something just fell on him out of the sky," she said. And I'm listening to this and I'm thinking, "Why are you telling me this? Why would anyone want to know this?"'

'How…' I choke. How is it said? How does anyone say anything? 'How long…?'

'How long does he have? Could be any time. Tomorrow, next week. Could be right this second while I'm sitting out here in the smokers' area, talking to you…' She shakes her head, laughs. Not her usual laugh. A brittle click, a hack.

'I'll come home,' I say.

'What? Oh. Well, all right. Please yourself.'

'I'll come straight home. I can be there…' But I don't know when I can be there. I don't even know where I am.

'Yeah, all right, but don't do anything drastic. You're at work. If you've got work to do, do it. I mean, there's no new news here. We always knew this was going to happen. He was always, as they say, on the path…'

Abruptly her voice becomes a staggered yodel; then it drains to silence. The screen jolts, fragments. A child's red and black building blocks, spilt from the toy box. Flickery cells, chunks of dripping comb.

'Alice?'

'– *jug* –'

'Darling? Alice? I'll come home. I swear. I'll come straight home.'

For an instant she's there again, as if entombed in living ice.

'– *view* –'

Then she's not there again. Nothing is there.

'Yes, Darling,' I tell the blank screen. 'And I love you. I love you too.'

I leave the storage shed and stand breathing in the dark. Then I see Ess and I start to run. I see Ess, tiny, remote, walking away onto the plain, and I run after him, shouting, calling his name, cursing his name. He's already so far away it's not possible that I can catch him up but I run anyway, run and run after him into the dark, the air smoothing my head, the earth thudding under my feet, until there's only the dark and the plain and the pain in my back and the flame in my lungs and the voice inside me and all round me shouting, calling his name, cursing his name.

16

Morning on the plain. Gnarls of distance, fathoms of sky.

Daniel is dying. Ess is missing.

But first things first.

Harry comes out of his tent and I'm waiting for him.

'You don't have to do this,' I say.

He looks tired, unprepared, but not especially startled. He nods, as if agreeing, but he's not agreeing. 'I beg to differ.'

'So you're just going to walk in there' – Tarik's cabin – 'and tell him all this stuff you think you know about his wife, and a photo, and a pile of rubble in Kolkata?'

'At lunchtime, yes. Midday. I'm just going to walk in there and tell him all that stuff.'

'But you don't *know*, do you? You don't know that any of it's *true*.'

'I'll take my chances.'

'You're going to upset people, you're going to confuse people. And people are already pretty upset and confused.'

'Sometimes that's just how it is.'

'I can't let you do it, Harry.'

'You know what, Steven? I don't think you can stop me.'

He's right. I think he's right. Is he right?

'Ess is missing,' I say. 'I don't know where he is.'

'Well then, you'd better get looking for him,' Harry says, and with a last shallow nod lumbers away to the latrine.

Asha is sitting on the ground, drying her hair in the middle of nowhere. The longer I look at it, her position, her placement on the earth, the more disturbing it becomes. She's not within the circle of the sheds, nor on its edge, nor especially beyond it – just *outside* of it. She must have been to the river to wash but she's not placed on a line that comes from anywhere or leads anywhere. She's somehow nowhere, in the middle of it, drying her hair section by section with a white towel and methodical rubs of her hands.

Creakily I walk up to her. 'Morning,' I say. She glances at me then glances away. But she doesn't seem especially hostile, so I sit down on the ground next to her. Her legs are crossed so I cross my legs also. 'I think we both got a bit frayed yesterday,' I say.

She shrugs, fairly loosely, which I decide to take as a good sign.

'I was out of order,' I say. 'On reflection I can see that. I was frayed, ragged at the edges... not that that's an excuse. I was a dick.'

She glances at me again. 'What do you want, Steven?'

She's right, I want something. But instead of telling her what I let out a long breath and say, 'Everything's got pretty fucked up here, hasn't it?'

'I'm sure I wouldn't know.'

'I think we've all got fucked up. Ess, Harry, Tarik, me... maybe even you.'

Asha tips her head to the side and begins rubbing a section of her hair vigorously as if trying to get a tune out of it. Her lips are clamped, cusped with effort. Until you look you've no idea what hard work it is.

I say, 'Ess is missing.'

She glances at me with sliding eyelids.

I say, 'He walked off. Last night. Didn't say where he was going or anything. He's not been back. I've been looking... but there's no sign.'

At last she stops rubbing her hair and begins scything at it with a tiny brown plastic comb. There is, I realise, no vanity in the way she does this: it is a chore, management – the management of a bodily mass. She says, 'I don't know where he is.'

'No.'

'Have you been up all night?'

'I have, yes.'

'You should've slept.'

'I'm sure you're right.'

She laughs, sort of. 'You look bad.'

I laugh, sort of, too. 'Well, Asha, I've got a lot on my mind at the moment.' I pause. Am I going to do this? But of course I'm going to do this: 'I talked to my girlfriend yesterday. You remember I mentioned my girlfriend?' She looks blank. 'Alice. She has this brother, and he's really ill. In fact, uh, he's going to die.'

Asha glares at me.

'This isn't a story or anything. My girlfriend's brother is dying. Right at this moment. This is what's happening.'

She glares at me. Then she looks away, scythes at her hair.

'So, you see, I have to go home. I have to find Ess and go home.'

'Finish your business, and go home,' Asha grunts.

'That's not...'

'I don't know where he is, all right?'

'No, no.'

'Probably he went to the village.'

'That's what I thought.'

'He'll come back.' She scythes at her hair. 'Or he won't.'

'Asha,' I say, 'I really need to find him.'

'Then find him. Go to the village.'

'I haven't slept...'

'Then sleep. Sleep then go.'

213

'You could help me. I was thinking... you could drive me to the village.'

'Why would I do that?'

'I don't know... because I'm asking you?'

'Why would I care that you're asking me?'

'Because you're that kind of person. Because you're a good person.'

'Is this how you make people do things for you?'

'Is this...?'

'In your work, in your *business*. Is this what you do? Tell people sad things about a dying brother, then tell them they're "good", so they will do things for you?'

'I'm not really that kind of business guy. I'm more like a secretary.'

She laughs – no doubt about it this time.

'I'm more or less a secretary. I don't spend my days making people do things for me. I answer the phone. I bring the coffee.'

'You bring the driver, you bring the car.'

'That's not what this is. I just want to find him and get us both the hell out of here. I just want to go home, and be with my girlfriend and her brother.' It's true, or it's mostly true: certainly I'm keen to find Ess and get him back here before midday, before Harry tells Tarik that his wife died a week ago in a building collapse in Kolkata.

'So you're finished here? No more business? No more Tarik? No more machine?' She widens her eyes in a parody of hurt. 'No more... India?'

'That's right,' I say. And it's true. And it's not true at all.

Asha grabs her hair with both hands, begins pushing it back, slotting it away behind her head like the blades of a penknife, and says, 'I'll make you a deal.'

'Okay.'

'I'll drive you to the village. I'll help you find him.'

'Okay, great.'

'And you'll give me half.' She smiles wonderfully. 'You'll finish your business here, Mr My Girlfriend's Brother is Dying, and you'll give me half. Half whatever you make from this transaction, Mr I'm Just a Secretary. Half of everything you make out here. From the machine, from Tarik, from Reva. From India. You'll give to me.'

'You're joking.'

'That's my offer. Take it or leave it.'

'Asha.'

'Think it over. Take as much time as you need.'

In the car, in the blazing, bouncing light, Asha grows excited. She laughs, slaps the wheel, shouts at me over the noise of the engine. Is it the money, the thought of the money? Or is it simply that now she's mad too – like the rest of us?

She says, 'It disgusts you. The whole place, the whole country. India disgusts you. Let me tell you, it disgusts me too. What is India but the world's whore, the world's favourite foreign fuck? So exotic, so authentic, so convenient, so *easy*... A country that's hardly a country at all. A country that will turn itself inside out just to give the world back its fantasy of limitless space, boundless possibility.'

'That's not what I think India is,' I say. 'That's what you think India is.'

We're still some way from the village when we see him, a stick-man isolated by empty fields and empty sky at the side of the road. Asha stops the car as soon as we see him, but I don't care. I get out and scuttle the last few yards to Ess's side.

From the car he resembled a short, slender tree – I made him out only because I was looking for him – but up close he blends with his surroundings much less successfully. He's not a rooted thing, impassive, eternal; he's a man wavering on his feet, trembling with exhaustion. Has he stood here all night? It's possible. He looks the way he looked that Saturday morning four years ago when I woke up in hospital and found him sitting in a chair next to my bed: red eyelids, glittery cheeks, an expression of perfect serenity.

By the time I get to him, he's already chuckling.

'How good of you to join me, Mr Strauss! There's no need, but I won't pretend I don't appreciate the gesture.'

'Okay,' I say, not sure how to say anything else.

'Naturally I'd have preferred to have given you the option, join me or don't join me, but I was myself taken unawares. Caught out by the unexpected urgency. Still, you're here now and that's the main thing.' He goes to slap my shoulder, but misses it completely. His face crunches up in a difficult sort of grin. 'I'm very glad you're here.'

I stand nodding for a while. I should say, *We need to go.* I should say, *I don't know about you, Ess, but I need to go. Alice's brother is dying and I need to go home. I need to go home right now.* But instead I say, 'You're expecting Reva.'

'Yes.' His grin clicks through a couple of rotations and becomes a broad, confident one. 'I daresay Tarik's good lady wife will be joining us at any moment.' He throws a salute in the direction of Asha, darkly outlined behind the windscreen of the Adventurers car, and says, 'And you've brought a driver and a car, no less! Do you know I didn't think of that? Just so caught up as I say by the quite unexpected *urgency*… I'm not sure what I would've done. Probably oiled a palm or two here, entailed the services of a couple of witless rustics. But you've spared me the trouble. How entirely marvellous.'

'Happy to help.' I nod and nod. 'So what's this "urgency"?'

'What do you think? The call, the call. The call from Fancy Bill confirming that he and Reva are almost here.' He opens his arms at the road and says it again: 'Almost here.'

'Great,' I say weakly.

'Not a moment too soon, if you ask me. When you think what I'm paying him… But most welcome news, just the same.'

'So Bill said he was bringing her here? This morning? To meet you?'

'Bringing her here, yes. To meet me, meet us all. Tarik especially, but… yes.' He drops his head and pushes it forward – that lunge of chagrin. 'They're just ever so slightly on the late side. I was expecting more like last night… but this morning, yes.'

'You've been waiting all night?'

'Delays. This is life. Brief intervals between unavoidable delays. But I think this morning, yes.'

I nod and nod. Then I say, 'I don't think she's coming, Ess.'

'No?' Calmly interested in whatever I might have to say.

'I don't think anyone's coming.'

'And why do you think that?'

'Harry has this story, he thinks Reva's dead, he thinks she was killed last week in a building collapse in Kolkata, so he thinks she's dead, and he thinks you've been had. By Bill or whoever. He thinks maybe you've been had.'

Ess stands blinking at all this with perfectly calm fascination. 'Does he really?'

'He does. And he says he's giving us till midday then he's going to tell Tarik. Which, you know, I think would be bad.'

'What do you mean, "giving us till midday"?'

'That's just what he said.'

'But what does that mean, "giving us"? "Giving us" what? What's he "giving us"?'

'Maybe we should ask him. We should go back…'

'Oh, no.' His frown now curls in a way that says he will indulge an idle fancy so far but no further. 'I can't go back. I have to be here. To meet Reva.'

I don't know about you, Ess…

I nod and nod. 'I don't think she's coming, Ess.'

'Bushwah. Bill called me. They're almost here.'

Nodding, nodding. 'I don't think anyone's coming.'

We're watching the road, watching the point at which the line of the road cuts off against the line of the horizon, Ess and I standing by the road looking a point that's not a real point at all but an accident of perspective, an effect of bodies in space, a conjuration of the eye.

I tell Ess we need to drink and eat, but he seems not to hear me, so I allow myself to drift into the village, along the deserted lanes, until at last I tumble by pure luck back into the courtyard where on our last visit we encountered Laxman and a great gathering of talkative villagers. Today it's empty. Funny: without people in it, the courtyard seems tiny. When it was full it seemed huge. Another trick of the eye.

Eventually I find a man at a stall who agrees to sell me tea and bread. The price he asks is astonishing, a provocation, a cold penalty, but I pay it anyway and scuttle back to the road. Ess accepts the food and drink when I offer it to him but he remains incapable of, or uninterested in, communication, wholly absorbed in his observation of the road.

I take the chai and the roti to Asha, too. She accepts my offerings through a scrolled-down window. She doesn't seem interested in talking to me either. I ask if she's okay in the car, if she maybe wants to get out, stretch her legs or something, and she tilts her head from side to side then seals up the window.

I return to Ess at the roadside. We eat and drink in silence. Again I imagine trying to tell him about Alice, about Daniel (*I don't know about you, Ess…*), but only the thought of it fills me with terror. I think of Alice's face in my tablet, the huge nakedness of her yawning mouth. She is so far away, sitting on a bench outside an English hospital, her brother in a bed with his stroke-twisted body and his fucked brain, the thousands of miles of planet between us all exhausting and intricate obstacle, and every vector of it washed in my coward's sweat and my idler's blood… But none of this is what terrifies me. What terrifies me is the thought that I would tell him, and he would simply nod, and turn away from the road, and say of course we must go. 'Of course, Mr Strauss. We must leave at once. Why on earth didn't you say anything earlier?' It feels like what he would do, sounds like what he would say. In only a very slightly different world he is saying it, he is striding away, phone clamped to his ear, already arranging flights as he waves to Asha to start the car and take us directly to the nearest airport, while I go on standing here, uncertain, immobile, no answer in me anywhere to his entirely pertinent question: *Why didn't you say anything earlier?*

I'm staring at the car, trying to catch a glimpse of Asha through the windscreen. If she got out and came to stand with us, I know, I would be able to tell Ess about Alice and Daniel. It wouldn't matter that she doesn't believe me, that she thinks the whole thing is a lie, a story, a business strategy; just her being with us would allow me to speak somehow. But she won't get out, won't stand with us. And I can't see her through the windscreen. A great burning hairball of reflected sun obscures her.

I heft my cup in the direction of the car and I say to Ess, 'I get a sense that things between you two have taken a turn…?'

He smiles. 'It's nothing. Just at the moment Asha is ever so slightly annoyed with me. No doubt you're aware that I clarified for her the place of Reva in our agreement…? Most odd. I explained the situation to her, in profuse and even pedantic detail, but it didn't seem to matter. She simply didn't seem able to find the... proper perspective on the arrangement.' He nods, then his smile tightens and he says, 'She'll buck up. You'll see.'

Midday is coming, with its heat and light. At the roadside there's no shade and I've forgotten my hat again and Ess has forgotten his. He's not wearing his sunglasses, either, no doubt afraid they will rob him of his first sight of the car, the distant lancing of sunlight reflected off bodywork, the vehicle in motion with Bill Fancy at the wheel, jaunty, jowly, in baggy shorts and a sweat-patched T-shirt, passing the time on the road with volleys of his decorative whistling, the trills, trebles and warbles of English birdlife, the woman scowling incredulously in the seat next to him, or maybe behind him, in a seat or a cot expensively customised to accommodate her physical fullness, the whole road movie of the two of them getting here, a story to be told and laughed over, backs slapped, heads shaken, puckered lips finally, ruefully kissed, on a scramble of rugs in front of Tarik and Reva's plain-hidden home... look long enough and you can almost see it, the faraway glint, the single rogue pixel that seems so little to ask, a request so modest it may already have been granted and you have to remember to check that it hasn't.

It hasn't. There's nothing there. There's not going to be anything there.

No one's coming. Reva's dead and Ess has been had.

'We have to go,' I say to him, as gently as I can. 'Harry...'

'I really don't think they'll be long now,' he says, mildly. 'I think not more than just a few minutes. Just a few more minutes.'

'Then we'll go back, okay?'

'Go back...?'

'Go back. Deal with Harry. Deal with Tarik. All that.'

'Yes, yes. If we must.'

We resume our road-watching for a while. Then I say, 'You mentioned something about paying him? About paying Bill Fancy?'

'Paying him, yes.'

'Did you mean you're going to pay him, or... you've already paid him?'

'Paid him.' He nods stiffly. 'Already paid him, yes. As I said, there were expenses. On account of Reva's extraordinary condition. And, and on other accounts.'

'And what was that? What did you pay him?'

'Everything. Everything I had left. Yes.'

He sits down. After fifteen hours on his feet, Ess sits down in the dust. The way he does this makes me suddenly desperate and when I look back at the road I'm not watching any more but willing, flinging out waves of telekinesis, trying by means of an obscure violent effort of the insides of my head to make it happen, to fill the empty eyelet of the vanishing point, to force the miracle, win that smallest of all mercies...

It doesn't come. Nothing comes. No one's coming.

I crouch down next to him. He's laced his fingers together and placed his hands over his head, like a hat. The face under it is red, burnt, burst, all splinter and scathe.

'We have to go, Ess,' I tell him.

The eyes in their crinkles, vast dead bloody ruts.

'It's midday. Midday gone. We have to go back.'

The eyes swim then find me and with a desolate effort he nods.

I help him to his feet. We're walking towards the car when I make two observations. The first is that I'm holding his elbow, leading him along by the elbow. The second is that something strange has started to happen to his face. Ess has noticed it too, and it seems to be causing him some alarm.

'Don't worry,' I say, in an absurd bright voice. 'It's okay. Don't worry, Ess, it's okay. It's all going to be okay.'

As we carry on towards the car, my hand lightly steering him by the elbow, he nods again, or anyway tries to. But it's difficult for him, with the convulsions wrenching at the tip of his sunburnt nose, dragging the splintery mask of his face down over his teeth, as if trying to make him eat it, trying to feed him his own face.

17

Asha drives slowly. It seems pointless to ask her to speed up. Midday has gone, and if Harry really means to take his story to Tarik, he's already done it.

I glance at Ess, sitting next to me in the backseat, looking out the window with a faint smile. The twitch has subsided but still his features have a pinched, precarious quality, as if it's only by a concentrated effort that he's keeping them from slipping loose, changing shape, drifting slackly over his face.

No one speaks. The heat, the glare, the rocking progress of the car lulls me into a heavy half-sleep full of the memory that I stayed awake all last night. I glance at Ess again then I look out the window too, at the seething dust, at the simmering scrub, at the brilliant red billow of a T-shirt above the grey stakes of a dry-dead bush.

Laxman stands behind the bush in his T-shirt and raises his arm in greeting. I have time to register this, to register also that there's someone with him – someone else huddling behind the bush – then the car rocks past and they're gone. It occurs to me that I should say something, do something. Stop the car, go back, speak to Laxman – but the moment has passed, the half-sleep is too heavy, the heat, the glare and the silence conspire to hold me in place, fixed among burning seat cushions at the end of the earth.

Harry is packing up his camp. Half of it has already vanished into his backpack, which sits up on the ground with pert independent life. He's winding a rope round his forearm as Asha brings the Adventurers car to a halt. He puts down the rope and rubs his hands on his shirt then stands, frowning about himself at the unpacked bits of his camp.

I open my door, stand, and I'm still thinking about how I'm going to get Ess out of the car, how I'm going to manage this whole situation, when I see Ess step quite briskly round the front of the car and set off in a determined way towards Harry. At this point he doesn't look mad or anything; he just looks determined. I scuttle to catch up with him.

'Leaving so soon?' Ess calls to Harry as we approach. 'Surely not. Stay, stay.'

Harry grimaces. 'I don't think so.'

'Won't you reconsider?' Ess says, with somewhat sinister cheer. 'What do you think, Harry? Can't we twist your arm?'

'No, I don't think so.'

'I'm sorry to hear that.' Ess sighs – a sound that has, too, its sinister clink and hiss. 'But as you've got your mind set on it, who are we stand in your way? It's been a pleasure, Harry. An honour and a boon.' He extends a hand. Harry looks at this hand warily, but doesn't take it. He goes on not taking it.

Then he looks up from Ess's hand to Ess's face and says, 'I'm not going right away.'

'Oh no? You don't think it's best to strike while the iron's hot?'

'I have some business first.'

'What business is that then?'

'I have to speak to Tarik.'

'Good lord, do you really?'

'Yes I do really.' Rubbing his hands again on his shirt, Harry starts with a lumbering step towards the cabin.

'Do you know, Harry, I'm not sure that's such a hot idea.'

'I'm sorry you feel that way.'

'In fact, Harry, I'm fairly sure there's no need for you to talk to Tarik at all.'

'I beg to differ.'

'No, Harry,' Ess says, striding after Harry and catching up with him easily, 'no, my dear chap, don't *beg*, don't ever *beg*,' speeding ahead and turning to block Harry's path to the cabin door, 'just do as you're told and keep your mouth shut, there's a good chap.'

Ess and Harry stand facing each other outside Tarik's cabin. Ess, smiling, looks as if he's perfectly willing to take a bite out of Harry's neck. Harry looks utterly miserable.

Then the door opens and Tarik is there. Ess starts to say something but it's too late. Harry has stepped past him into the cabin and there's nothing for Ess and me to do but follow.

The first thing I see is the flowers. The workbench at the end of the room has been tidied up, the mess of tools and parts cleared away and replaced by a stubby glass vase with three dainty pink flowers in it. For some reason this blows my mind. Where did Tarik find flowers? When did he go to get them? Why has he tidied his workbench and replaced his tools and parts with a vase of pink flowers?

Tarik moves to stand in front of his little altar of flowers, to place his body between us and it, protecting or hiding it. His expression is unclear, but he appears both to want us to leave him alone and to assume that we won't do anything he wants.

Harry is standing next to him. Ess, still going forward, seems about to walk right into Harry – to try to walk through him, to demolish, dematerialise him. With a startled look Harry puts his hands up and pushes on Ess's chest. Ess allows himself to be halted. And it's funny, obviously, because Harry's this great big guy and Ess is this delicate teeny-weeny but still that's how it happens. Tarik looks worried by all this and I guess I probably do too.

'We're here to *talk*,' Harry says, with an entirely mysterious emphasis, glaring at Ess. 'Everyone's just here to talk.'

'We're all going to have a marvellous chat,' Ess says, his emphasis ferocious and unmistakable. 'See if we can't unproblem a problem or two.'

Tarik seems frozen, looking at neither Ess nor Harry but at some point in between them. He edges backwards against his flower altar.

'Can we sit? Is that acceptable, Tarik? Are there chairs? I think if maybe we can all just *sit down*...'

Tarik seems frozen. He frowns slightly then sits down on the floor. So the rest of us sit down on the floor.

Harry frowns, knits his fingers together and starts to speak. The voice he starts to speak in is nothing like the voice he's been speaking in since we first met him. 'Tarik, what I have to say to you now is hard, and I don't know how to say it other than all-out and up-front. If my talking that way makes you feel like you want to give me a slam on the nose, you just slam away, you just go right ahead and have at it, you'll find no quarrel in me.'

Harry glances in the direction of, though not quite at, Ess and me. He smiles, with wet bits of teeth in his beard.

'The same goes for you gentlemen. I know you've reasons of your own for preferring me not to pipe up on this matter, and I understand that you too may wish me some corporeal harm. Well, sure. Let me speak and when I'm done if you gentlemen need in some way to harm me you go right ahead. Only, you know, not too corporeally.'

'You piece of shit,' Ess says to Harry, folding his arms, conversational. 'Oh you fucking piece of *shit*.'

Harry squints inside his specs. 'That's as maybe.' Then he returns his attention to Tarik. 'I need to talk with you about your wife. About Reva, Tarik.'

Tarik looks at Harry. His face in the cabin's low light is handsome, sculpted, smooth. He's dispensed with the rockstar stubble at some point.

'I have reason to believe, Tarik, that your wife was recently in Kolkata.'

'Balls,' Ess says.

'Not balls. I believe Reva was recently in Kolkata, at an office block on the outskirts of the city and I have evidence to support this belief. I have…'

'Absolute balls,' Ess says.

'That is not so. Tarik, I have evidence which I can show you and which you can see with your own eyes. I don't pretend to know the intimate details of what these gentlemen have told you…'

'"Don't pretend"?' The contempt in Ess's voice doesn't quite carry. 'All this is is pretending! All of it! Pretending! *Lying!*'

'If these gentlemen have told you they are in any position to, to, to convey Reva to your *presence*, then I have to say that is not true. No sir.' He shakes his head. 'That is not true. I don't know…'

'No,' Ess snarls, 'you don't, you don't know a fucking thing…'

'… Assuming somewhere along the line there was some confusion, or error, or some form of other willful deception beyond the control of…'

'Deception!' Ess takes a desperate in-suck of breath. 'Like you're anyone…'

'… But however that may be, the truth is, Tarik, Reva is not coming here. No one is bringing her here. She's not coming, Tarik.'

Tarik looks at Harry. He's like a photograph of himself thirty seconds ago – a replica, a stand-in, while the real Tarik attends to important business elsewhere. It's not possible to say that this is not in fact precisely what's happening.

Tarik has dispensed with his stubble and tidied his workbench and replaced his tools and parts with a vase of pink flowers because he thinks his wife is going to arrive. He thinks at any moment an engine will rasp on the plain and the rasp of the engine will become a distantly bucking vehicle and the vehicle will become a slapping-open of doors, a pale skirt of disturbed dust and stepping through that skirt or within it, wearing it like a bridal train, his wife, his Reva, her face and her forgiveness displaced into his future by no more than hours or minutes, no more than moments, close enough now almost to see, to touch.

'I don't know any way to say this but all-out. Reva went to an office block in Kolkata last week and the building collapsed…'

'Oh balls,' Ess says, with a gasp that wrenches his whole frame. 'You don't have to listen to this, Tarik. You don't have to *believe*…'

'… And Reva didn't get out… She was found, I'm sorry to say. Somewhat later.'

'Fucking *balls*,' Ess says, and takes a huge gasp.

'I'm sorry, Tarik. But it's true. It's the truth. And I'm just so sorry about that, I really am.'

Ess gasps, stares down at the floor, does not or cannot speak.

If he could speak, he would say something like: *A likely story.* Something like: *Ask yourself one question, Tarik – where's this coming from? Who's this holier-than-thou colonial to speak anyway about deception, when it's perfectly clear that it is he who is bent on deception? He who is inventing distasteful stories for the sole purpose of confusing you, of exploiting you, and cheating us while he's at it? No, it is only as I told you. Reva is alive and well. She has been staying with family in Goa and even now my trusted associate, my Fancy Bill Fancy, is bringing her to join us. Lend no ear to these vicious fantasies. Your wife is coming back to you. She's almost here.* But he can't speak. I can speak, I could say it for him. But I don't and only go on sitting on the floor while no one says anything.

Tarik looks at Harry.

His face, the face of the real Tarik, would show the terrible workings of denial and disbelief through which his soul must now penetrate. But we're not looking at his face. We're looking at a photo of his face from a minute ago, the colours already growing lurid and archaic, the textures seeping, curdling.

Ess is right: Tarik doesn't have to believe Harry. He doesn't have to consider Harry's evidence. What is evidence? Anything can be faked by anyone. The technology required is so primitive it's scarcely even technology any more – it's life, it's instinct, the sinewy hardwire of the contemporary animal. Not all the pics and docs and live feeds in the world will add one atom of weight to what Harry has already said and done.

Then the life-size photo we're looking at, the Tarik image bullioned with imperfection, stutters into motion. The eyes twitch like eyes inside a mask. Like the eyes of horses, with their sepia inner lid, their roiling whites.

'Get out,' Tarik says.

Harry nods, uncrosses his legs, prepares to stand. He's still mostly on the floor when Ess springs at him. Lightly, silently, Ess springs across the floor and throws himself on top of Harry. For a while neither of them makes a sound. Whatever struggle occurs between them is loose-limbed, weak-jointed. Ess reaches for Harry's face. Harry removes his hands not by pushing them away but as it were peeling them off, one after the other, patiently, over and over again. Ess's hands waver above his head then drop and then the rest of him drops too. Harry slips back and props himself against the wall. Then there's a gusting sound, a hovering sound. It seems to be above us, all round us, this sound, then it is only the sound of Ess breathing, of Ess gasping for breath. Harry seems to be cradling him in his arms, but I don't think this is really what's happening.

'A likely story,' I say. I say, 'Ask yourself one question, Tarik...'

'Get out,' Tarik says. 'All of you. *Get out.*'

I stand, go towards Ess and Harry, try to help Ess to his feet. But Harry shakes me off with strange violence. I am still absorbing it, this violence, when Ess himself climbs up between us, white-faced and wide-eyed, manoeuvres us both aside with the points of his elbows, and barely keeping his balance strides across the cabin to the door and disappears outside. We all watch him go, or at least Harry and I do. Then Harry stands, lumbers to the door and steps down and passes outside also. I look after them. Behind me I know there is a clean-shaven man sitting on the floor and behind him a workbench with a vase of deadly pink flowers on it. If I turned and looked I would see these things. But I don't turn, I don't look. I go forward on the tap-tapping wooden feet of a fairground puppet and step through the door and pass outside into the useless sluice of the afternoon sun.

Ess is standing in front of the cabin, squinting with a faint sickly half-smile at the far edge of the plain. Harry is standing what appears to be a carefully considered distance away from him, staring at the bit of ground immediately in front of him with no expression whatsoever. I walk straight past them, not looking at them, not acknowledging them in any way, and I go up to the Adventurers car in its patch of swirled silence and pull at the passenger-side door, not expecting it to open, but it opens and I thrust myself inside, pack myself in through the opening like a horrible parcel for speedy delivery.

Asha is sitting in the driver's seat, where she is always sitting, has always sat. Her hands are crossed at the top of the steering wheel, which I have some memory of being something you're supposed not to do. I don't really know. I've never learnt to drive. I've never had the presence of mind to take lessons, never had the imagination to picture myself sitting in that seat, operating the life-and-death controls.

We don't look at each other or speak to each other. I gaze at the sky, one faraway section of it, crossed loosely and intermittently by a blue light and a gold light. After a while she passes me a water bottle and I drink. Then I rest my forehead on the dashboard, lulled by contact with the hot and pitted plastic. Then I sit up and drink some more and eat a piece of roti that Asha produces from somewhere, hard, dry, surely not a piece of the fleshly fresh bread I brought her earlier, then I go back to gazing at the sky. A blue light and a gold light, rhythmically swinging, like vast pretentious desk-toys, like the executive playthings of absent and outdated gods.

Asha says, 'He asks you a question about yourself and even as he speaks you feel the opening of a chamber inside him into which he will take the answer you give him, where he will repose it and cherish it and seat it on cushions and drape it with veils. A Regency chamber, all glitter and plush, all English space and rest. He will keep the answer you give him here forever. Even when both of you are gone, dead, decayed, unstrung into your DNA, you know this chamber will remain. He leans towards you and he smiles and his voice is the voice of the smiling face in the gilt-edged mirror and he asks where you were born, what your parents were like, any brothers or sisters, how many, where you went to school, which lessons you liked, which you didn't, why, what were your dreams when you were sixteen, who did you love, who loved you, who hurt you most and who was most hurt by you, how did you come by this line of work, why do you do it, how much do you earn, how much does it excite you, why, where do you see yourself in five years' time, and it doesn't matter what he asks because he makes sure you know the only thing that matters is your answer, the answer you alone could give, the answer he will seat on cushions and drape with veils and preserve in that English space, and you know this is worth everything, he makes sure you know this too, what he gives you when he takes your answer is worth everything.'

'I've no idea what you're talking about,' I say.

The day is almost over when a sound of commotion causes me to sit up again, to raise my forehead from the dashboard and see Harry and Ess, still standing outside the cabin, now arguing, or anyway shouting at each other. I see also that I am alone in the car. The driver-side door is open and Asha is striding on bare feet towards the shouting men. As she calls out and starts to remonstrate with them, I slowly push open my door, step outside and begin walking towards them also.

Everyone is shouting. I stop walking several paces away and put my hands over my ears. I don't need to hear them to know what they're shouting about. Asha is shouting that this is no way for grown men to behave. Harry is shouting that he is sorry. Ess is shouting that he wishes to die, that all he wishes is to be forgotten and to die.

After a while Ess falls silent. Harry goes on shouting and so does Asha. Ess waves a hand at them, turns away. He folds his arms and holds them in front of him as if they're a terrible burden. His head hangs forward, as if it too is unbearably heavy. Then he looks up and there's his face, with closed eyes and downturned lips, a straining rictus, an ancient carving of grief. It's the face of those people you see on TV, keening next to craters where their homes used to be, next to heaps of Kolkata rubble in which their loved ones have been carelessly entombed. Except, obviously, it's not that face at all. It's the face of a humiliated businessman. It's the face of a middle-aged executive who has blown the biggest business deal in history and lost all his money to boot. Except, obviously, it's not that face at all.

He sees me, starts to traipse towards me. I stand with my hands over my ears.

Then we hear the shot.

The report seems to get louder and louder, amplified by the vast echo chamber of the plain. Even with my hands over my ears I can hear it getting louder, louder. Ess stops traipsing towards me. His eyes widen. The fibres of his woodcarving rictus swivel and stir. He looks like a man at the point of death – that surprise, that innocence.

Tarik is standing in the doorway of his cabin. He is holding his gun, gripping it in both hands, blinking behind his specs and pointing his gun through a sheet of white smoke. The heavy air keeps trying clumsily to whisk this sheet away, but fails, only tugging at it, rippling it, causing it to shimmy. The expression on Tarik's face is intricate, flickering with thought, though he is also weeping continuously. He has shot someone but it's not Ess.

Harry turns so suddenly he almost unbalances himself. He teeters then stands with a hand shading his eyes, looking away across the plain.

Asha runs at Tarik. She knocks the gun from his hand and knocks him backwards through the doorway into the cabin. She too disappears into the cabin.

Ess stands, eyes wide, his face a mass of wavering filaments. He drops his hands over his head, laces his fingers together, goes on standing there, quietly, patiently, almost happily, like a child awaiting further instruction.

I look at Harry then look at what Harry's looking at. Far away across the plain, two dots: one black, one red. The red of the red one is brilliant, familiar. Then it billows slightly and I know what it is. The red of a T-shirt, too big for its wearer's body.

At last I take my hands from my ears. I shout: 'Laxman!'

Tarik has shot Laxman. But Tarik is nowhere in sight.

Harry standing with a palm shading his eyes.

Ess wearing the hat of his joined hands, patiently waiting.

I start to run. I shout again: 'Laxman!'

As I run the dots on the plain slowly become people – teenagers, young men. The one dressed in black is flitting from side to side of the one in the red T-shirt lying flat on the ground. The one in black seems to be trying to raise the lying-down one. But the lying-down one is not getting up, is not capable of getting up.

Then my back fires. No click, no needly pain, but an explosion of impact, crumpling everything. As if part of the impact of that car four years ago in Yeovil didn't quite reach me at the time and catches up with me only now. The explosion, the crumple, the spiral of fiery agony carries me off my feet and throws me down in the dust.

I try to get up, but I can't. The agony bids me hold still. I stare at a pebble, small and white and covered with fine cracks on one side, very close to my face. After what seems an incredibly long time I move my head and I see Harry shading his eyes, Ess standing under his hands. Then I move my head again, look in the direction of the two human dots, the two young men, Laxman and his black-clothed friend, but the plain is empty; they've gone.

18

By the time I can stand and move and walk back towards the cabin, Harry is crouching over Ess, who is now lying on his side on the ground. He appears to be asleep, though his eyes are open. Harry keeps muttering to him, stroking his arm, but Ess gives no indication that he's aware of any of this. Then Harry says to me, 'We should move him.'

I look at Harry. I tolerate the idea of smashing his head open, of finding a rock and stoving in his skull. But I can hardly stand, hardly move. Crouching, with trembling calves, Harry manages to turn Ess on his back, then work his hands in under his arms and pull him up onto his feet. Ess wavers, sinks against him, threatens to unbalance them both. I put my hands on Harry's back and push, as firmly as I can, to support them. Briefly the two men totter from side to side then they stabilise and Harry begins to lead Ess towards the storage shed in which we've been sleeping and I hobble after them.

Harry drops Ess onto his sleeping bag. He doesn't mean to, he tries to lower him, to let him down gently, but at some point his grip fails and Ess slips away from him and falls in a sitting position onto his sleeping bag then slumps over on his side. His head rolls and knocks hard against the shed's planks. Harry says, 'Fuck.'

I stand leaning against the wall. Harry looks at each of us then coughs and says he should check on Tarik. I don't say anything. Then Harry goes out and leaves Ess and me alone in the shed.

After a while I can sit again, and I sit. I take hold of Ess's head and turn it towards me as carefully as I can. His eyes are still open, but he doesn't appear to be in pain. There is a livid patch on his forehead where he knocked against the planks. Otherwise his face is blank, slack, unoccupied.

For a long time nothing happens. Then I hear noises from the cabin – the muffled rumble of raised voices. The voices grow louder, sharper. One gives way to shouts. The other voices subside. The shouting voice gives way to cries then subsides also. Then there are other noises from the cabin, not the noises of voices.

I wait until nine then open my tablet and log into my Skype account. The wifi icon flickers, the circles ping. I stare at them for as long as I can bear to, which is about the same length of time it takes me to realise that I'm crying, shaking with grief.

I log out of the Skype account and log in to my email. All this takes a while, with the way my crying makes my hands quake and my fingers skid about on the screen, painting it with zigzags of tears and snot. Then my email opens and straight away I see there's a new message from Alice. The subject line is: 'Daniel'. I tap on it to open the message and, with a dubious fillip, the message opens:

Dear Steven,

I'm afraid I have bad news. Daniel died last night. It happened quite early in the evening and I was still at the hospital at the time so I was quite glad about that.

He didn't seem to suffer. He seemed to be sleeping and he was breathing through a respirator and all that happened was that for a while his breaths got heavier and heavier then they started to space out then the spaces between the breaths got longer and longer and then there were only spaces and no breaths. For a long time after his last breath it kept looking like he was going to take another one but he didn't.

I'm all right. As I told you yesterday, there's really no new news. Daniel was on the pathway all his life and last night he came to the end of it and no one can be surprised that that finally happened.

Sorry if this isn't making sense. Sierra says I'm probably in shock. I don't feel like I'm in shock, but probably that's the shock talking. I'm only writing to you because when we talked yesterday you seemed pretty fired up about coming home and I thought you should know what the situation is before you make any arrangements you can't change. Finish your work and come back when you can. It would be nice to see you. What I mean is you don't need to rush any more. You know what I mean.

Speak to you later,
I love you,
Alice

I watch my fingers as they close my email and re-open my Skype account. The circles ping and I watch them. All they have to do is reach across the earth and find Alice and bring her to me. They ping and ping and I watch them.

Daniel has died. I understand this but at the same time it means almost nothing to me. What does it mean? It means that he's gone, as Alice said, that he's vanished down the pathway – the pathway out of life, from the realm of the living to the region of the dead, to the shadow sphere, the weightless world. But I don't know what that means either.

I stare at the screen. The circles ping, ping. Then the wifi icon shrivels, the circles dim then blip to nothing and the screen holds nothing but futile light.

Somewhere on the face of the earth Alice is staring into her laptop. She's waiting for it to conjure me, to incarnate me. But the magic has failed. She is there and I am here and the curve of the planet turns stubbornly, irreducibly between us.

I stare at the screen. And then, at the same instant that I realise I'm howling – that my mouth is wide open and I'm howling – I raise my tablet in both hands and smash it down on my knee. The thing crunches and I feel a jolt of pain. I smash the tablet down again, again, the pain convulsing my leg, my whole body, until the tablet breaks. A lot of mysterious flexible internal stuff keeps the pieces linked together, but I twist and wrench at them until they separate, tear apart like a hunk of dense bread. The piece still in my hand I fling against the wall. It taps lightly on the planks then drops rustling among the other crap back there. Another piece, to which the screen is still attached, a warped misty sheet, like a gigantic fingernail, I kick away with my heel.

Then there's nothing else to do. I look at Ess. He blinks. I watch him closely, almost holding my breath, waiting for some other indication that he's still alive, still in there. But he only blinks, breathes.

'Ess?' I say. The croak of grief in my voice is faintly surprising. I say, 'You should have killed me. I've been thinking about it and I think it would have been better. I think it would have been better if you'd just killed me.'

In Toulouse in 2011 Ess said, 'It's hard to believe, isn't it?'

We were sitting in the balcony of his executive suite in the dusky evening. We'd spent the day on a walking tour with the charming Skycoach representative, and the hours in the sun had left us dazed and reflective. Now, with an imperial gesture, he waved a hand at the view from the balcony – picturesque central Toulouse, and by extension all France, all civilized Europe. At that time such gestures still seemed entirely appropriate to him.

'Hard to believe that it's real,' he said. 'You see it, but some part of you rejects it. Don't you find? You'd think I'd be used to it by now, but let me tell you, Mr Strauss: I'm not. I feel the same way every time I come on one of these jaunts. Doesn't matter how often I take the flight, hail the cab, check in at reception, unpack my suitcase, then move at last to the window, the balcony… Every time that frisson of rejection. The unreality of France, the unreality of Spain. The unreality of South Africa. The unreality of the United States of America. I sit in my balcony and I'm expected to *believe*… A wee lad from Yeovil, from the mizzle and the mud, from the green and the brown. That's what I am, you see, even to this day, a wee Yeovil lad with grass stains on his knees and a completely black scab on his elbow and tiny crisscross sort of wounds on his cheek where he once got stamped by a cow into a cattle-grid, horrible experience, probably the defining moment of my life, the coalescing trauma or what-you-will, you can still see them, faint red lines, just here…?'

I looked: the graph-paper scar. 'Barely.'

'Really? Well, the marks may fade from the surface, but inside I bear the scars yet. Have no doubt about that. Mud and mizzle and a cow's hoof stamping my head into a cattle-grid. The filth down there, shiny pebbles, stones, grit, but also bloody wool and torn-off nail and bits of bone gone black and grey. That's reality, the look of it, the taste of it, the feel of it that you carry round with you everywhere, a little heap in the base of your stomach, and then you sit in a balcony like this and you see a view like that… and something doesn't quite make sense, does it? It doesn't *add up*.'

'We're lucky,' I said. I laughed. 'Lucky devils.'

He looked at me. At that time his look was still like the look of a vastly powerful alien being – an extraterrestrial emperor or god. Then he smiled, gradually, gracefully, a smile to be etched in marble and displayed as the central monument of an idealistic community of the far future, and he said, 'It's not luck. Do you really think luck did this?' He chuckled fantastically. His humiliation by Skycoach was still eleven hours away. 'No, I'll tell you what did this. Heroic madness. A kind of, if you will, divine lunacy. That celestial derangement that allows a man to preserve his own reality – to hold fast to that kernel, so to speak, that rough cluster, the bloody wool and nail of his own reality – when the world surrounding him is wholly and irremediably unreal.'

'So, what you're saying is, we're mental.'

'I'm afraid so. The pair of us. Irremediably cracked.' He laughed and I did too.

Toulouse was settling into the grain of its woodcut dusk. Ess took a sip of brandy then sat whirling the glass in his hand.

'One other thing.' He frowned into his glass, then up at me. His eyes were sharp with drink – not misty, not clouded, but oddly piercing, far-seeing. 'While we're talking. Sometimes, just occasionally… you know you are here, don't you?'

'How do you mean?' I asked, grinning.

'You know you are here. You know you are now. You take a breath and you draw down the air of this momentary heaven. You sit and you apply pressure to surfaces. You lean back and the bones of the chair creak.'

'Sorry, Ess,' I was grinning, 'no idea what you're talking about.'

'You know you are real, don't you? That you are a person…'

'Yeah, obviously I do. Obviously.'

'Yes. Of course you do.'

I wake to sunlight and murmuring. I sit up on my sleeping bag. Ess, lying next to me on his, has finally closed his eyes. He's breathing, softly snoring, in a way you could almost believe is peaceful.

On the ground in front of me are some of the ragged bits of my tablet: shiny crinkly black squares, irregular-edged, like the parts of a dully impossible jigsaw puzzle.

My back feels numb, solid, without give or flex. It doesn't hurt to move it; only I can barely move it. Awkwardly I stand.

I put a hand on the wall. I pick up my water bottle, drink, then go back to standing with a hand on the wall. I listen to the murmuring, the muttering from the cabin.

I shuffle to the open door and stand in the doorway, in the flood of morning sunlight. I scan the plain, left to right, my eyes in the morning heat seeming to wiggle on their sticks. Harry's camp has now completely gone, leaving not even a mark on the dusty ground. The netted obelisk of his backpack has gone too; I assume he came out in the night at some point and took it into the cabin. The Adventurers car is still where I expect it to be. In fact everything looks more or less as I expect it to look, barring only my surprise that our being here has made so slight an impression. Frightening, how slight the impression we make. In a city, a town, maybe this truth would be less obvious (though no less true). But the plain conceals nothing. The great inhuman dream of it will shake us from its bones and its teeth, grind to atoms our every trace. Soon there will be nothing to prove we were ever here at all.

Something's wrong – something other than the plain's vast denial of our presence or consequence. I listen to the murmuring, muttering, buzzing from the cabin. Then I realise what's wrong. The sounds I can hear, the sounds I've been hearing since I woke up, are not coming from the cabin. They're coming from somewhere else.

At first I think they're coming from the plain, from the plain itself, from its heat and mass, its gnarled static and bleached wavelength. Then I look and I see where they're really coming from, the row of figures blurring into visibility on the horizon, slowly materialising from the ripply distance and heat haze. A row of tiny dark human shapes: five, six men, no seven, no eight.

Even at this distance I can see that their hands are not empty. Their silhouetted arms seem to have grown slender tapering branches, but I know what this means is they are carrying the same strange farming gear I saw them wielding on our first visit to their village – rods, staffs, sickles, scythes.

Eight men from Laxman's village are marching on Tarik's cabin. Marching towards us through the light and heat and distance and dust.

I rebound into the storage shed as if struck – as if again struck by a large vehicle in rapid motion. I bend over Ess, shake his shoulder, call his name, do everything I can think of to rouse him. But he will not be roused. 'Ess,' I wail, 'Ess, Ess.' His snoring stops, his breathing shifts its pitch. His eyes spongily open then spongily close. I shout at him, yank his arm, slap his face. But he will not be roused.

'Ess,' I wail, 'I'm not messing about. People are coming, people who are very, very pissed off with us. We've got to go. Do you hear what I'm saying? We've got to wake up and go.'

I wait for his eyes to open again but they don't. Then I straighten up and scuttle over to the cabin and start banging on the door.

'Wake up!' I shout into the cabin. 'You bastards! You *bastards*! Wake up and get out here! Get *the fuck* out here, you bastards!'

The door opens and Harry leans out with a windswept look. He squints at me, then his head judders back and he squints past me, over my shoulder. I have a pretty good idea what he's squinting at, though I turn to look too anyway.

The marching men of the village have almost reached us. They are so close now it's possible to see that they are not in fact even really marching – they're walking, not quite strolling, not quite ambling, moving with steady but somehow shuffle-footed purpose. They have sticks in their hands, bladed tools, spindling instruments.

Harry nods, once, and withdraws into the cabin.

'What?' I shout after him into the hot gloom. 'What are you doing? Can't you see…'

Then Harry comes out again, leading Asha by the arm, gripping her arm in one hand, pointing at the men with his other.

Asha allows herself to be led. As she goes, she narrows her eyes on the walking men. She presses her lips together in a sneer of disapproval, of disavowal, the single most violent expression I've ever seen on the face of a human being.

Together Harry and Asha somehow go towards the approaching row of men. How do they do this – oppose the wave, the force, the magnetic repulsion of that approach? The same repulsion that seems about to lift me off my feet and hurl me bodily into the back of the cabin, under a blanket, under a table? I can't imagine how they do it. I need all my strength only to keep on standing by the doorway, in the sunlight, in full view of the men.

Abruptly Asha stops walking. Harry, taken by surprise, stumbles over his own feet then stops also. Without looking at him, without noticeable irritation, Asha shakes his hand off her arm. She raises her chin, squares her shoulders.

The advancing men cease their advance only a few feet away from the point at which Harry and Asha stand waiting for them. There's no special ceremony to the way the men do this; a couple of them shuffle to a halt, then a couple more, a couple more, until they're all standing still, the row, if it was ever really anything so orderly as a row and not just a trick of perspective. Only a clear space is left round the two men who halted first, an elderly guy with a neat short white beard and a younger guy with a pair of glamorous chunky headphones slipped round his neck like a futuristic brace. I assume the older guy is the village headman, the younger an advisor of some sort, but the truth is I don't know who or what either of them is. They could be Laxman's grandfather and father. Laxman's doctor, Laxman's teacher.

Of Laxman himself there's no sign. I don't know why I thought there would be, but anyway there isn't one. I picture him back at the village, in a soft bed in a cool hut, some part of him in plaster while all the other parts of him play a handheld computer game. This is the picture I need to see, the story I need to believe, the story of the bed and the hut and the computer game and the boy with a major but fundamentally non-serious injury.

Harry takes a half step towards the two men who I think are the village headman and his advisor. He begins to speak, in stammering American, but it's clear that the two men have no idea what he's saying. Raising his palms in a gesture pleading forbearance, he starts again, this time with quick turns of his head and meaning glances at Asha. He seems to think that Asha is going to translate for him. But there never seems any real possibility of this happening and Asha, ignoring him, takes plunging strides forward into the proximity of the two men and starts to roar at them in rapid-fire Hindi.

Funny: there is very visibly no language barrier between Asha and the two men from the village. And yet they seem to have no idea what she's saying either.

While she goes on roaring, Harry stands with a grave expression. Now and then he nods, as if to underline some excellent point she's made. But I'm not sure he understands her any better than I do, and I don't understand her at all. To my ears, and possibly also to Harry's, Asha could be proposing to the men what is in her view the best, most efficient way of killing us and getting rid of our bodies.

The men's reactions to her speech are no reliable indication of anything either. The older man seems to be sourly considering Asha's perspective, his lips pinched and cheeks sucked in within

244

his beard, while the younger keeps flapping a hand at her, as if directing traffic, signalling her to move on. Asha aims at this guy an especially vociferous cluster of shrill syllables, and both men flinch with indignation. Quickly this indignation flares to anger. And then all the men are angry, shifting their feet in the dust, voicing the same restive vowel. The way they do this brings back into prominence the various objects in their hands, the glistening antennae, the bow-like blades.

Now several things happen at once. Harry takes an unwary gallant step forward. The guy with headphones round his neck raises the staff in his right hand until its ornate point soars above his head. And exactly as these things are happening there is a sudden crash next to my head, a sudden blur in front of my eyes, a thready flip of sweated fabric and straining muscle.

I blink. Somewhere in this blink there is the sense of a flash of blue lightning. There is a sense that this flash issued not from the sky but from the point of the staff raised above the headphones guy's head. There is a sense also that this flash struck Harry's body. But I don't know, didn't see, because I blinked somewhere in the middle of it.

Then several things have happened. Harry is lying in the dust with a flat frozen look. The headphones guy is gleefully examining his staff, appraising it from end to end, flicking at what looks like a sort of handmade control panel mounted on its side. The other men are shouting, some at Harry, some at Asha, some at the older guy, some at the younger headphones guy posing with his scifi staff, some at each other. And Tarik is running. Tarik has run out of the cabin, run past me, run away on to the plain. I turn and look and I see him running. He appears to be running towards the test site. And he appears to be carrying something, cradling something in his arms.

'Tarik!' I shout after him. But he only carries on running.

Asha is leaning over Harry, pressing her fingers to his neck, pressing her ear to his lips. A couple of the men totter towards her and her head snaps back and she roars at them and the men shamefacedly retreat. Another couple appears to be remonstrating with the headman, indicating his advisor with gestures of accusation and cancellation. And yet the final couple of men seem to be remonstrating with this group, flinging their palms in similar gestures of derision and dismissal.

Tarik has reached the test site. The white streak of his kurta disappears into a gap between two blocks.

'Asha!' I shout. 'Can you see this? Can you see what Tarik's doing?'

Harry lets out a low groan. His face is grey-blue, depthless; his eyebrows and beard have a compressed, vacuum-packed sort of appearance. He groans again and Asha leans back from him. She climbs to her feet, shouting at the men standing over her.

One of the blocks at the test site flickers, as if something has fallen away from it. I keep looking and I see it again, the same but different: a flicker at the block's other side, only this time something flying up, something slender, a strand, a hair.

'Asha!' I shout. 'Are we seeing this? Are we seeing what Tarik's doing?'

Still lying on the ground, Harry moves a grey-blue hand to his grey-blue face. He pushes his specs round on the bridge of his grey-blue nose.

Asha is arguing with the headphones guy. She pushes him on the chest. He takes a step back then a step towards her again. She knocks the staff out of his hand and they both stand looking down at it.

A dot, a speck bubbles up on top of the block. The speck lengthens into the shape of a man. Tarik is standing on top of the block.

Carrying something.

A flicker at one side then the other. Slender somethings falling away, flying up.

He's untied the rope. He's retied the wire. And he's standing on top of the block.

Cradling something in his arms.

'Asha!' I shout. 'Oh Jesus fucking Christ, Asha…'

And then, all at once, no one's shouting. I look round and for a second the men from the village seem to be staring at me. Asha, pivoting away from the headphones guy, seems to be staring at me. Harry, sitting up on the ground with his frozen look, seems to be staring at me. Then I realise they're not staring at me but past me.

The block has risen into the air. As I watch – as we all watch – it shrugs off and drops the huge impediment of its shadow. The block goes on rising.

Tarik is standing on top of it.

He's untied the rope. He's retied the wire.

'Oh Jesus fucking Christ…'

Now Asha is running, kicking up the dust as she sprints towards the test site, towards the block rising unstoppably into the vertiginous blue sky. I open my mouth to shout again, but there's nothing left to shout. There's nothing left to do, either, but Asha goes on running anyway, as the block rises and rises and then melts to a spot of black in the highest part of the sky, then a dot, then a speck, then nothing at all.

Epilogue

The Teardown

19

Harry was right.

At Chhatrapati Shivaji International Airport I've been waiting for almost two hours when I look up and she's there, standing on the walkway with a lopsided smile and a suitcase propped behind her. I start towards her, not sure how this is going to pan out, whether we're going to hug or shake hands or nod *hello* to each other or whatever, then she laughs and throws her arms round me and laughing I throw my arms round her.

She's there, she's right here, pressed against me, in my arms.

It's strange, all of it, for quite a long while. The reality of her presence is hard to take in. It seems I can manage only bits of her at a time: her hair, then her lips, then her eyes of unearthly substance – her eyes like portals to another earth.

We kiss then I say, 'How are you? How was the flight?'

'Like seventeen hours in a pub toilet. How are you?'

'I'm fine.' Then I say, 'I'm so sorry, Alice.'

'Mmn. You're sorry, I'm sorry, everyone's sorry.' She shrugs: the clarity, the pristine wonder of her shoulders.

Moving on down the walkway, we come in sight of a gigantic banner – urban dusk, dangling feet – and pause, arm in arm, to look at it. Alice blows through her lips and says, 'How're we feeling about that?'

'We're not feeling anything about that. It's nothing to do with us.'

'But you don't think…'

'No, I don't think.' I smack a kiss onto her mouth, which she seems quite pleased about. 'I don't think.'

Back at his place, Harry shakes only the very tips of her fingers. He looks as if it were crossing his mind to curtsy. Then Alice gives him one of her big, silly hugs – she turns you round and round, like she's looking for something – and after that he loosens up and we are able to talk more or less naturally. He says of course Alice is welcome under his roof for as long as she pleases to stay under it, and of course for the duration of her stay his room will be ours; he will himself be perfectly comfortable on the couch. Alice begins to object, but I cut across her, maybe somewhat sharply, with, 'Don't worry about it. Let the old fucker suffer.' And Harry nods, meekly, almost gratefully.

Later we go to the spare room to look at Ess. He seems to be asleep. We sit on the end of the bed looking at him and Alice says, 'Can't anyone do anything?'

'There's a doctor who comes. He says we just have to wait for him to come out of it in his own time.'

Elderly, slab-haired Doctor Sharma visits the flat very regularly. Harry seems to have given him a key, because sometimes I find him sitting in Ess's room, applying an ointment or a cream, talking to Ess about the cricket or the economy. At some point I got used to the sight of the growing colony of jars and tubes and bottles and packets on Ess's bedside table. At some point, also, I got used to the sight of Doctor Sharma's face in the sick room or the sitting room or the kitchen, everywhere in the flat, Harry somewhere nearby, both of them laughing with their high, hooked, old-guy teeth.

But what I think is: *No, Darling. No one can do anything.*

'Well, here we are,' she says, and breathes a sigh of mysterious contentment. She laces her fingers with mine, their cool wax, their supple life. 'What do we do now?'

'We could go out. We could go to bed...'

'No, not "now". I mean *now*. What do we do *now*?'

After Tarik ascended into the sky Asha kept running until she herself was no more than a dot on the horizon. Before she came back the men from the village had stood for a long time in wonderment, begun to show expressions of perplexity, of something akin to grief, and then with laborious hand gestures and sharp shoves in each other's sides shuffled their feet and started to move away. Before Asha came back the elderly guy who I thought was the village headman took hold of my hands and pressed them between his then nodded with mercurial tears flying free at the ends of his eyes.

Two of the men stayed with Harry, checking he was all right, and I stayed with them too, and the rest of the men departed with shuffling steps for the village. Soon there was no one else in view anywhere on the plain. At last the distant human dot that was Asha started to get bigger and some time later she was standing with us again, her hair covering her face. I don't know whether she was crying or not. I'm tempted to think not.

Harry recovered quickly. None of us knew what had happened to him. After a rest and plenty of water he was able to stand, and talk. His face looked frostbitten from the inside out. He spoke to you quite normally but then every few minutes a fit of icy shudders would descend and all he could do was stand there hugging himself while his eyes bluely glared and his teeth chattered.

I went to check on Ess. He was still lying on his sleeping bag in the storage shed, as if nothing had happened. I didn't try to talk to him, didn't try to wake him but only checked that he was still breathing (he was) and that he seemed comfortable (he did) and then I went back to the cabin where Harry was sitting on a chair by the workbench while Asha examined him and poured water down his throat and kept taking his pulse.

I have to admit that at this time also I made a thorough search of the cabin. I wasn't subtle about it, and made a big mess. I saw right away that Tarik's laptop had gone, but nonetheless I turned the place upside down in my hunt for the machine's schematics, for any scrap, any clue to the machine's marvellous functioning. Harry and Asha were careful not to watch me while I did this, as if they knew before I did that I wasn't going to find anything, though in fact there's no way they could have known this. Anyway, I didn't find anything. I smashed a couple of things – the workbench, a cupboard or two – then Asha took hold of me bodily and forced me sit down on the floor next to Harry while she poured water down my throat and listened to my chest and took my pulse.

That night Harry and Asha slept in the cabin. I slept in the storage shed next to Ess. There was some talk between Harry and Asha about moving Ess, about picking him up and bringing him into the cabin, but I rejected these plans, somewhat fiercely. 'We're going to have to move him sooner or later,' Harry said. This was obviously true. But at that time I wasn't yet ready for us to start moving him. So I slept next to him in the storage shed.

In the morning we moved him. At the instant that I woke him he opened his eyes and seemed to smile at me with a loopy wide smile, then he closed his eyes and went on smiling that strange smile with his eyes shut while Harry and I picked him up and carried him across to the Adventurers car and fitted him into the backseat and put the seatbelt on him. While we did this Harry kept up a weird one-sided conversation with him, which seemed to me both disgusting and crazy, though I managed not to comment on it. All that morning I felt dry, light, flammable, dreadfully ashamed of my behaviour the previous evening, looking for the schematics and wrecking Tarik's cabin.

While we packed the car I asked Asha if the men from the village had said anything about Laxman. With eyes pinched tight by suspicion of me and my motives, she said they had. She said she had asked the headman if Laxman was badly injured, and the headman had said he wasn't – he was recovering in the clinic from a superficial wound to his shoulder. She said the revelation of this fact had been her main point of contention with the men. It was what she'd been arguing about with them when Tarik began to ascend into the sky.

Then we drove back to Mumbai. During the journey Ess relieved himself, silently and helplessly, many times. Soon the car reeked of his piss and shit. We wound the windows down, stuck our heads out in the blasting air when we could, and didn't talk about it.

We arrived in the city late at night. Asha drove us to Harry's place, a large and wildly luxurious ground floor flat not far from the causeway. Then she drove away and Harry and I picked up Ess and carried him into the flat and put him down on the couch, where he went on sitting and smiling with his eyes shut until Harry and I came back and picked him up and carried him to Harry's spare room and laid him down on the bed. That night he slept in the bed and I slept on the couch and we carried on sleeping in those places until Alice arrived at the airport with her suitcase.

'You were right,' I said to Harry, when it all started to happen. 'Have you seen this? I mean, you were really right. You were right about everything.'

*

After dinner at Leopold's one night we're walking back along the causeway when Alice says, 'It makes sense though, doesn't it? If we're doing this.'

'We're doing it,' I say.

'We'd have our own space but not be too far away. We'd have to get jobs for the lease and such like. Don't know what we're eligible for, but we'd find something. Cleaning windows, scrubbing pots…'

'What about your work? I mean your *work*? Your…'

'I can do that anywhere. That's the beauty of it.' She grins at me. And she's right. Her work, her *thinking*, it is her core, her brilliant viscera, and it comes with her everywhere. 'We could keep up with Ess, pop in whenever, see how he's doing. Keep up with Harry, too. Only not so much cramping his style.'

'Oh, Darling,' I chortle, 'I'm not sure there's much style there to cramp.'

'Maybe not. But at least he'll have more time alone with his boyfriend.'

We continue walking along the causeway for a while. Then I say, 'What?'

'Harry and his boyfriend. When we move out, they'll have more time together.'

'Harry and his *what*? Harry doesn't have a *boyfriend*.'

'Yes he does. Doctor Sharma is Harry's boyfriend.' Patiently she blinks at me. 'You didn't see that? The whole flirtation, coded-courtship thing they've been doing? For like *a month*? Jesus, Steven, you need to open your eyes. You know, take a look round once in a while.'

It's late afternoon and I'm walking on Chowpatty Beach when I'm startled by a familiar sight: the white flash and boxy build of the Adventurers car. There are some people standing by it, youthful, European – paying Adventurers. There's a guide, also, addressing the group, pointing to one end of the beach then the other. At last the young Adventurers move off to explore the beach and the guide stands leaning against the car, arms folded. Now I get my first proper look at her. And obviously she's Asha.

My immediate instinct is to run – to pelt down the beach and throw myself at her feet. Instead I walk towards her slowly, creakily, over the ridges and lumps, the tidelines of trash. I halt a short distance away then painfully clear my throat and say, 'Hi. Uh, hello.'

She looks at me. She looks away. She says, 'Hello, Steven.'

'I wanted to say...' I've no idea what I wanted to say. My hands rise from my sides and clutch either side of my face, as if I'm concentrating on something, which I'm not. 'How are you? These days? Asha?'

'I'm very well.' She looks at me again. 'How are you?'

'I'm fine. Alice is here now. I mean in India, in Mumbai. Actually we're talking about staying, you know, "making a new life" here.' As soon as I've said it I hear how unlikely it sounds – that we could stay; that we could make a new life, here or anywhere. I start to nod. 'We're just talking. Airing the possibility.'

She looks away again.

'Do you ever think about what happened?' I say.

She frowns, as if a wholly unrelated thought has occurred to her.

'I do. I think about it all the time. I think about Tarik, about that block going up, up, until I feel sick with it. I wonder what happened to him. I wonder where he is. In the sky somewhere. In space. Way up in the, the high channels... And Reva. Sometimes I wonder what happened to Reva. Do you ever think about that?'

Asha stands there, arms folded, leaning against the car, not looking at me. Then she says, 'Why do you think something happened to Reva?'

'Didn't it?'

'Why does something have to have happened to Reva?' She looks at me again. 'I'll tell you what I think. I think Reva is watching us, right now. Watching us, and laughing at us, laughing at us all. Like god.'

'Is that what god does?'

'Watch. Laugh. Other things.' She looks away again.

A while later I say, 'I keep thinking. I should've...' And that's all I say.

'You did what you do. What you always do. You people, you English.'

'Maybe,' I say. And I nod and then I turn and walk away and I never see Asha again.

Harry was right.

The Swiss got there first.

Nineteen days after Tarik Kundra ascended into the sky and vanished, taking with him not only the machine's sole working prototype but also its schematics and his laptop and every other clue to the thing's marvellous functioning, a team of physicists at CERN held their press conference to announce to the world that they had developed a viable antigravity technology. As you know. Not that the scientists made the nature of their work immediately apparent: no doubt fearing incredulity, they called the conference stating only that they had a 'major breakthrough' of 'international significance' to present.

We all saw Prof Hesse give that brief and baffling speech from that plastic lectern on the edge of Lake Geneva before introducing three young associates who, he nervously promised, would 'make plain by their actions what I may only muddy in words'. These youngsters, wearing what looked like climbing helmets and hockey pads, and each equipped with a lightweight backpack – the ones containing a parachute – then began to bounce about the air, leaping over the trees, cartwheeling above the lake. Footage of the conference pretty well preserves the reactions of the unsuspecting press, the shrieks, the technical fumbles, the continual failure to focus on something moving very quickly very high up in the sky.

So the reality of antigravity technology has begun to sink in. Commentators began using phrases like *antigrav tech* and then *AG-tech* ['ay-gee tech'] and now, *agtech*. Current affairs programmes began debating things like *agcommerce* and *the agmarket* and *the agfuture*. The reticent Prof Hesse himself became a conspicuous media presence and pop icon, his woolly, canine face appearing on screens and T-shirts and bedroom walls everywhere.

Agtech is not yet available for purchase. It will be soon, though. And anyway, we all know how it works, more or less. Or at least, we've all been able to find out, since on the day of the press conference the CERN team published the essence of their research online and distributed those several hundred prototypes of their device to colleagues round the world. Yes, certain individuals and bodies made efforts to have the team's work taken offline, citing reasons of public safety and whatnot (conjuring up images of unwise teens soldering together agdevices and levitating themselves into the wide blue yonder), but none of it came to anything. The schematics are still there for all to see. You can log on and have a look at them right now. And besides, you'll own a unit yourself soon enough.

In the meantime those ads are everywhere. Every time I step outside there seems to be another one – or, rather, another copy of the same one, a banner of an ideally attractive young Indian couple gazing into each other's eyes as they float together through the orange urban dusk, the sun dimmed and blurred behind them, the Queen's Necklace spread like expensive fire beneath their dangling beautiful bare feet.

One morning I go to Ess's room and he's not there. The bed is empty, the sheets are on the floor, and he's not there.

I search the flat, every room, every wardrobe, of which it turns out there are many, though Ess is not in any of them. I try the back door, find it unlocked: not open, at least, but unlocked. Is it always unlocked? I can't remember. I call Harry but he doesn't answer. I call Alice but she doesn't answer either. I go back to the front door and stand looking up and down the street. But the dusty glare in each direction holds no sign of him. I wonder who I should call now. Doctor Sharma? The police?

I search the streets in the immediate vicinity of Harry's flat. Then I begin to search more widely, leaving the broad pavements of the familiar tourist circuits for quieter, narrower streets, alleyways that terminate against walls of clammy brick or the caged refuse of shops or tearooms. In desperation I head back to the causeway and mill backwards and forwards in the sluggish crowd, in the hopeless mash of humanity. But it's no use. Even if he were here I would have no way of seeing him, of distinguishing him from so many of his brothers and sisters. I buy a bottle of water at a stall and drink it in one go, standing by a wall full of huge and beautiful cracks. I try Harry again. I try Alice again.

Then my phone rings in my hand and it's Harry. 'He's here.'
'Where's here?'

It's almost midday by the time I arrive at the building site. Only it's not a building site any more but a school, with freshly painted white walls and wooden shutters and orange tiles glowing on the wide and sloped roof. On the bright, clayey ground in front of the school several dozen tiny children – the first intake of pupils – are sitting in circles or pools. Harry is there, with his boyfriend Doctor Sharma. And Alice is there too. And Ess is there too.

'It's fine,' Harry calls out to me, 'I've talked to the teachers, they say there's no problem.'

'What's going on?'

'Seems he just came in this morning. Walked right in, started making friends with people.'

I go up to him, up to Ess. He's sitting on the ground with a couple of the teachers, and with Alice, a little way away from the circles of children. Still, he keeps calling across to the kids, pulling faces, waving his arms.

I sit on the ground in front of him. It takes him a while to realise there's anyone there. Then he looks at me, and squints and smiles.

'Hello,' he says.

'Hello, Ess,' I say.

Weeks indoors have left him pale, his skin almost blue, almost translucent, under the dark splashes of forehead freckles I've barely noticed before. His eyes are watery, dazzling, shapeless, only just contained by the cup-like lines of their crinkles, into which it seems they may at any instant flow, and flow, and finally drain away.

'We've been learning songs,' Ess says.

'Yes,' I say.

He leans forward confidentially, and I lean forward also, so he can pour his secret directly into my ear. 'We learn them, then we sing them. It's a terribly good system.'

'Yes,' I say.

'You should try it. We'll be doing another one in a minute. Give it a try. If you've got time, and you can stay.'

'Yes,' I say, 'I can stay.'

He smiles, then goes back to pulling faces and waving his arms at the children, who shriek and clutch each other delightedly.

He's right. Soon one of the teachers stands and begins to explain the rudiments of a song: a song about rings of roses, about falling down, about fishes in the water, fishes in the sea… Ess listens entranced, eager to learn, desperate to start. I watch him for a while then I look up and I see a flight of birds passing overhead, graceful, effortless, gliding towards the sun, beginning to blur, to melt, to break up, like specks on a ceiling, things imagined in air.

ACKNOWLEDGEMENTS

I am grateful to Priya Bradshaw and Eddie Moore, who gave me the best possible introduction to Mumbai and to India.

Thanks also to my agent, Emma Herdman, and to Alice Lutyens, Sophie Harris and everyone at Curtis Brown who supported this book.

Also to Sam Jordison and Eloise Millar of Galley Beggar Press: exemplary readers, editors, publishers.

To my mum, and my sister, and my brothers.

And to Gemma.

Friends of Galley Beggar Press

Galley Beggar Press would like to thank the following individuals, without the generous support of whom our books would not be possible:

Christine Waddington

Lucy Beresford

Bianca Winter

Angie Creed

Gavrielle Groves-Gidney

Jeremy Biggin

Karen and Kat

Karim Rashad

Ashley Tame

Anthony Trevelyan

Steve Finbow

Michael Spoor

Rachel de Moravia

Lauren Razavi

Rosie Morgan

James Miller

Joy Molyneaux

Diana Jordison

Luke Scott

David Hebblethwaite

Emma Strong

Stephen Walker

Philip O'Donoghue

Polly Randall

Max Cairnduff

Tory Young

Max Cairnduff

Catherine O'Sullivan

Colleen Toomey

Chris Wadsworth